RAVE REVIEWS FOR
FRANCIS RAY

THE WAY YOU LOVE ME

"As always, Ray leads her readers on a mesmerizing journey of drama and love . . . *The Way You Love Me* confirms the fact that Francis Ray is, without a doubt, one of the Queens of Romance." —*A Romance Review*

"Fans of Ray's Grayson and Falcon families will be thrilled with the first installment in the new Grayson Friends series . . . Told with such grace and affection that this novel is a treat to read."
—*RT Book Reviews* (4 stars)

"A romance that will have readers speed-reading to the next tension-filled scene, if not the climax."
—*Fresh Fiction*

ONE NIGHT WITH YOU

"The steam the lovers create is a pleasure to behold. Ray never disappoints!" —*RT Book Reviews* (4½ stars)

WITH JUST ONE KISS

"Heartwarming and fun." —*RT Book Reviews* (4 stars)

NOBODY BUT YOU

"A story that tugs at the heartstrings."—*RT Book Reviews*

"Fast and fun and full of emotional thrills and sexy chills. Everything a racing romance should be!"
—Roxanne St. Claire

"Not only does Francis Ray rock in this book but you also see a whole different side of racing that will keep you on the edge of your seat." —*Night Owl Romance*

"A wonderful read." —*Fresh Fiction*

UNTIL THERE WAS YOU

"Ms. Ray has given us a great novel again. Did we expect anything less than the best?"
—*RT Book Reviews* (4 stars)

"Crisp style, realistic dialogue, likable characters, and [a] fast pace." —*Library Journal*

ONLY YOU

"Francis Ray's graceful writing style and realistically complex characters give her latest contemporary romance its extraordinary emotional richness and depth." —*Chicago Tribune*

"It's a joy to read this always fresh and exciting saga."
—*RT Book Reviews* (4 stars)

"The powerful descriptive powers of Francis Ray allow the reader to step into the story and become an active part of the surrender . . . If you love a great love story, *Only You* should be on your list."

—*Fallen Angel Reviews*

"Riveting emotion and charismatic scenes that made this book captivating . . . a beautiful story of love and romance." —*Night Owl Romance*

"A beautiful love story as only Francis Ray can tell it."

—*Singletitles.com*

"Readers will find a warm and wonderful contemporary romance with plenty of humor and drama. Adding a fun warmth and reality to these characters and a plot that moves quickly add all the needed incentive to read this fun book."

—*Multicultural Romance Writers*

IRRESISTIBLE YOU

"A pleasurable story . . . a well-developed story and continuous plot." —*RT Book Reviews*

"Like the previous titles in this series, *Irresistible You* is another winner . . . Witty and charming . . . Author Francis Ray has a true gift for drawing the readers in and never letting them go."

—*Multicultural Romance Writers*

DREAMING OF YOU

"A great read from beginning to end, it's even excellent for an immediate re-read." —*RT Book Reviews*

"An immensely likable heroine, a sexy man with a heart of gold, and touches of glitz and color, [this] is as unapologetically escapist as Cinderella. Lots of fun." —*BookPage*

YOU AND NO OTHER

"The warmth and sincerity of the Graysons bring another book to life . . . delightfully realistic." —*RT Book Reviews*

"Astonishing sequel . . . the best romance of the new year . . . the Graysons are sure to leave a smile on your face and a longing in your heart for their next story." —*ARomanceReview.com*

"There are three more [Grayson] children with great love stories in the future." —*Booklist*

SOMEONE TO LOVE ME

"Another great romance novel." —*Booklist*

"The plot moves quickly, and the characters are interesting." —*RT Book Reviews*

ST. MARTIN'S PAPERBACKS TITLES BY FRANCIS RAY

The Falcon Novels
Heart of the Falcon
Break Every Rule

The Taggart Brothers
Forever Yours
Only Hers

The Graysons of New Mexico Series
Until There Was You
You and No Other
Dreaming of You
Irresistible You
Only You

The Grayson Friends Series

The Way You Love Me *With Just One Kiss*
Nobody But You *A Dangerous Kiss*
One Night with You *All I Ever Wanted*
It Had to Be You *All That I Need*
A Seductive Kiss

~

Trouble Don't Last Always
Someone to Love Me
I Know Who Holds Tomorrow
Rockin' Around That Christmas Tree (with Donna Hill)

Anthologies
Rosie's Curl and Weave
Della's House of Style
Welcome to Leo's
Going to the Chapel
Gettin' Merry

All That I Need

FRANCIS RAY

St. Martin's Paperbacks

This is a work of fiction. All of the characters, organizations, and events portrayed in this novel are either products of the author's imagination or are used fictitiously.

ALL THAT I NEED

Copyright © 2013 by Francis Ray.
Excerpt from *All That I Desire* copyright © 2013 by Francis Ray.

For information address St. Martin's Press, 175 Fifth Avenue, New York, NY 10010.

ISBN: 978-1-250-02381-0

Printed in the United States of America

St. Martin's Paperbacks edition / July 2013

St. Martin's Paperbacks are published by St. Martin's Press, 175 Fifth Avenue, New York, NY 10010.

10 9 8 7 6 5 4 3 2

Chapter 1

Fallon Nicole Marshall had always considered herself cool under pressure. After all, she was a well-respected travel writer for some of the top magazines in the country. She routinely dealt with tight deadlines, demanding editors, computer glitches, and uncooperative people. She'd baked in 107 degrees, frozen in 6 below, to get a story and just the right photographs. She had the patience of Job and the tenacity of a terrier. Nothing—if you didn't consider her need for two cups of coffee each morning—got the best of her anymore. She'd been there, done that.

Or so she'd mistakenly thought.

Slowing down on the highway, Fallon put on her signal and turned her rental onto the paved road three miles out of Santa Fe. Her slim fingers flexed on the steering wheel of the late-model Taurus. She was only marginally pleased that they weren't damp with perspiration. She might be a bit nervous about obtaining information for her next story, but at least she wasn't showing her frayed nerves on meeting Lance Saxton again.

It was perfectly understandable that she felt apprehensive—after all, she had been, well, rather abrupt to Lance Saxton two weeks ago when they'd first met. She'd practically accused him of being a thief and walked away from him in self-righteous indignation. Although he had to share some of the blame for that crack about "not handling their financial responsibilities correctly," she had to take her share as well.

She freely admitted that since her mother had been swindled by the unscrupulous owner of an auction house and Lance owned an auction house she had judged quickly and harshly.

And she'd been wrong.

She hadn't discovered her mistake until recently. Naomi Reese, her friend and neighbor, had insisted Fallon read an article about Lance in *Fortune* magazine. Fallon had turned up her nose and ignored the sudden thump of her heart on seeing a picture of Lance in an expensive navy pin-striped suit standing in front of Saxton Auction House, but she'd read the article.

In less than a minute she'd known she'd been wrong. She'd handed the magazine back to Naomi, thanked her, and gone home, telling herself if the opportunity ever presented itself she'd apologize, fully aware that she wasn't going to initiate the contact. That changed a few days ago.

Now she needed Lance Saxton to gain access to the Yates home for the article she planned to write. He might toss her out; then again, he might not. There was only one way to find out.

Moments later the red-barrel roof of a house came into view; then as she rounded a curve she saw the sprawling Yates house. She slowed and came to a complete stop. It was simply beautiful with the afternoon sun shining on the roof and the adobe exterior. She could easily imagine coming home from work or a trip and catching the first glimpse of the house. She didn't even live there and yet she felt a sort of calming peace. One day she'd have a house, a family, but for now she enjoyed her job. She loved to travel and was paid well to visit and write about some of the most exciting places in the world.

The last thought had her squaring her shoulders. She was good at what she did. Nothing had ever stopped her in the past, and she wouldn't allow Lance Saxton to be the first.

Putting the car into motion, she continued down the mile-long road and parked on the circular driveway in front of the massive red double doors, reasoning if Lance threw her out, she wouldn't have far to go to her car. Getting out, she again studied the sprawling two-story house.

The home was originally built in the 1920s by oil mogul Thaddeus Yates. He liked the Southwest and chose Santa Fe as his base when he wanted to relax and get away from Lubbock, Texas. After his death, his only child and daughter, Colleen, expanded the six-thousand-square-foot home another five thousand square feet to include a loggia and pool house. Her son did more renovation on the house plus extensive landscaping, turning the usually parched grounds of the area into a verdant paradise with lush green grass and a rainbow of flower hues.

Fallon hadn't seen grass so lush since she'd left her hometown of Austin four months ago. She was tempted to slip off her sandals and let the grass tickle her toes. She refrained. All she needed was for Lance to see her and think she was a nutcase. Still, with less than twelve inches of rain yearly in Santa Fe, it would cost a small fortune to maintain the grounds.

Through research she'd learned that the single male heir and last owner had died six months ago from injuries sustained in a skiing accident. Banks sometimes paid for minor upkeep, but nothing more.

Fallon realized she was stalling, and with good reason. She wasn't looking forward to ringing the doorbell and meeting Lance Saxton again. She didn't mind admitting she was wrong so much as she didn't like the idea of making that admission to a man she had a mild attraction to. She'd like to think he'd caught her at a weak moment, but that would be a lie. She traveled so much she didn't have time for a relationship, and she valued herself too much to have meaningless affairs.

Yet her girlie antenna had zinged the instant she had looked into Lance's midnight black eyes. He had the "Y" yummy factor in spades: at least six feet four, in sinful jeans and a white polo that delineated hard muscles. She had almost fantasized about the naughty things he could whisper in her ear—until she learned what he did for a living. And went as cold as an iceberg on the man.

Sighing, Fallon removed her camera from the case, looped the strap around her neck, and grabbed her notebook. Standing there wouldn't get the job done. Closing the car door, she followed the paved path to the wide double doors, all the time telling herself that this was a story like all the hundreds, probably thousands, she'd written in the past.

It was her job as a travel writer to point out the new and unusual, the best places to make that vacation or staycation exciting, fun, and memorable. Reading about the auction in the newspaper had given her an idea for a story—that of leaving time on the schedule for something unexpected, like an auction.

The Yates home was a piece of history that would soon be gone . . . just as her family's heirlooms and antiques were gone. She'd never forgive the owner of the auction house who had cheated her mother and made their lives miserable when Fallon was seventeen, but she'd been wrong to lump Lance with the crook.

The Yates possessions weren't going to be low-balled as the Marshalls' had been. Lance Saxton, although new to the auction scene, had a sterling reputation as a savvy businessman with a Midas touch. Whatever he touched succeeded in spades. The Yates auction would only be his second in the three months since he'd opened Saxton Auction House. The other had been in Tucson, where his office was located, and hugely successful. The retired movie star's possessions had sold out after the second day of the four-day sale.

Fallon realized she was stalling. Again. She hadn't called for an appointment. She honestly hadn't known what to say. *Hey, I'm sorry I accused you of being a thief, but I have this great idea for a story and two editors are interested, so let's forget about our first meeting.* If the positions were reversed, she would have thrown him out. She had a bit of a temper—which had gotten her into this mess.

So, she'd taken the coward's way and asked his cousin, Richard Youngblood, if he thought Lance would be at the Yates house working. Richard had been at his fiancée Naomi's apartment that morning eating breakfast and discussing wedding plans. They were as giddy as teenagers and so much in love. Fallon was happy for both of them, especially after what Naomi had gone through.

Declining the offer of breakfast, Fallon had gone back to her place next door to leave them alone. Or as much as possible with Naomi's five-year-old daughter, Kayla, with them. Neither Richard nor Naomi seemed to mind. That had been hours ago. It was almost two. It had taken Fallon this long to work up the courage to drive out.

Blowing out a breath, Fallon rang the doorbell.

In the small library of the Yates house that Lance Saxton had taken for his office, he slowly lifted his head when he heard the doorbell. He'd been waiting for the sound since Richard called that morning to tell him that Fallon had asked if he would be there.

To Richard's "Don't blow your second chance," Lance had said nothing.

Since Lance didn't have any other appointments and he wasn't expecting any deliveries, he reasoned it was Fallon Marshall. His hand flexed on the pen in his hand. It didn't take much to visualize the stunning woman with long curly hair, bedroom brown eyes, model cheekbones, and lips to drive a man crazy. For some reason—perhaps because Richard was in such a great mood and Lance could tell his cousin was finally interested in a woman—the moment they'd met Lance had found himself attracted to Fallon.

It was the first time in months he'd had more than a passing interest in a woman. He'd honestly thought he had written women off except for the occasional ones he took to bed. It was purely physical for both of them: easily had and easier forgotten.

The chime came again. This was the housekeeper's half day off. The people he'd hired to help catalog the house contents for the auction had driven into town for a late lunch. There was no one there but him. If he didn't answer, Fallon would leave and he wouldn't have to worry about forgetting his long-ago promise of steering clear of women he couldn't easily walk away from. Yet he found himself coming to his feet and leaving the office. Fallon was just a woman.

Opening the front door, he had to revise his earlier thought about Fallon. She was stunning in a raspberry knit top and white walking shorts. Her eyes were just as captivating as before, her mouth just as tempting. His hand clamped on the doorknob as they continued to stare at each other. He wouldn't be the first to speak. She had called him a thief.

"Hello, Lance. I guess you're surprised to see me."

"That's putting it mildly."

Before saying "I'm not sure if you remember or not, but I'm a travel writer," Fallon ran her tongue over those lips he'd dreamed about.

Since his mouth was dry, he simply nodded. Fallon was too much of a temptation. As soon as possible he was sending her on her way.

"I read about this place and the auction you're having. I came up with the idea for an article." She glanced around the yard. "This house might not be on the historical society's register, but it has a lot of history that will be lost once the auction is over. I'd like to preserve that."

"By doing a story," he said, unable to keep the derision out of his voice. Another person who wanted to profit from the misfortune of others. And she'd thought *him* heartless.

Her eyes narrowed briefly; then she shifted back to him, inadvertently making her breasts in the knit top jut forward. Lance gritted his teeth and opened his mouth to tell her good-bye, but she finally spoke.

"Not just a story. I want to bring the history of the house and the people who lived here to life. I also want to let readers know that it's all right not to plan every second of a vacation. Wonderful opportunities like this auction might present themselves. I've done a bit of research on the house already."

"Don't you think that was a bit premature?" he asked, glad his voice was normal even if his heart rate wasn't.

"Yes, but knowledge is never wasted." She stepped back and looked up at the window overhead. "Do you know that some of the timber in this house came from Yates's grandparents' property in Louisiana? He was a bit of a sentimentalist." She sent Lance a quick grin. "The stained glass in the window overhead is from Paris and the chandelier in the living room is Waterford. They're his wife's selections."

"Women like the finer things." Lance had learned that lesson the hard way.

Fallon's brow arched. "So do men. Thaddeus spared no expense to build this house. It took three years. His daughter expanded it even more. From the little I was able to find, she doted on her son and wanted the house to last for generations. It's a shame that her dreams died with him." Fallon gave Lance her full attention, her expression so heart-rending he had to lock his knees to keep from reaching out to comfort her. "It would be wonderful if that didn't happen, if the family history could be preserved and be the impetus for other family dreams and legacies."

His gaze narrowed on her. So, she wasn't just beautiful and brassy. It was rare to meet someone not in the business who really understood the value and importance of beloved furniture and accessories being a legacy.

There were times when he thought of his own mortality, even at thirty-six. He never planned to marry. What would he leave behind? Who would mourn him? The answers weren't comforting, so he continued to study Fallon. Unlike most people, his direct stare didn't make her fidget.

He'd been devastatingly wrong about women before, but something told him that Fallon was telling the truth. This was more than a story to her. Watching her hair dance in the breeze, her steady gaze, he came to a decision.

Instead of being annoyed with Fallon, he really should be thanking her. If she hadn't put a stop to things that afternoon they met, they would have probably ended up in bed and his life would have been in turmoil again. Besides, he'd like the Yates history and legacy to be preserved as well.

Stepping back inside, he watched her eyes widen, her mouth open. He realized she thought he was going to shut the door in her face. It annoyed the hell out of him that she believed he was that rude. "Come in."

Her mouth hung open for a second longer, before she snapped it shut. She quickly stepped inside. "Thank you."

He noted that perspiration dampened the flawless skin on her forehead. Perhaps he was rude to keep her out in the heat. "Would you care for something to drink?"

"No, thank—" Her eyes widened and she was across the room. Reverently her hand grazed the top of an oak-finished chest of drawers. "This is one of Thaddeus's pieces, isn't it? His daughter used this for her hope chest."

Lance joined Fallon. "You did your research well, I see."

"I wanted to be prepared." She smiled over her shoulder at him, then turned back to the piece that was as tall as she. "He was a furniture maker before they struck oil on his property. A picture of this chest was the only one I could find of the contents of the house."

"There are other pieces he made mixed throughout with the more famous makers like Chippendale," Lance said. "The house is a treasure trove of furniture, artwork, and crystal."

Her eyes glittered with hope, one hand clamped on the camera, the other on the notebook. "Then you'll let me do the story?"

He was probably crazy, considering he barely could keep his eyes off her lips. "You can do the story." He motioned toward her camera. "Feel free to take as many photos as you like. You seem to understand and appreciate the furnishings—that they meant something to the Yateses, they aren't just things or possessions," he said.

For a second, her eyes darkened with pain. "Yes."

He wondered if she was thinking about the incident that had caused her to brand him a thief.

"Feel free to look around. I'll be in my office." He pointed to an open door to the left. "Just let me know when you're leaving."

"Thank you."

With a brief nod, he returned to his office, hoping he hadn't made a terrible mistake.

Fallon caught herself admiring Lance's muscular build, the easy way he moved—all right, his butt—and quickly turned away. Now wasn't the time to go all girlie over a good-looking man. Lance had been gentleman enough to overlook her bad manners in the past, and she had a story to do.

However, twenty minutes later she wasn't so sure anymore. The house was as fantastic inside as it was outside, the furnishings beautiful. Thaddeus's wife had liked English antiques, and so had their daughter. There was none of the heavy masculine stuff Fallon had half expected. The only leather she had seen was in the game room, a pool table. To do the story, she needed to be able to talk about specific pieces of furniture and what they meant to the family.

If she had had her mind on the article instead of on a certain part of Lance's anatomy, she wouldn't have forgotten that important detail. There was only one way to correct matters. She started down the elegantly curved staircase with a mahogany handrail and didn't stop until she was in front of the door Lance had indicated. She knocked.

"Come in."

Plastering a cheerful smile on her face and hoping she wasn't disturbing him, she opened the door. He sat behind a massive desk in a room filled with bookshelves. This room had been the Yates library.

Lance lifted his dark head, his gaze direct and his expression patient. On either side of him were undraped floor-to-ceiling windows. Framed by sunlight, he was gorgeous. The thought ran through her mind that he didn't smile as easily as the man she'd met weeks ago. A pity.

"Yes?" His voice, once warm and tempting, was now coolly professional.

"I'm sorry to disturb you, but were there any diaries that might put significance on the individual pieces of furnishings or household articles?" she asked, crossing to stand in front of his desk. "As I said, Mr. Yates was said to be sentimental. The house is a showcase, but I want my readers to know the why and the how."

"Yes. Thaddeus Yates and his daughter left notes, but they're part of the auction and I'd rather they not be handled," Lance explained, removing his eyeglasses.

Disappointment slumped her shoulders. "I see."

He seemed to hesitate, then came to his feet and around the desk. " 'I've read the notes and am familiar with everything. If you'd like I could give you a brief tour."

"Lance, thank you." He really was a nice guy. "That would be wonderful."

"We could start in here." He turned toward the built-in bookcases on the walls. "Thaddeus had these made in New Orleans. Some people just purchase books to fill out a library because of their binding or size, but Thaddeus loved to read and so did his wife and daughter. Each book was selected by one of them."

Fallon lifted her camera and took a couple of shots, then walked over to the shelf and pulled out a slim book. "*Wuthering Heights*. I wonder, was the mother or the daughter the romantic?"

"Safe to say it wasn't Thaddeus. Men know better."

Fallon frowned. "You don't believe in romance?"

"Not many practical men would." Lance opened the library/office door. "We can continue upstairs. You'll note that, although extensive remodeling has been done, the original wood molding around the fireplaces and walls remains. This way."

Fallon wasn't ready to leave the conversation on romance, but she wasn't given a choice. Replacing the book, she turned to follow Lance.

As they went through the house and as she listened to him talk, she realized he cared about the furnishings. It wasn't just money to him. He seemed to understand what the house meant to the mother and daughter who had acquired most of the furnishings.

Back downstairs, Lance led her to the dining room. "Surrounding this late Georgian dining table is a suite of Empire chairs. It can comfortably seat twelve. Thaddeus's daughter, Colleen, personally picked this out on a trip to England."

Fallon snapped a photo, then lowered the camera. "Clearly she intended this for large family gatherings."

"Her son, Herbert, was two at the time," Lance said. "While traveling she wrote that she and her husband wanted more children. Her son understood the legacy. Ten years before his death, he had his last name changed to Yates."

Fallon's fingertips grazed the table's polished surface. "Like the sterling flatware you showed me in the linen closet, she wanted these things to be handed down to the next generation, but it didn't happen."

Not a flicker of emotion crossed Lance's face. "No, her son never married."

"I hope the new owners love and appreciate the house and the furnishings as much as Herbert's mother," Fallon said.

"Why would you say that?" Lance asked with a frown.

She hunched her slim shoulders. "She just put so much into this place, had such hopes. It's sad that they had to die with her son. Maybe with the next family living here, that won't happen."

Fallon heard a door open, then close. Voices.

"That will be my employees returning from lunch," Lance explained.

Fallon glanced at her watch and gasped. Her gaze quickly lifted to Lance's. She'd been there almost two hours. It had been easy talking and listening to Lance. But he hadn't given off any signals that he was interested in picking up where they'd left off—before her unfair accusation.

She had to admit, she was disappointed. She'd certainly messed up. Perhaps it was for the best. She was leaving in less than a week. "I didn't mean to take up so much of your time."

"It's all right." He lifted his long-fingered, manicured hand toward the door. "I'll show you out."

Fallon followed Lance out. In the open area, she saw two young men and an older woman going up the staircase.

Opening the front door, Lance stepped back so she could pass. As soon as she did he said, "Goodbye. If you have any more questions, or want to come back, you're welcome."

"Thanks." She tossed her notebook in the car and placed her camera in the case, then straightened. Lance still stood on the wide porch. He could just be being polite, but maybe he'd been thinking about what might have happened between them just as she had.

"You want to meet at Brandon's restaurant for dinner around seven?"

Lance's gaze narrowed. She'd caught him off guard and it pleased her immensely. "It will make up for my poor behavior when we met, and thank you for not holding it against me today."

He stared at her a long moment, as if trying to figure her out. She'd like to think she was one of a kind.

"I'll see you at seven."

She grinned and felt like dancing. She hadn't realized how important the answer was to her until he'd agreed.

"Seven it is." Waving, she got in her car and pulled off. Through the rearview mirror she saw Lance still standing there. He was such a dichotomy. Who was the real Lance, this self-composed man or the flirtatious one she'd met weeks ago? She was determined to find out.

Chapter 2

Fallon tried to convince herself that it was just a business/thank-you dinner. Not even changing her dress twice before settling on an off-the-shoulder raspberry-colored dress convinced her otherwise, nor did the three changes of sandals and earrings. However, she gave up trying the moment she saw Lance, tall and mouthwateringly delicious, waiting outside the restaurant for her.

Her heart did a crazy jitterbug; her legs weren't quite as steady as they'd been moments earlier. He stood a few feet from the long line of people waiting to enter the Red Cactus.

She was ten minutes early. She'd told herself it was to allow time to park and not because she was anxious to see him again. She rolled her eyes. It was bad when you started lying to yourself.

Lance reached her in seconds, his dark brows furrowed. "Are you all right?"

So he was perceptive. "Just thinking," she said. At least that was the truth. "I tried to make reservations, but they were booked. You want to wait?"

"I admit, I'm not the patient type when waiting for a table," he told her. "Fortunately, I took the precaution of calling and making reservations, just in case."

She smiled up at him. "Thanks."

Long, lean fingers gently took her arm. Her skin heated, tingled.

They continued inside the restaurant, past the stares of those waiting in line. Fallon was almost compelled to explain that they weren't cutting, they had reservations.

Lance didn't appear to notice. He stopped in front of the hostess's podium. "Reservations for Saxton at seven."

The pretty young woman in a slim-fitting black dress smiled and picked up two oversized menus with red boots and cacti on the front. "Certainly, Mr. Saxton. If you and your guests will follow Lacy, she'll seat you at your table."

Smiling, Lacy accepted the menus. "This way, please."

Lance's hand moved to the small of Fallon's back and she almost yelped. Heat radiated through the cotton fabric as if on bare skin. Lance could really be a problem—if she let him.

"Here you are," Lacy said.

Lance pulled out a chair at the table for two for Fallon, took the seat across from her, and accepted the menu. "Thank you."

"Your waiter, Shawn, should be with you shortly. Can I get you anything to drink?" Lacy asked. "Wine, cocktail, or flavored tea perhaps?"

"Fallon?" Lance asked.

Fallon wasn't much for alcohol, but tonight seemed to be the one to be a little daring. "Black mojita."

"Pomegranate iced tea."

"I'll get those right out," Lacy said, and left.

Fallon propped her arms on the table and hoped she wasn't too obvious, but the man certainly was easy on the eyes. "How are things shaping up for the auction?"

"Good. The catalog with the most expensive pieces arrived this morning," he told her. "The employees you saw this afternoon are finishing up listing the smaller items."

"From what I saw, you all have a humongous task ahead of you," she said. "The glassware alone is extensive and impressive."

"It will get done." The words were clipped, final.

Fallon believed him. Lance wasn't a man who impressed her as tolerating excuses—and that included himself. "Then you deserve a night to relax. Have you eaten here before?"

"No. I spent summers here growing up, but I haven't been back since I graduated from college." He glanced around the crowded restaurant. "Brandon has done well for himself. I hear the food is delicious, but I guess you can tell from the long line and the restaurant being booked."

"I've seldom tasted better," she told him. "One of the first stories I did on Santa Fe was on the Red Cactus."

"How long have you been a travel writer?" he asked.

"Since my junior year at college," she related. "I get to travel to exciting places and get paid for it."

His dark head tilted to one side. "But I don't think money is your motivating reason."

Surprised delight swept through her. "It's not."

"Your drinks. I'm Shawn. I'll be your waiter." A tall, slender man dressed in a white shirt and black pants placed the glasses in front of them and took out a pad and pencil. "Are you ready to order or do you need a few more minutes?"

"Fallon?"

"I already know I want the triple sampler and the onion rings, but I don't think you've had time to study the menu." Fallon closed her menu.

Lance opened the menu, briefly glanced at it, and said, "I'll have the porterhouse, medium, with a baked potato, butter only, asparagus, and house salad with ranch dressing." Lance handed the man his menu.

Frowning, Fallon followed suit. "How did you do that?"

"Speed-reading." Lance picked up his drink. "So what drives you?"

She realized two things: Lance didn't want to talk about himself, and there was definitely more to him than his sexy good looks. "Growing up in Austin, I dreamed of being a news correspondent and traveling all over the world." Her fingers closed around the stem of the glass. "When that didn't work out, this sort of just happened when a magazine wanted a fresh article on Austin. The story led to another and another. By the time I graduated from college, I had logged a lot of miles on my mother's car and written over fifty articles. I like traveling and discovering things people might have overlooked. After graduation, I just kept going and writing."

"Where were you before you came here?" he asked.

"Where the rich and famous play, Martha's Vineyard." She laughed. "Besides the historic fishing villages, it has breezy beaches, adorable towns, delicious food. The lobster was out of this world."

He gazed at her over his glass. "The wealthy are here as well. Is that what drew you?"

"No," she answered. She would not be miffed with him. "People and places draw me. Martha's Vineyard and here can be expensive, but both can be enjoyed by families on a budget, one of the things I take great care to point out."

He placed his glass aside. "You're different."

"Good or bad?" she asked.

"I haven't figured it out," he said, staring at her intently.

Butterflies took flight in Fallon's stomach. She reminded herself that she was leaving in less than a week and hoped she listened.

"Your food." The waiter served them both. "Is there anything else I can get either of you?"

"Fallon?"

Fallon mentally shook herself and looked at her plate. "I'm good."

"Same here. Thanks."

Fallon tucked her head to bless the food, then reminded herself this was a thank-you dinner. Finished, she reached for her quesadilla and took a generous bite. Moaned. Savored. She did love good food. When she opened her eyes Lance was staring at her. The heat in his eyes almost singed her. He wasn't being distant now.

He broke contact first and reached for his knife and fork. "Why didn't the news correspondent dream work out?"

Fallon wondered how he could revert back to being impersonal after eating her with his eyes, then realized it took practice. But why would he have learned such self-control? Her natural curiosity to see what others didn't kicked in.

He looked up when she didn't answer. "I hope I'm not being too personal."

She reached for her drink. She sipped and studied him over the rim of her highball glass. He didn't fidget, just kept her gaze. That took practice as well. There was definitely more to Lance than met the eye. Perhaps he deserved the whole story, but not tonight. "Something tells me you wouldn't care if you were."

The corners of his sensual mouth quirked. "How is your food?"

"Delicious."

"That's always good to hear."

Fallon glanced up to see Brandon Grayson, owner of the Red Cactus, a wide grin on his handsome face. "You couldn't cook a bad dish if you tried."

Brandon's grin widened. "If you ever have trouble getting a table, ask the hostess to find me."

"I'll do that," Fallon said, pleased. She'd met Lance and Brandon at a late luncheon at his wife's family-owned hotel, *Casa de Serenidad.*

Brandon shook Lance's outstretched hand. "Good seeing you again."

Lance nodded toward Fallon. "Thank Fallon. She suggested we eat here."

"But Lance was smart enough to get reservations," she said, amused. "So this is a joint effort."

"Faith taught me that two is always better than one." Brandon glanced between Lance and Fallon.

Fallon hoped she wasn't blushing. She didn't dare look at Lance. "Your wife is wonderful. Naomi is so excited about the wedding reception at her hotel. She still can't believe she and Richard were able to obtain one of the smaller ballrooms."

"Nothing Faith likes better than planning events for special friends and family." Brandon shook his dark head, the long braid hanging down his back moving sensuously. "She, Mama, and Catherine were on the phone early this morning talking about place settings and flower arrangements for the tables."

"This morning Richard and Naomi were going over the final guest list," Fallon said. "His parents arrived yesterday, and tonight they're going over it to finalize everything."

"It will be good seeing Uncle Leo and Aunt Gladys again. When we talked last night, they sounded just as happy as always," Lance mused. "I bet they never thought they'd come home to find Richard planning his wedding."

Fallon's brow lifted. "You sound as if you never expected him to get married."

"Marriage isn't for everyone," Lance said, the amusement gone from his face.

"Maybe not for everyone, but I'm glad I found Faith," Brandon told them. "Enjoy your dinner."

Fallon picked up a taco but watched Lance. If she didn't miss her guess, there was a certain woman in Lance's past and it hadn't ended pretty. Fallon continued eating for a bit but couldn't resist asking, "You don't approve of Richard marrying?"

"I never said that." He polished off his steak and shoved the plate aside, his annoyance obvious. "I haven't gotten a chance to know Naomi very well, but she appears sweet and loving. Exactly the type of woman for Richard."

It was on the tip of Fallon's tongue to ask Lance about the type of woman he thought suitable for him, but thankfully she caught herself before blurting it out. "Yes, she is and, after what she went through with her first marriage and a few days ago, she deserves to be happy."

"Richard will see to that, and that her ex never bothers her again," Lance said with a hint of anger in his voice. Any man who hit a woman was scum—no matter the provocation. For all the hurt

Ashley had put him though, physically harming her had never entered his mind.

He picked up his glass and saw Fallon watching him with those bedroom eyes of hers. She was trying to figure him out. He'd also caught her watching him during dinner. She was still interested in him. If he was honest, he was more than interested in her. But if things went further, she had to know it would be purely physical. No emotional involvement or happily ever after.

"What about you?" he asked abruptly. Fallon might be the kind of woman who wanted forever.

She straightened, her tempting breasts jutting forward. Lance tried not to stare and worked not to let his body go into overdrive. Nothing was happening tonight—if ever.

"I beg your pardon?"

"What's your view on marriage or are you engaged already?" he asked, irrationally angry at the thought of her marrying anyone.

"I fully intend to marry one day and have a family, but it's difficult with traveling so much," she told him. "I'm seldom in one place longer than a few months. Hardly long enough to have a lasting relationship with anyone."

So, she wanted forever. That left him out. Even without traveling, lasting relationships were difficult. He should know. "Would you like coffee or dessert?"

"If I eat another bite I might pop." She wrinkled her nose. ' "I'll have to get the cheesecake another time."

Lance signaled the waiter. "The bill, and please add a slice of cheesecake in a to-go container for the lady."

"Certainly, sir."

Fallon reached for her purse. "My invitation. My treat."

"My reservation." He reached for the bill presenter as soon as the waiter approached. Lance barely glanced at it before shoving a large bill inside and handing it back to the waiter. "Thank you."

"Thank you, sir, and a good evening to both of you."

It would be better if it ended with both of them in a bed, but that wasn't happening. Lance stood, picked up the to-go container for the cheesecake, and reached for her chair. "I'll walk you to your car."

Fallon came to her feet and glanced at him over her shoulder. "That's not necessary."

"Since I plan to follow you home, I think it is."

Fallon kept looking in the rearview mirror. First dates—if they went well—usually ended with a good-night kiss. But considering theirs had started out as a business/thank-you, Fallon wasn't sure what to expect at the door. Lance had certainly sent out mixed signals. She couldn't get a handle on him.

For once, the parking spot in front of her door was vacant. She pulled in next to Naomi's SUV. There was a light on in both of their apartments, but since it was barely eight thirty Fallon was sure Naomi and Richard were still at his parents' place.

Shutting off the motor, Fallon got out of her car with the cheesecake and searched the parking lot for Lance. She saw him seconds later. It was easy to pick out his muscular build, the easy stride of his walk. He appeared self-assured, but there was something there that she couldn't quite put her finger on. With her leaving at the end of the week, she wouldn't have time to figure out what.

"Sorry to keep you waiting. I couldn't find a parking space."

"That's all right," she said, horrified to hear the breathlessness in her voice. She quickly reached into her bag for her key and turned to open the door. It opened on the first try despite her shaking hand.

"Most women have to search for a key." Lance shoved his hands into the pockets of his dress slacks. "I should have known you're too smart for that."

"Comes from traveling and moving so many times," she said. Then she faced him and took the plunge. "Would you like to come in?"

"I should get back," he told her, his expression bland. "There's still a lot of paperwork and tagging to be done before the auction."

She honestly didn't know if she was disappointed or not. Starting something with Lance might feel good, but she wasn't sure it would be good for her. "Good night, and thanks for today and dinner tonight. And this." She held up the dessert.

"You're welcome. Good night."

She entered her apartment and couldn't help one long, last tempting look at him. She'd see him at Richard and Naomi's wedding, but somehow Fallon knew if she and Lance didn't connect now they never would. She started to swing the door shut.

The flat of his hand stopped it. His hand flexed on the door as if he wasn't sure of himself. "It goes without saying that if you want to come out to the house again, you're welcome. I'll be working there all day tomorrow."

Fallon couldn't keep the wide grin off her face. "I'll be there the same time. I want to write up my notes."

"I'll see you then." Reaching out, he closed the door.

Fallon threw the dead bolt and headed to her bedroom. She hadn't gotten the kiss, but tomorrow was another day.

Fallon woke up with a smile on her face. She didn't even think of denying it was because she was going to see Lance. He intrigued her as much as he made her want to take a bite out of him. Laughing, Fallon bounded out of bed and hit the shower. She'd never had such a crazy thought in her life.

Twenty-three minutes later, she was knocking on Naomi's back door. In Fallon's hands were two mugs. One held a mixture of coffee creamer and sugar. The other mug was empty. She might bum coffee, but she always came with what she wanted in it.

It was seven ten, but Fallon knew her neighbor and friend would be up and alone. Naomi taught kindergarten and would be up getting ready for work. And since her ex was no longer a threat, Richard wouldn't be spending the night.

Fallon heard the locks disengage seconds before the door opened. "Good morning," Naomi greeted. "Help yourself to coffee."

"Bless you." From long practice, Fallon prepared herself a cup of coffee, then sipped.

"I fixed extra waffle batter," Naomi said. "If you hurry you can tell me about your date before Kayla joins us."

Taking another sip, Fallon went to the stove to check on the sizzling sausage patties. She picked up a metal spatula. "Nothing to tell."

Naomi closed the lid to the waffle maker and faced Fallon with a frown. "Richard said he asked about you a couple of times before you went out there yesterday."

"That was then and this is now, as the saying goes." Fallon lifted two turkey patties from the skillet.

The whistle of the waffle machine sounded. Naomi removed the waffle and added more batter. "How do you feel about that?"

"I'm leaving at the end of the week."

"Don't remind me." Taking the spatula from Fallon's hand, Naomi removed the other patties. "If you weren't coming back for the wedding in six weeks, I'm not sure I could stand it."

Fallon hugged her, then leaned her head against hers. "Same here. Like I said, the apartment gods were smiling on me this time. It's been great living next door to you these months."

Naomi straightened. "You and Catherine helped me stop being afraid and reach out for Richard.

You've been wonderful with Kayla. I'd say it was the other way around."

"Yeah, it's been nice." Fallon removed the waffle when the alarm sounded. "Mama and Megan are anxious to have me home before I leave for my next assignment."

Taking the platters of meat and waffles, Naomi placed them on the kitchen table. "If you weren't leaving, would it make a difference with things between you and Lance?"

"I'm not sure." Fallon sipped her coffee. "Bad timing. I'm going out there today to take more notes."

"Then there's still a chance."

Fallon shook her head. "Lance is a hard man to read."

Naomi placed another plate on the table. "So it will take more effort. Won't the end results be worth it?"

All Fallon had to do was think of the searing look Lance had given her the night before. "Yes."

"Then go get him."

Late Tuesday afternoon Lance finally heard the sound that he had waited all day to hear, the chime of the doorbell. So, she had finally come—if it was her. She was almost two hours later than the day before. He'd begun to worry about her fifteen minutes past the time he thought she should be there.

Bad. Very bad.

No matter how much he told himself to keep it professional, some part of him—the stubborn part that had helped him succeed in business if not his personal life—wasn't listening. He'd almost called Richard to check on her, then reasoned that if something had happened Richard would have notified him.

If Richard knew.

Lance threw his pen on the desk and came to his feet. He hadn't done a solid ten minutes of work all day. Women messed up a man's orderly life. He knew that better than most. Yet—

A knock came on his office door. "Mr. Saxton, your guest, Ms. Marshall, is here."

Relief, excitement, uneasiness—so many emotions crowded Lance's brain he couldn't sort all of them out. He'd never been this conflicted about a woman or anything else in his life. He tended to see things in black and white—no gray—since the year his mother had married another man and made Lance feel like an outsider in his own home.

"Mr. Saxton?"

Letting go of the resentment, Lance unclenched his fists. The past needed to stay in the past. "Come in."

The door opened. He caught a brief glimpse of Carmen, his housekeeper; then Fallon stepped into the room and she became his entire focus.

She was stunningly beautiful and off-limits. Before he knew it, he was moving. He didn't ask or hesitate; he just took her into his arms, his mouth finding hers. He expected a mild resistance—which he was fully prepared to overcome. What he didn't expect was for her to melt in his arms, to soften and wrap her arms around his neck, letting her sleek, elegant body mold itself against him. He was a bit shocked by his behavior, but passion was stronger than caution.

Heat and desire shot through his veins. He took the kiss deeper, his tongue thrusting and sliding across hers and feasted off her incredible soft, sweet mouth as one hand swept down her elegant back. Finally he lifted his head and swept his mouth across hers, intending to kiss her again.

"That's some hello," she said, but her voice trembled as much as she did in his arms.

He couldn't recall a woman being that shaken by a kiss, but staring down into Fallon's deep brown eyes, he had the feeling again that she was different—and therefore more dangerous to his peace of mind.

Still, his thumb traced over the dampness of her lower lip. Before now he would have thought himself a cautious man—life had made him that way. Yet—"I regretted I didn't kiss you last night."

"So did I," she admitted.

His head dipped. She pushed out of his arms. He let her go—for now.

"I'm leaving Sunday on the seven-thirty morning flight to Austin," she said, her voice steady, her gaze direct. "I don't do affairs."

He believed her. His bad luck with women was holding. After three years of going through the motions, he'd finally met a woman he'd like to get to know better out of bed and she wasn't available. "I wish you weren't a woman of principle."

She tilted her head to one side. "Which means you've been around the wrong type of women."

Since she was right, he didn't comment, just went to stand behind his desk. He needed to put some distance between them. "You're late."

"Naomi's coworkers gave her a surprise bridal shower after school. I went to pick up Kayla." Fallon grinned, quick and easy. "The principal was concerned that some of the gifts might be of the adult variety, and she was right. I'm here now."

"So you are." He took a seat and picked up his pen. "They're still doing inventory, but feel free to roam and take pictures."

Her eyes widened, her hand went to her chest.

He came out of his seat and crossed to her. "What is it?"

Her gaze went to him, then skittered away.

He'd seen that evasive look from women too many times in his life. He'd hoped never to see it again. He started for his desk. "I won't keep you."

"I was hurrying and forgot my camera," she said softly, but he heard and swung back around.

"At your apartment?"

Folding her arms, she looked out the window over his shoulder. "The car."

He stared at her. She'd been that anxious to see him?

"Don't get the big head," she told him, lowering her arms. "The house has a lot of appeal as well."

"Yes, it does." Not only could he get a big head, but he also could lose it over the woman with a half smile on alluring lips whom he was beginning to crave.

"I better get to it." She went to the door.

"Do you have any plans for dinner?" he asked, hoping to sound casual.

She wrinkled her pretty nose. "Two-day-old spaghetti."

"I think I can do better than that," he said.

"You cooking?" Folding her arms, she leaned against the door.

"Not one of my talents," he told her. "Fortunately, Carmen is an excellent cook, although I'm not sure what's on the menu tonight."

"I'm easy."

His brow lifted.

She flushed. "I meant—"

"Believe me, I know full well what you meant." The laugh just slipped out. It was rare to see a woman blush, even rarer to laugh in the company of one.

Eyes narrowed, she came away from the door. "You're laughing at me."

"It would seem." He pulled a folder closer to him. "Carmen prepares dinner for me before she leaves at six. Usually it's something I can reheat since I have a tendency to get buried in my work, so any time after six we can eat."

She returned to the door. "I can get involved as well. One or the other of us will come find the other if the other gets hungry."

"Ah, I think I understood that," he said, smiling. She really was fun.

She grinned. "Later."

The door closed and Lance stared after her, his smile slowly fading. Fallon Marshall was proving to be more than a pretty face and incredible body. He just hoped she was as open and as honest as she appeared.

Chapter 3

Fallon had told Lance the truth regarding becoming engrossed with work and forgetting the time. She thoroughly enjoyed the hunt, as she called ferreting out information and places that others might have missed or presenting them in a different way to people to give them an entirely new perspective. She wanted to do that now. Very much.

Lowering the camera, she stared down at the graceful lines of a Regency table crowded with delicate-colored crystal in various shapes in front of the window in the master bedroom suite. Thaddeus's daughter had collected crystal. Fallon's fingers traced the curves of the intertwined heart-shaped red crystal paperweight.

"First-anniversary present from her husband."

Fallon looked up to see Lance, arms folded, long jean-clad legs crossed as he leaned against the doorframe. She accepted that he'd always make her heart race. The man certainly packed a wallop. To give her heart time to calm, her body not to want what it couldn't have, she glanced back down. "They're beautiful and stunning."

She sensed rather than heard or saw him move. "According to her journal, she'd hoped her son's children would collect as well."

Sadness swamped Fallon. In spite of what had happened, her family still had one another to talk to, to be there for one another. "She and her father had so much hope for a legacy that will never happen."

Lance's wide-palmed hand gently swept down her arm in a comforting gesture—which surprised and pleased her. "Perhaps not her family, but another family. I'm selling the collection in one lot, so the chances of that happening are good."

Fallon frowned and picked up the paperweight. "I don't know about crystal, but since everything I've seen is of the highest quality I have to reason that this collection is also."

He nodded his dark head. "They are. Most are Baccarat like the one you're holding."

"Wouldn't your chance of selling all of them be better if they were sold separately?" she asked.

"Possibly, but they'll present better in a group." His hands slid into the pockets of his jeans. "Dinner is ready."

She didn't think that was his only reason, but she let it pass. She replaced the paperweight. "You help the house come alive for me. I—" Her eyes rounded as a thought struck.

Spinning sharply, she grabbed his arm, felt the warm muscles flex beneath her fingers, and tried to keep her mind on what she'd been about to say. "What if you put details about the furnishings on discreet cards? It would do the same for a lot of the buyers coming, and give people time to think about purchasing and starting their own tradition."

"It will be on the auctioneer notes."

She was shaking her head before he finished. "Some will buy on impulse, but others need time to think."

"Then they'll miss out." He took her arm and started from the room. "It's almost seven."

"If you had an open house—possibly invite the local historical society, prominent collectors, to get a nice buzz—it would be great."

Lance threw her a skeptical glance before starting down the stairs. "The auction is in less than two weeks."

"To get an unhurried view of this place, they'd clear their schedule if they had to." Fallon sniffed the air as they stepped off the last rung of the spiral stairs. "Something smells good."

"Roast chicken, garlic roasted potatoes, asparagus, yeast rolls." Lance led her through the kitchen with deep mahogany cabinetry and six-inch crown molding. At least he tried to.

"This is almost as big as my entire apartment." Fallon stopped and turned in a circle. "I love the contrast of the white window frames and curtains against the dark wood."

"The kitchen was modernized two years ago with Miele ovens, a Viking cooktop and grill, and Rohl sinks with Dornbracht fittings," he told her.

Fallon grinned. "Only the best."

"Exactly." Lance opened the back door and stepped onto the loggia.

"It's beautiful out here." Fallon followed him onto the vine-covered bricked area and admired the many potted plants in varied hues, the green lawn, and the deep blue waters of the rectangular pool a short distance away.

"Herbert did some updates like the kitchen and baths, but where he really shined was in his vision to turn the dry, unforgiving land around the house into a verdant garden." Lance pulled out a chair at a round rattan table with a glass top.

Fallon placed her camera on a low table nearby and took her seat in one of the rattan chairs. "Thank you." Once he was seated, she blessed their food and served them. "So what do you think of my idea?"

"It has merit."

Getting used to Lance's short or monosyllabic answers, Fallon plunged ahead. "I could help write them up. I think handwritten notes would be more personal, don't you?"

What he thought was that Fallon was proving to be as smart as she was stubborn, but then so was he. "Yes."

She wrinkled her nose and handed him his plate loaded with food. He noticed with pleasure that she had healthy portions on hers as well. She seemed to enjoy food. He could only wonder if she enjoyed more carnal appetites, since he was doomed never to know the answer.

"It's impolite to stare." Fallon cut into her chicken.

Since she had caught him, there was no sense

denying the fact or looking away. "I enjoy looking at beautiful things."

Her head came up sharply. Her eyes went dreamy; then she shook her head. "Stop that."

"I'm not sure I can," he admitted, then wanted to kick himself. Telling a woman that she had any kind of power over you was a recipe for disaster.

She sat back in her chair. "I can't figure you out. One moment you're all business, the next you're the flirtatious man I first met, then next you're somewhere in between. Which one is the real you?"

"Somewhere in between," he said. "How is the chicken?"

"Delicious, and you're evading. But since I'm hungry and this is your home—" She broke off.

"What is it this time?" he asked, getting used to her thoughts hopping from one subject to the other.

"This house. Usually no one lives on the estate in a case like this, yet here you are and the grounds are spectacular and the house is spotless." She laced her fingers together and propped her elbows on the table. "So, give. Who bought this house?"

Lance took another bite of his asparagus. "Smart, but perhaps the person wants to remain anonymous."

Fallon popped a potato cube into her mouth, chewed, and studied him. "Perhaps."

He didn't like the way she was scrutinizing him. As smart as she was, she might figure it out. For the time being, he didn't want anyone knowing he'd purchased the house. "How long does it usually take to write an article?"

She picked up her fork. "Depends on if I'm able to get reliable and full information."

His mouth twitched. So she knew he was trying to throw her off track. "I'm sure the piece will be excellent in any case."

"Like the Yateses, in my writing I don't settle for anything but the best."

He could see that. "Being the best requires a lot of skill, determination, and time. It doesn't leave room for much of anything else."

"No, it doesn't," she agreed. "I miss my family, but this is what I want to do—at least for now."

"And later you'll have that family you talked of," he said, annoyed at himself for the irritation in his voice.

She picked up her wineglass and stared over the rim. "A family is in the far distant future. I love what I'm doing, but if one day I wake up and can't stand the thought of getting on another airplane, renting another car, or writing another story, I'll quit and find something that does excite me. What about you?"

"Like the unfortunate heir to this place, everyone isn't meant to get married. I found his diary that will not go in the auction. He spent lavishly trying to buy happiness and wasted his life. He died a sad, lonely man. I'd like to think I'm smarter and face facts: marriage isn't for me," he told her. "I'm happy for Richard, but I've stopped looking."

"I'd say there's truth in the old saying 'until the right woman comes along,' but that isn't what I meant." She set the wineglass aside. "You've been able to move from one business venture to the next, each more successful than the last—is this, the auction house, what you've been searching for?"

He didn't know how to answer her question, and that irritated him. "I'm not searching for anything," he snapped.

Her brow lifted. "All right, but could you please send the charming Lance back? The night is beautiful and I'd like to take a walk, and if he doesn't return I'm not helping clear the table or wash the dishes."

"I'm perfectly capable of doing both," he told her.

"You probably are, but it will be quicker if we both do it, and I've never met a man who liked washing dishes." Standing, she picked up their plates and started for the kitchen.

Stacking the serving dishes, Lance slowly followed. Instead of leaving in a huff, she was helping. He was right. He'd never met a woman like her. He might be confusing her, but she was doing the same thing to him. "I was rude."

She took the service ware from him. "Yes, you were."

"But you didn't leave," he asked. "Why?"

"Because I misjudged you once and regretted it." Folding her arms, she leaned back against the countertop. "My natural curiosity is to ask questions, find answers. I forget that sometimes the answers aren't easy or pleasant." She straightened. "Please bring in the other things. I'll try to find a container for the chicken."

"On the countertop by the refrigerator," he said, then, "Unlike you, I haven't found anything that holds my attention for a long period of time."

"Yet you've been able to make a success of every business venture you've ever been in." She shook her head. "Lance Saxton, you're a remarkable businessman. If you ever find what you're passionate about, the world had better look out. Now, let's get this kitchen cleaned so we can take a walk."

He'd expected sympathy, not admiration. She'd taken him aback again.

"The table won't clear itself, Lance."

"Going." He was halfway out of the kitchen before he realized Fallon was giving him orders and he was carrying them out. He gave orders; he didn't take them unless they suited him.

In righteous indignation, he marched back toward the kitchen empty-handed, reached for the door, and stopped abruptly. His breath snagged. Through the glass door he saw Fallon bent from the waist holding the refrigerator door open, her hips swaying from side to side, causing the material of her Bermuda shorts to tighten and his body to harden. Faintly he heard her humming "Rio" by Duran Duran.

Need and desire pulsed through his veins. His breath shuddered out over his parted lips. When he could get his feet to move, he went to the table instead of to Fallon.

If it took taking orders to taste her again, to feel her soft and clinging in his arms, so be it. But before the night was over he was going to be doing some taking of his own.

* * *

Silently Fallon and Lance walked side by side on the meandering paved path on the grounds, their way lit by wrought-iron lanterns. "It's so quiet and peaceful here. It's almost as if we're the only people for miles."

"We practically are," he said. "The house is a mile from the highway and sits on four acres. Yates liked his peace."

Fallon's fingers fluttered though the leaves of a Japanese maple, one of several in large pots interspersed with boxwoods clipped into globes. "These might not make it though the winter."

"Then they'll be replaced."

Fallon stopped beneath a lantern to see his face. "I forgot: the rich don't think about money as much as the rest of us."

"You'd be surprised," he said, his hands sliding into the pockets of his jeans. "Once you have it, there is the matter of keeping and managing your assets."

"Assets. Most people have little or no acquaintance with the word," she told him, and continued back toward the house.

"You have something against people having money?"

"Of course not." She stepped onto the loggia. "Unfortunately, there are people out there who don't care if they have to cheat or use others to get that money."

"Like the man who cheated your mother."

"Sorry, you're nothing like him. It's just that the

incident creeps back at times." Impatiently she threaded her fingers through her thick, curly hair. "My parents loved working in the garden together. We had a potted Japanese maple by the front door they planted the year my younger sister, Megan, was born."

Taking Fallon's hand, Lance tugged her to a lounge chair. "What happened?"

"It's a long story."

"We have time."

She blew out a breath. "My father was a wonderful man. He loved his family and worked hard to own his own printing company. Six years later, he developed liver failure. He always thought he was infallible. He had insurance, but it wasn't enough. Medical bills quickly mounted. Medical tests and doctors' visits needed a co-pay up front." She moved her shoulders uneasily. "I was in my junior year of high school. My sister a freshman. We knew Daddy was sick, but not how serious until our parents told us they were going to sell the family antiques."

"They were trying to protect you."

"I know. I realized we must be in serious financial straits when I saw Dad with his baseball card collection that had once belonged to his grandfather." She swallowed. "All he wanted to do was provide for his family, and that was taken away from him."

"What happened?"

Her fingers intertwined with his, flexed. "Unfortunately, my mother signed a contract with an unscrupulous owner of an auction house. Instead of the fifty thousand dollars plus my parents were expecting, the check was for less than two thousand."

Lancer's face hardened. His arm went around her stiff shoulders.

"My mother had signed a contract to get forty percent of the sale price, and Charles East, the slime owner, was quick to show Mama what each item sold for at the auction," Fallon said, bitterness rolling off her tongue. "An eighteenth-century cabinet in mint condition sold for fifty dollars."

"He sent in a ringer and lowballed everything," Lance said.

Fallon's hand clenched and unclenched. "We didn't figure that out until later. The police couldn't do anything. In a month, he was gone. Two months later my father died thinking he'd failed his family."

Lance's arm tightened around her shoulders. "No wonder you wanted to take me on. I'm sorry."

"I'm the one who's sorry." She twisted her head to look at him. "You're nothing like the man who cheated us. It's just that losing Daddy was difficult enough without losing practically everything we had. I hope you understand."

"I do. My dad died in a construction accident when I was nine." Lance gazed out into the night. "I didn't want to believe it. He hadn't been gone an hour. We'd had breakfast together and talked about the softball game I was pitching in that afternoon."

"Sounds as if you had a great father as well," she said.

"I did," Lance said, facing her. "To me, he was

all the superheroes rolled into one. There wasn't anything he couldn't fix around the house or on a car. But I liked best the times we went fishing and hunting, just the two of us."

"For me and my sister, it was story time." Fallon smiled at the memory. "Daddy loved doing all the character voices and sounds. We always went to bed with laughter."

"Whatever the criminal took, he couldn't take your memories. Remember that and honor your father."

She nodded. "That's what my mother said. Above all, Daddy wanted us happy. He was so proud of his family."

"Did he know you wanted to be a travel writer?" Lance asked.

"He knew I wanted to be a journalist," Fallon told Lance. "But when we lost the house and had to move, I had to enroll in a different school and lost the scholarship I was counting on."

Lance cursed beneath his breath. "Your family went through a lot."

"'And survived,' my mother is proud of saying."

"She must be a very special woman."

"That she is. She's even found it in her heart to forgive the man who stole from us, but I'm not so forgiving," she said, anger creeping back into her voice.

"What did you say the name of the man was?"

"Charles East. Why?"

"He shouldn't have the opportunity to ruin another family's life," Lance answered.

He made the statement with such conviction she kissed him on the cheek, then got to her feet. "Thank you. Now I have to be going."

Still holding her hand, he came to his feet as well. "I don't suppose I can talk you into staying longer."

"Afraid not. Thanks for a wonderful dinner." She started for the table with her camera. "My notebook is on the table in the living room."

"Are you coming back tomorrow?" Lance asked.

"I promised Naomi to go with her to look for a wedding dress," Fallon told him. "I just hope we have better luck this time than we did looking for a dress for her the other time she wanted to look good for Richard."

Lance's hands bracketed Fallon's waist. "Since you always look good, that's a problem you'll never have."

"T-thank you." Her heart skittered. He was too close. His mouth too tempting. She'd wanted to kiss him again since that morning. The kiss they'd shared wasn't nearly enough.

"There are your eyes that grab a man, and lips that tempt and beckon." Lance's hand threaded though her hair, arching her mouth upward, taking it.

Fallon sighed at the first brush of his mouth, opening for him, giving him full access. He took his time, thoroughly ravishing her mouth, inciting her passion to get closer, to join in the mating of tongues.

When he lifted his head, his heart was pounding as fiercely as the blood rushing though his body. "I want you."

Fallon's eyes opened slowly. He glimpsed the desire even if he hadn't felt it in the trembling of her body. "I—I can't."

He could take the decision from her. He knew it as surely as he knew his name. The thought cooled his passion as nothing else could have. Women always had a choice with him. The thought of anyone, including himself, taking advantage of Fallon angered him.

But that didn't mean he was ready to release her. "It's not easy letting you go."

"For me, either, but I don't do this."

His arms tightened; then he stepped back. "I know. That's why I'm letting you go."

Her eyebrow lifted. "Pretty sure of yourself, aren't you."

"Yes, but if I pushed I'd lose so much more." He picked up her camera. "I saw your notebook on the chest in the great room. We can pick it up on the way out."

"Your hands aren't steady, Lance." She grinned. "I'd say you aren't the only one with a little power."

Lance followed her back inside to pick up her notebook, then out to her car. In spite of the need clawing though him, he liked that Fallon gave as good as she got. As soon as she unlocked her car he handed her the camera. "I'm following you back to your place. Give me a minute to drive my car around. No arguing."

"Who's arguing? I assume you plan to see me to my door and not just drive off once I get there."

"Of course. What kind of man would do that?"

"Plenty. Considering the benefits, I'll wait for you."

Would he ever get used to the way she talked? "What benefits?"

She grinned and got inside her car. "Kissed good night twice."

Fallon fully intended to get another good-night kiss until she pulled up in front of her apartment and saw the small group of people outside of Naomi's door. Fear kicked in until Fallon recognized Richard and his parents with Naomi and Kayla. Fallon's hands unclenched from the steering wheel. The last time people had been congregated in front of Naomi's door, she'd been kidnapped.

The parking gods were with Fallon and she parked only a few doors down. Getting out, she waited for Lance. Through the rearview mirror she'd seen him park a few spaces across from her.

"Looks like we're just in time." Catching her arm, he continued toward the group. Introductions were quickly exchanged.

"Aunt Gladys. Uncle Leo. It's so good to see you again." Lance hugged the petite gray-haired woman before reaching for the older gentleman, who was easily six feet tall. "It's good to see you."

"Lance, I'm so glad to see you," Richard's mother greeted him, her hand on Lance's arm. "We'd planned to come out tomorrow."

"You're looking good. Almost like old times." Mr. Youngblood patted his nephew on the back. "It's been a long time since the four of us were together."

Lance's smile slipped a bit. "Sorry I wasn't able to make it any of the times you invited me back."

"We understood." Mrs. Youngblood gently touched his cheek.

"Of course we did," Mr. Youngblood agreed. "You're here now at the best time and that's all that matters."

Mrs. Youngblood turned to her son, sniffed, then looked at Naomi and Kayla. "I can't believe Richard is getting married and I'm going to be a grandmother."

"And I get to call you Nana," five-year-old Kayla piped up with a wide grin.

Everyone laughed. "What about me?" Mr. Youngblood asked.

"Gramps," Kayla promptly answered. "And when school starts and they have grandparents' day, you get to come."

"We'll be there," Mrs. Youngblood assured the little girl.

Naomi sniffed. "I—I never dreamed. You—" She hugged Mrs. Youngblood. "It is as easy loving you as it is to love Richard."

Fallon blinked away tears, then glanced at Lance. His expression was closed, so she couldn't tell what he was thinking.

Richard threw his arms around the women embracing. "My two favorite women."

"Come on, Gladys, and let's get going," Mr. Youngblood said. He spoke to Lance. "We've been trying to leave for the past hour so Naomi can put Kayla to bed."

"I'm not sleepy," Kayla said with a shake of her head.

"You will be." Naomi turned in Richard's embrace and placed her hand on her daughter's shoulder. "Tomorrow we go shopping for my wedding dress."

"Whatever you select, you'll be beautiful," Richard said, kissing Naomi on the cheek. "So don't stress over it."

"Spoken like a man in love." Fallon grinned. "Always knew you were meant for each other."

"And you were so right." Naomi smiled up at Richard, then at his parents. "I'm glad we have you. My parents . . ." Her voice trailed off.

Mr. Youngblood caught Naomi's hand. "You make our son happy. We were beginning to think he'd never find that special someone."

"I was just waiting to find the best," Richard said.

Mrs. Youngblood spoke to Lance. "I wouldn't mind helping plan another wedding."

Lance started, "Marriage isn't for me."

Sadness touched Mrs. Youngblood's attractive face. "With everything within me, I hope you're wrong."

"Come on, Gladys. It's after nine. Night, everyone." Richard's father gently urged his wife toward a black pickup truck.

"Wait, honey," she said, then, "Lance, your mother isn't sure about coming. Perhaps you could call her. I'd like my only sister to be here."

"You have more influence over her than I do," Lance said, his words bitter.

"That's where you're wrong." Mrs. Youngblood touched his arm. "We'll talk. Good night. See you at ten, Naomi."

As the good-byes were exchanged, Fallon noticed Lance's stiff posture, his stoic expression. There was something going on between him and his mother.

"I'll see you to your door."

Fallon caught back a sigh on hearing the cool politeness in Lance's voice. He didn't even take her arm. Ignoring the frown on Naomi's face and the curious look on Richard's, Fallon went to her door and unlocked it. "Thanks for dinner." She wasn't going to waste her breath inviting Lance in. Out of the corner of her eye, she saw Richard, Kayla, and Naomi enter her apartment.

"Good night," Lance said with none of the warmth he'd shown earlier.

"Good night." Fallon went inside her apartment and closed the door softly behind her. Not only had she not gotten a good-night kiss, but she also wasn't sure if she hadn't just seen Lance for the last time.

Chapter 4

Lance didn't want to answer his ringing cell phone. He knew who was calling without looking at the readout. Parking his car in the three-car garage, he went inside the house to turn off all the lights and reset the alarm. He left though the back door. The ring came again.

He'd reprogrammed his cell phone to ring ten times before going into voice mail. With his new business he hadn't wanted to be out of touch with his employees or potential clients. *Probably two rings to go,* he reasoned. All he had to do was wait a few more seconds and he'd be off the hook . . . and up most of the night with a guilty conscience.

Taking a seat on the lounge chair he and Fallon had shared earlier, he answered his cell phone. Respect and love won out, as he knew it would. "I'm fine, Aunt Gladys."

"I'm not so sure about that," came his aunt's quick answer.

Lance blew out a breath. She always knew him better than anyone other than his father. Lance had mistakenly thought that person would be his mother.

"You and Irene need to stop dancing around each other and talk."

"Aunt Gladys, I don't—"

"She's my only sister and you're my only nephew," Mrs. Youngblood cut him off. "It hurts to see that you've grown so far apart since Luther died."

"Her doing, not mine." Too restless to sit, he came to his feet.

"Lance, honey. Marrying Jim didn't mean she loved your father any less."

Lance swallowed the anger. A month before his mother started seeing Jim Banks, she'd gotten rid of everything that had belonged to Lance's father, including the fishing gear and the comic books they'd begun to collect together. Two months later—a year after Lance's father died—she'd remarried. She'd acted as if Luther hadn't mattered, as if Lance didn't matter. That hurt. It still did.

"It's done and over."

"If that were the truth, you would have been home in the past five years more than a couple of times," Gladys reasoned. "She wouldn't be anxious about coming to the wedding."

He paced. "What do you want me to do? She wants nothing from me—not even a simple cell phone."

"Lance, she's retired now and stays at home. She doesn't need a cell phone to keep in touch with people. What she needs is her son's love."

"She has Jim," Lance shot back.

For long moments there was nothing but silence. His aunt was a loving woman with a tender heart who loved her family. She wanted them to be close, but it wasn't going to happen.

"Just call her. Please. For me. I want her here for Richard and Naomi's wedding," Gladys said, her voice unsteady. "Family comes first."

He opened his mouth to remind his aunt that to his mother it didn't, then decided it wouldn't do any good. His aunt tended to see the good in people. The one and only time she'd met Ashley in Atlanta Gladys had thought her "a wonderful young woman." To his undying regret, Ashley had fooled both of them.

"I'll think about it," he finally answered. It was the best he could do. Conversations between him and his mother were stilted and awkward, the visits more so. They didn't seem to have any common ground. She'd remarried when he was ten and proceeded to take her new husband's side in every argument until Lance felt like an outsider in his own home. The following summer, and every summer until he went to college, he spent with Richard and his parents in Santa Fe.

"The wedding is in less than six weeks," Gladys said with mild annoyance. "Richard wanted to get married right away, but luckily Naomi understood that his father and I wanted more of a celebration, since this is Richard's first, and it's necessary to give family and friends time to make arrangements to get here."

Lance and Gladys were back to his mother. Their family was small. His father had been an only child. Richard's father had a retired widowed sister in

Las Vegas. She had three children in the same city. Since they owned their own business, Lance didn't see a problem about them traveling or taking the Saturday off. "It's a short plane trip from Oklahoma to here."

"Then you'll call her?"

Lance looked up at the sky, then chuckled. "You're still as stubborn as they come."

"With my size, I've had to be," she said, and he heard the laughter in her voice. "Good night, Lance."

"Good night, Aunt Gladys." Lance disconnected the call and retook his seat to stare up at the faint stars sprinkled in the moonlit night. He supposed before too long, to make his aunt happy, he'd call his mother. As he'd told his aunt, he had no influence over Irene. Her decision rested on what her husband, Jim, wanted.

Girls, then women, Lance had discovered as he went from high school to college and then into the workforce, seldom considered him in their long-range plan or thinking. He was a disposable convenience. With Ashley, he thought he had finally met someone to whom he mattered. She had proved more deceitful than any woman before her and hurt him the deepest.

He wasn't going to go put himself at risk for that heartache ever again. He was alone and that was the way it was always going to be. Images of him and Fallon locked in a heated embrace flashed in his mind. They both knew whatever it was between them wasn't forever. She had her life; he had his. For him to forget was asking to be trampled beneath a woman's spike heel again.

Not in his lifetime.

Coming to his feet, Lance headed for the guest quarters and his solitary bed.

Fallon had a restless night. She'd dreamed of Lance. Not a passionate dream, but a disturbing one of him standing alone and lonely. She'd tried to go to him, but the more she strained against whatever force kept them apart, the farther away he seemed to be. She'd awakened with a headache, feeling blue. She might not want to have an affair with Lance, but she wanted to see him again.

Admitting to herself that that wasn't likely to happen until Richard and Naomi's wedding, Fallon got out of bed and got dressed. This was a big day for Naomi. No matter how miserable Fallon might feel on the inside, she wasn't going to let it show.

She was reaching for the door when someone knocked. Thinking it was an anxious Naomi, Fallon opened the door with a grin to find she was right.

"You're seven minutes early."

A bubbling Naomi grabbed Fallon's hand and pulled her out the door. "Mrs. Grayson and Catherine sent a limo to pick us up. Mrs. Youngblood is already inside."

Fallon had recently met Mrs. Ruth Grayson. She was president of the Women's League, a charitable organization that helped women in need. Naomi had once been one of those women and now volunteered. Mrs. Grayson's son Luke was married to Catherine Grayson, a noted author and child psychiatrist.

Catherine was a very close friend of Naomi and Kayla. Catherine had even made Kayla the main character of her book, *The Guardian*. It was at the celebration party of a successful book signing benefiting the Women's League that Fallon had met Lance, Ruth Grayson, and four of her five children, Luke, Morgan, Brandon, and Sierra, and their spouses.

When Fallon, Naomi, and Kayla arrived, Richard had been waiting at the valet stand at Brandon's wife Faith's family-owned hotel, *Casa de Serenidad*. Lance had been with his cousin. The attraction between Fallon and Lance had been immediate but, because of her accusation, had died a quick death.

"Come on, Fallon," Kayla cried, taking Fallon's hand. The little girl's other arm was wrapped around the waist of her teddy bear. "Teddy and I have never ridden in a limo before."

Adjusting her red leather cross-body bag, Fallon locked the door. "This is what I call doing it in style."

"I can't believe this. Mrs. Grayson and Catherine have been so wonderful already." Naomi pressed her hand to her chest. "They're meeting us for breakfast. The driver is taking us there.

"Well, let's not keep them waiting." Naomi hurried them to the limousine.

Fifteen minutes later they arrived at their destination, Santa Fe Municipal Airport. Fallon's mouth gaped when they were escorted on board the private Gulfstream belonging to Sierra's husband, Blade Navarone. Ruth Grayson, Catherine Grayson, and Ruth's daughter, Sierra Grayson Navarone, were already there.

"We wanted to help you find the perfect wedding dress," Ruth Grayson said. "Sierra had a few ideas. So we're taking a little trip to Los Angeles."

"And since Mrs. Grayson has had experience with five brides in the family, I accepted her help," Mrs. Youngblood told Naomi. "I hope you don't mind."

Naomi blinked back tears. "Mind?" She hugged each woman, leaving Catherine last. "You helped me to become the woman I always wanted to be; thank you."

"As I said, I might show you, but you had the courage to take your life back." Catherine smiled. "I'm proud of you."

"Fallon, I see you have your camera," Sierra said.

"I try never to leave home without it." Fallon lifted the Nikon, then glanced around. When she'd met Sierra and her billionaire real estate mogul husband, Blade Navarone, their bodyguard Rio had stopped Fallon from taking a photograph of them. Catherine's husband, Luke, explained it was a family outing, but looking into the unblinking gaze of Rio, Fallon hadn't been sure. "Is it all right if I take pictures?"

Ruth Grayson answered, "I'm sure Naomi would like photographs of the trip to share with Richard later."

"I would," Naomi agreed. "And perhaps you can get a travel story out of it."

Fallon had thought the same thing. Once again she looked at Sierra. It was up to her.

Sierra hooked her arm though her mother's. "As a businesswoman myself, I'm well aware of taking advantage of opportunities when they present themselves. I'm also aware that not everyone has integrity. Fortunately, you're not one of those people, so have at it."

Fallon quickly turned to snap a photograph of Naomi standing by Catherine and Mrs. Youngblood with Kayla. The next shot was of Sierra and Ruth. "You do know that a lot of media outlets will want the pictures of you, Sierra."

Sierra's eyes narrowed. "Because I'm Blade's wife. But one day they'll want mine because of what I've accomplished in real estate."

"I don't have a doubt that will happen." Fallon grinned. "In the meantime, you get to enjoy all the benefits of being married to Blade."

"That's a fact." Sierra grinned and slapped hands with Fallon. "Ladies, have a seat and I'll tell the pilot we can take off."

Naomi hesitated. "Sierra, there's something I have to tell you first. You might not want the plane to take off, but I can't put it off any longer."

"If it's about you not needing the house you put the contract on, I'd already figured that out." Sierra seated her mother, then sat next to her and fastened her seat belt. "With the wedding you and Richard won't have time to finish the remodeling—which is a good thing. The next buyer might not like your ideas."

Naomi frowned. "I don't understand."

"Richard already has a house and I don't see you two as wanting rental property, so you'll want to sell the house you were going to buy. I'm hoping you'll consider me to be your Realtor to sell it for you."

"Gladly. I can't think of anyone better." Naomi took her seat beside Kayla.

Sierra spoke to the flight attendant standing to one side. "Please tell Frank we're ready to leave. As soon as we level off, you can start serving breakfast."

"Yes, Mrs. Navarone," the young woman said, and left.

"Ladies," Sierra said. "Prepare yourself for a fantastic day."

Lance buried himself in work all the next day. He didn't want to think about missing Fallon or the eventual call he'd have to make to his mother. By six that night, he figured accomplishing one of the two wasn't bad. He'd had lots more practice shoving his mother to the back of his mind and none missing a woman who intrigued him, irritated him, and excited him as no woman before her had.

Lance rolled his shoulders more in irritation than to loosen the stiff muscles in his back and shoulders. He'd been meticulously going over the catalog entries for the past two hours. And no matter how many times he'd come to an item that he had shown Fallon and his traitorous mind pictured the wonder or the laughter on her beautiful face, he kept his eyes on the page.

He was not going to turn into one of those men who daydreamed about a woman. Especially a woman who would be gone from his life in a few days.

His cell phone rang twice. He let it ring for a third time before he glanced at the readout. He told himself he wasn't disappointed that it wasn't Fallon and answered, "Saxton speaking."

"Very distinguished and professional sounding," Richard said, laughter in every syllable.

"Practice," Lance said, and leaned back in his chair. "Naomi must be back." He assured himself he was not trying to find out if Fallon was home.

"Their plane is landing in twenty minutes."

Lance straightened. "Plane?"

"I couldn't believe it, either," Richard said. "Mama, Mrs. Grayson, Catherine, Sierra, and Fallon flew to Los Angeles. I'm sure they could have found a dress here instead of flying to California on Blade's private jet."

Lance whistled. "Your fiancée moves in some very high financial and social circles."

"Not exactly," Richard said. "She was blessed to befriend Catherine Grayson. I instigated her meeting Ruth Grayson. Since the Grayson family is so close, when one takes you under their wings the others do as well. But Naomi and Kayla are so wonderful and lovable, it's easy to see why people want to be there for them."

Lance's lips twitched. Richard was a goner and didn't seem to mind a bit. Lance hadn't found that lasting happiness, but he was happy for Richard and his soon-to-be family. "It's also easy to see you're a man deeply in love."

"And each time I see them I fall a little deeper," Richard agreed. "I'm heading to the airport instead of waiting for the limo to drop them off. I've already been instructed to wait in front so I won't see the dress."

"So you're just picking up Naomi and Kayla?" Lance rolled his eyes, aware he hadn't fooled Richard.

"Yep. That's the reason I called. Seems we—the men—were calling our women all day. The last time Naomi and I talked before the plane took off to return, she said only Fallon hadn't received a call."

Something twisted in Lance's chest. He knew what it was to be an outsider.

"At first the women made a game out of trying to decide who would call next—me, Daddy, Blade, or Luke—until Catherine noticed that Fallon wasn't as bubbly as she had been when Blade called next. It was only for a moment, but Catherine is good at reading people. Afterward, I was the only one allowed to call."

"Wait. Ruth Grayson is a widow, and from the way she almost teared up at the luncheon over her deceased husband I can't believe she's dating." He hoped not, at least. He wanted one woman to love her husband even after he was gone.

"No, just work. The president of the Board of Regents at St. John's, where she teaches. Blade's event director needed more information on a project scheduled at their castle in September. One of her students about the merits of a doctorate program he's interested in registering for."

Lance muttered beneath his breath. Learning what Mrs. Grayson's calls were about had probably made Fallon feel even more like the odd man out.

"I can give you Fallon's cell phone number or you can get your behind out here and meet her."

"She's leaving on Sunday." He mustn't forget that, no matter how much he wanted to.

"She's here now, and you have the financial means to go wherever she's traveling."

"I can't."

"Can't or won't? Seventeen minutes."

In spite of himself, Lance glanced at the crystal clock on his desk. "You know better than anyone why I don't want to become involved."

"I hurt and cried and cursed with you. I'll always remember the rainy night you called, the long plane ride to get to you," Richard said, his voice tight. "Don't punish yourself because of Ashley's selfishness. You deserve a life with a loving woman."

"Whoa." Lance stood. "We're just talking and

getting to know each other." He raked his hand over his head. "I've barely kissed the woman."

"Sometimes one kiss is all it takes," Richard said with conviction. "If you didn't think it could progress further, you wouldn't be so afraid of continuing to see her. Now get your butt out here. You don't want Fallon feeling as if no man cares about her."

Lord help him, he didn't. It was that he could never give her what she needed and deserved. "Maybe Catherine read Fallon wrong. You said it was only for a moment. She could have blown this whole thing out of proportion."

"Catherine Stewart Grayson has two Ph.D.'s and was up for the department chair of psychology at UCLA before deciding she'd much rather be married to Luke."

No help there, but Lance wasn't giving up. "People make mistakes. Things will even out once they land. You might be starry-eyed in love, but Luke's probably not coming and I'm sure Blade isn't."

"I saw Luke go into the terminal with Blade and Rio while we were talking, and before you ask, Daddy rode out here with me. Don't worry; he left to catch up with Luke and the others. Neither he nor Mama knows about Ashley. You gonna let her ruin your life or be the badass everyone thinks you are and go after what you want and are so afraid to have?"

"You're pushing it, Rich."

"'Cause I love you. So get out here or I'll be

forced to introduce Fallon to a man who'll appreciate her."

"No!" Lance snapped. There was a click and he saw "end" on the screen. His fingers tightened, his anger escalated. Richard had hung up on him. If Richard thought he could manipulate Lance into going to the airport, he was wrong.

Placing the phone aside instead of flinging it against the wall, Lance went back to the catalog, but this time he couldn't focus. Instead he saw Fallon with one of Richard's vet friends. The man was all teeth, leering at Fallon, his hands the size of dinner plates, ready to . . .

A possessive anger rushed though Lance. Standing, he reached for his phone and headed for his car. First he would see Fallon and make sure no other man touched her; then he would strangle Richard.

"Sierra, you lived up to your promise and more." Naomi hugged the other woman. "You made the day one I'll never forget."

"And you found the perfect dress." Sierra leaned closer and whispered, "One Richard can't wait to get you out of."

Naomi blushed, then turned to the other women. "Thank you all for being my friends, for sharing this day with me."

Fallon snapped the shot, sniffed. "You're going to be a beautiful bride, and thanks for not putting me in a yucky bridesmaid dress."

The words were barely out of her mouth before

a cell phone rang, quickly followed by two more, then a fourth. "Looks like your men are anxious to see you," she said with a real smile. She'd gotten over her initial spurt of melancholy of missing Lance and wishing they had more time.

"They probably want us to know they're here." Catherine, the matron of honor, picked up the wedding gown in the heavy plastic cover. "Naomi, Richard is waiting for you outside so he doesn't see the dress. You, Kayla, and Gladys go on."

"I'll help with the wedding dress." Fallon picked up the full skirt.

Naomi nibbled on her lower lip. "Perhaps I shouldn't have gotten one so elaborate."

"Nonsense," Mrs. Youngblood said. "You loved it the moment you saw it, and you looked beautiful in the ball gown. If you hadn't gotten it, you would have regretted it. Now let's go see that son and husband of mine."

Naomi took Mrs. Youngblood's hands. "Thank you for sharing your son with me and Kayla. We love him, too."

"And I get to call him Daddy once the minister says they're man and wife," Kayla interjected. "And we'll live in the same house and I can help him take care of the horses every day."

"Mrs. Navarone, Mr. Navarone asks if there is a problem," the hostess said, her lips twitching.

"Please lower the door," Sierra instructed, then turned to the two bodyguards who had stayed out of the main cabin until they landed. "Aaron, please take the gown from Catherine and Fallon and put it in the limousine. Paul, take Catherine's and Fallon's dresses, then come back for the other bags with Naomi's name and Fallon's name and instruct the driver to wait for Fallon. After he takes her home, he is to deliver everything else to Catherine's house."

Naomi's phone rang again. Catherine and Fallon urged her toward the door. "Go."

Hugging the woman, Naomi took Kayla's hand and went down the steps, her future mother-in-law following close behind. The two bodyguards followed with their second load.

Fallon picked up two bags. "I can help carry things out. Blade and the others are probably anxious to see you."

"No more than we are." Catherine picked up two bags.

"That's always nice to hear," Luke said.

"It certainly is," Blade agreed.

With squeals that would have done a high school girl proud at meeting her teen idol, Sierra and Catherine ran to embrace Blade and Luke. The kiss that followed was hot enough to singe asphalt. Fallon glanced at Mrs. Grayson to gauge her reaction and saw her smiling. Apparently she wasn't bothered any more than Rio, who wore his usual closed expression.

"Would all those be yours?" Blade asked, nodding toward the shopping bags and clothes in garment bags.

Sierra chuckled. "Mama and Catherine have a few things."

"Em-m-m." Blade reached for Fallon's bags. "You might need your hands free going down the stairs. After you."

Having a billionaire take her bags, especially one as gorgeous as Blade Navarone, momentarily caught Fallon off guard. Then she realized he probably wanted to rush her along so he and Sierra could go home to continue where they'd left off.

For the first time in a long time Fallon wished there was someone special in her own life. Images of Lance flashed in her mind. She firmly pushed them away. That wasn't likely to happen.

"Of course." She started out of the plane.

She wouldn't think about Lance. She'd seen the last of him. Head down, she grabbed the rail and went down the steps and walked into a solid wall of muscle. She opened her mouth to apologize and glanced up into Lance's intense black eyes. He held a red rose in front of him.

"I didn't know your cell phone number."

So she hadn't been as poker-faced as she'd thought about the men's frequent phone calls. She guessed it was probably Catherine who noticed. She'd probably called Luke, who had called Richard, who in turn had called Lance. It struck Fallon again how close they all were and how they looked after family and friends.

In her traveling so much, she'd missed making those deep, lasting friendships—until she had moved next door to Naomi. "Would you have called?"

"I'm not sure." He shifted. "I just know I had to see you again."

"Why?"

"To do this." He pulled her into his arms, his mouth finding hers.

She didn't do public displays of affection and was annoyed when seeing others kissing outside of airports. But protest or resistance never entered her mind. She simply melted.

Her arms went around his neck, drawing him closer, taking, giving. The last thing she recalled before her brain fuzzed was that Blade had been right: she did need both hands free.

Chapter 5

Lance gradually became aware of the noise surrounding him and lifted his head. The dazed look on Fallon's face, the desire in her eyes, almost had him pulling her back in his arms. "You make me forget."

Her eyes widened. He realized he'd spoken the words out loud. His mind sought a way to mitigate the damage he'd just done. Never let a woman know she had power over you. He knew that as well as his name.

"You seem to have the same effect on me." Her fingertips stroked his chest through his shirt. "I don't kiss in public."

His hands flexed on her arms. "I keep reminding myself you're leaving on Sunday."

"So do I."

He stared down at her. She up at him. Both knew their time was limited, but neither was walking away. He bent to pick up the rose he'd dropped and handed it to her.

"Thank you."

"Richard's idea," Lance felt compelled to say. "I always thought flowers were overdone."

"Since I love flowers, I'd have to disagree." She motioned toward the limo and the uniformed man standing by the driver's door. "He's waiting for me."

"Do you want to go someplace tonight?" Lance asked

"Are you asking me on a date?"

He frowned down at her. "I suppose I am."

"No." She started for the limo.

He was so stunned by her answer that she'd gotten several steps away before he caught up with her and took her arm. "No?"

"No," she repeated.

He wasn't going to ask again or even ask why. He was going to take himself back to the Yates house, because if he saw Richard now he might really strangle him.

"The driver is waiting."

"Why?" Lance bit out, annoyed at both of them. Not even his aunt was this stubborn.

Fallon's chin lifted. "Because of the way you asked, as if you're being forced to take me out. Is Richard behind that as well? Well, let me tell you, I'm not that hard up." She took off for the limo again.

He was quicker this time and caught her in a couple of steps. "Richard didn't tell me to take you out. But he was going to introduce you to some guy."

"So you're one of *those* men?"

"What?" Fallon could really give him a headache or a complex, perhaps both.

"You don't want me, but you don't want anyone else to have me, either," she snapped out.

He wanted her, but it was a close enough accusation to make him glance away.

This time he didn't catch her before she reached the car and got in. He considered reaching for the door, but then what? On the tarmac was no place to have a discussion. He watched the limo pull away, then turned and saw Blade, Sierra, Luke, Catherine, and Rio at the base of the stairs watching. Lance wasn't sure how much they'd heard, but from the displeased expression on the women's faces they weren't too thrilled with him.

Blade probably regretted getting him through Security. At least Luke looked sympathetic. Rio's face was unreadable. Lance continued inside the airport. He'd forgotten Ruth Grayson had been with the women until he saw her in the terminal. She headed straight for him.

"The things we often value the most are the things that take the greatest effort to obtain," she said. "You know that better than anyone."

He'd always been a private person. Now his friends seemed to know he couldn't keep a woman happy. Again.

Mrs. Grayson patted his arm in reassurance. "She kept the rose. I'd say, 'Good luck,' but some men make their own."

Lance stared after her as she walked away. He could have told her he wasn't giving up, but maybe she knew it already. He and Fallon weren't finished talking, and this time she was going to listen.

*   *   *

Fallon had calmed down considerably by the time the limo driver pulled up in front of her apartment. She knew Lance was leery about relationships. He'd made it no secret he wouldn't mind taking her to bed, but it ended there. It was her fault for thinking he might regret as much as she did that she was leaving in a couple of days.

Gathering the handled shopping bags, she stepped out when the driver opened the door. "Thank you. Please bring the dress."

"Certainly."

Moving ahead of the driver, Fallon went to her door. Setting the bags down, she inserted her key to open the door, then entered. "Please put the dress on the sofa." Placing her shopping bags on the other end of the sofa, she reached into her bag for a tip and heard the door close.

Her head came up. Instead of the driver, Lance stood there.

"I tipped the driver. Where do you want me to put this?"

"Anywhere, and then you can leave." Removing the straps of the camera and cross-body bag, she placed them on the sofa cushion. She knew he hadn't gone; she could sense him. And, heaven help her, she wanted him.

"Can we start over?"

Folding her arms, she turned and tried to look uninterested. No one had to tell her that Lance didn't run after women. He was too self-contained for that. "I can't think of one reason why."

Placing the dress carefully on the green floral sofa she detested, he came around the coffee table to stand in front of her. "I can."

"Lust isn't a basis for anything except misery and heartache."

Something flashed in his eyes; then it was gone. "I want to show you that I'm not the jerk you think I am."

"And why would you think I'd care to find out?"

"You still have the rose I gave you," he said. "You took it from the airport, and it wasn't in the limo. I checked when I passed."

She could have kicked herself. Even angry with him, she couldn't throw away the one and only thing he'd ever given her. "I said I liked flowers."

He shook his dark head. "You're too independent to want anything from a man you don't like."

He had a point. She stepped around him and opened the door. "Please leave."

"Shouldn't you put the rose in some water?"

"Maybe I'd get more enjoyment over watching it wither and die, sort of like whatever was going on between us."

He blinked. "Why don't you want to go out with me?"

Annoyed at him, she slammed the door shut. He had no right to look so . . . wounded.

"Is there someone else?"

Her head jerked up. "If there was, you wouldn't be standing here getting on my last nerve."

"Does that mean you aren't angry with me anymore?"

That she could answer. "Not by a long shot. You acted as if it were some sort of privilege to be asked out by you, and at the same time as if the request was dragged out of you. You can't make up your mind about me, and I don't have the time or patience to wait around until you do."

He looked shell-shocked. "Fal—"

She held up her hand. "Leave. I'm hoping you're enough of a gentleman to leave without me calling the police. You're not wanted here."

He stiffened. For a long moment he stared at her. "I apologize if my presence offends you."

The loneliness in his voice shouldn't pull at her. She'd caught enough of the conversation last night to know he and his mother didn't get along and that he hadn't seen his aunt and uncle in years despite obviously loving them. What had made him stay away from his family, to be so self-contained?

"You won't have to see me again."

All she had to do was keep quiet, but the results would hurt people she'd come to care about—including the infuriating but compelling man standing in front of her, his broad shoulders slumped, his eyes bleak.

"That's going to be tricky, since we're both in the wedding."

"I'll explain to Richard that I have business obligations. Good-bye." He started for the door.

"You can't hurt Richard and his family like that just because we can't get along," she protested. "Let's just pretend that this afternoon never happened, and each wish the other well."

"You were right about me earlier." He glanced over his shoulder. "I'm not sure what to do about you or how you make me feel."

"Who was she?"

His eyes widened in shock. He actually took a step backward.

"Studying people and trying to figure them out is a hobby. I'd say a successful man like you wouldn't be this conflicted if something major hadn't happened in the past to make you leery." She went to the first handled bag and pulled out the rose. He'd come a long way; perhaps he could go further. "I better get this in some water. While I'm doing that, you can figure out a nice way to ask me out or you can leave. Either way, you're staying in the wedding as a groomsman."

"I'm not going to talk about it."

Relieved, though her curiosity was not satisfied, Fallon pulled a pitcher from the cabinet and filled it with water. Despite everything, she was beginning to care about the stubborn, lonely man. He needed her, she thought, then rolled her eyes. She wasn't going to be one of those women who talked themselves into being some man's savior only to lose a part of themselves in the process.

"Your choice, but don't confuse me with her. Since I had trouble dealing with the past, as we both are aware, I'll cut you some slack." The silence was so oppressive that she half-expected him to be gone when she turned.

He stood by the front door as if he wasn't sure about staying. Placing the container on the coffee table in the living room, she picked up her rich chocolate-colored gown. "I need to hang this up."

"Fallon."

"Yes?" She paused, her expression cordial as she faced him.

He looked wary, as if he wasn't sure of himself. "I'd like to take you out tonight," he said, then added, "It would be a date."

"Any idea where we're going?"

"No, but if you say yes I'll figure it out by the time I pick you up," he told her, his body visibly relaxing.

She smiled to put him at ease. "Since I have to know how to dress, it would be a good idea to tell me before then."

Lance hadn't dated in years. Since he'd walked out on Ashley three years ago it wasn't difficult finding women who only wanted the same thing he did, sexual release without obligation. Once the encounter was over at her place, never his, they never saw each other again. Now, staring across the candlelit table for two, he readily admitted he'd like to see Fallon again.

She was breathtaking in a little black dress that made his blood heat and his heart pound. The five-inch heels caused her slim hips to sway enticingly and her sexy legs to appear incredible long. He could easily imagine them wrapped around his hips as he drove into her satin heat.

"Want some?"

"What?" He jerked upright.

Grinning, Fallon held out a spoonful of key lime pie. "You were staring."

Dessert wasn't what he wanted. "No, thank you. When you're finished, we can try out that nightclub I told you about."

Swallowing her last bite, she pushed the plate aside. "El Paradise. I heard about the place, but I spotlight places families can go to together."

He signaled the waiter for the check and paid the bill. "What about after the children have gone to bed?"

"Depends on if they're old enough to stay by themselves," she told him. "Some of the more exclusive hotels might have sitter arrangements in advance, but not the smaller ones. Besides, most parents want to know who is keeping their children."

Standing, he reached for her chair and took her arm. His mother hadn't cared that he spent summers elsewhere. "I suppose." He threaded their way through the elegant restaurant to the valet and handed the young attendant his ticket. In a matter of minutes he and Fallon were on their way to the nightclub.

"How are things shaping up for the auction?" she asked.

During dinner she'd regaled him with funny stories about her travel, as if both wanted to keep things light. "The last of the items were listed today. Tomorrow we'll double-check everything."

"Have you given any more thought to the personal notes with the auction pieces or the preview get-together?"

"Frankly, I haven't had time to think about either." Flicking his signal, he pulled up to the valet. Attendants were there immediately to assist them. Rounding the car, Lance took Fallon's arm and walked beneath the dark maroon awning.

"I don't hear any music." Fallon tilted her head to one side. "When I was in college the way to tell a good club was if the music slapped you in the face a block away. How about you?"

"I worked my way through college at the auction house I recently purchased. There wasn't much time to party."

She leaned into him. "Then we'll have to make up for lost time tonight."

A broad-shouldered man in a black suit opened the red door. The hard rock sounds of Van Halen blasted.

Lance covered one ear: Fallon laughed and quickened her steps. "Sounds as if the place is jumping."

"Perhaps we should find a quieter place."

"Not on your life." Grabbing his arms, she pulled him farther inside. Strobe lights bounced off the wall. On the floor couples danced and sang along with the music. There were two levels and the DJ on the third. "Quick. I see a table."

Lance let himself be pulled. He was enjoying watching the excitement in Fallon's face. The "table" was an eighteen-inch circle. Somehow they got the attention of a waitress and ordered drinks. Beside him, Fallon swayed to the pulsing beat of another song.

"Something tells me you're a good dancer."

"I can hold my own," she answered with a grin.

"Your drinks. Tonic water and a cosmopolitan."

Lance handed the waitress a large bill. "Thanks. Keep the change."

Fallon picked up her drink and sipped. "This brings back memories."

"Your college days were fun, then?"

"Yeah." She grinned. "You wouldn't believe some of the crazy things we did."

"Like what?" Lance reached for his tonic water.

"If I told you I'd have to kill you." She giggled. "We swore each other to secrecy. Oh!" She placed her glass on the table, took his, and did the same. She came to her feet, pulling him with her. "We *have* to dance to this song."

"We can't leave our drinks or the table unattended," he protested.

"With the large tip you gave the waitress she'll watch the table. Stop stalling and let's go bump hips."

Lance's eyes narrowed. Fallon rolled her eyes. "Not that way."

"Pity."

Fallon almost felt sorry for Lance. He had absolutely no rhythm dancing to the upbeat tempo. If the dance floor hadn't been so crowded she might have insisted they take their seats. Although she had to give him points for trying and not giving up.

"If I'm embarrassing you, we'll go to our table."

She danced to him, then away. "Everyone has to learn."

"Not in public." He did an awkward bounce from one foot to the other.

He was right. Aware that Lance didn't put himself out there, she realized he was making the effort for her. Her heart melted a little bit more. When the song ended and flowed into the slow tempo of an old Teddy Pendergrass tune she walked into Lance's arms.

"This I can do, and more like it."

Fallon had to agree as he held her. She placed her head on his chest and listened to the erratic beat of his heart and just enjoyed the tender way he held her, the easy movements of his body. "I'd say you've done this a few times."

"Mrs. Hendricks liked to dance."

Her head lifted. "What about Mr. Hendricks?"

The corners of Lance's mouth curved upward. "He's a worse dancer than I am, believe it or not. On Sunday afternoons, when there were no auctions, I'd go over for dinner at their house. Sometimes we'd play dominoes or cards, but the evening always ended with dancing."

"That sounds nice."

"It was, although at first I resisted. But after a couple of months, she wore me down," he told Fallon.

"How?"

"She said that I was her last chance for a dance partner," he recalled. "She was in her sixties and as kind as she could be. I realized it was something I could do to make her happy after everything she and her husband had done for me."

"You really are a nice guy."

He pulled her closer instead of answering. Fallon almost sighed. He didn't take compliments any better than he answered questions about himself. Questions swirled in her mind that she knew would go unanswered if she asked them. Perhaps he was giving all he could. If she wanted to get to know him better, and she did, she had to accept that there were details of his past that were off-limits. To a curious person like her, that wasn't easy, especially since she was beginning to care about him.

"You go to sleep on me?"

Her head lifted. Even in the darkened club she could feel the intensity of his hungry eyes on her, beckoning her just as much as the heat of his body, the strength of his arms. "Not a chance."

The music stopped, and another song began to play. The tempo was slow enough for Lance, but he continued to stare down at her. "You ready to go or you want another drink?"

Fallon shivered. She'd debated all evening whether she should ask Lance inside her apartment when he took her home. Each time he kissed her it was harder and harder to pull back, and with each kiss she wanted more.

"Fallon?" Her name was a husky whisper on his lips.

"Let's go."

* * *

Opening her apartment door, she stepped inside almost hoping he'd take the decision from her. Although he hadn't moved, she could tell he was as tense as she was. "Do you want to come in?"

He stepped inside, closing the door behind him. She hadn't moved away, and with his incredible sexy body so close, she didn't want to.

"Would you like something to drink?" Her voice sounded thready.

"I think we both know what I want." He wrapped his arms around her. "Let's see how close we can go to the edge without going over."

"Let's."

His mouth took hers, the heat building slowly. He wrapped his arms around her waist, holding her slim body to his as his mouth devoured hers. His hand swept over her hips, pressing her against his hard arousal. She moaned into his mouth, her arms tightening around his neck. Finally, he lifted his head, his breathing as labored as hers.

"Tomorrow is your last day here." He brushed his hand tenderly over her cheek. "You want to go someplace?"

"I promised Kayla I'd take her to the carnival tomorrow afternoon. She let it slip that Naomi is planning a going-away dinner."

"So how about breakfast at the Yates house and afterward you can see how things are shaping up for the auction?" he asked.

"I'd like that."

"Nine all right?"

"Perfect."

He wasn't ready to say good-bye. Business always came first. He needed to call a couple of buyers, go over all the plans to ensure everything was on target. "Do you mind if I join you and Kayla?"

"I don't mind at all. In fact, I'd like that a lot."

Lance had never been around small children and wasn't sure how he'd get along with Kayla or she with him. Ten minutes after meeting the energetic Kayla, he'd ceased worrying. She'd promptly said he was going to be her cousin and gave him a hug.

"Let's go have fun," Fallon said.

He'd planned for her and Kayla to enjoy themselves, but it was a shocker to him that he did as well. They ate their way through the high-caloric foods with gusto and grins. One unexpected delight was the kiss tasting of cotton candy Fallon gave him after he tried and failed to win her a stuffed animal.

"I couldn't lug it on the plane with me anyway," she said to console him. "And Kayla already has Teddy."

"I wanted to win one for you," he said, still not appeased. He should have been able to knock the bowling pins down. Although he hadn't pitched in Little League since after he'd lost his father, Lance had been a pretty decent pitcher.

"I have something better for both of us." That was when she'd kissed him.

There was applause and "Go, man," from those

standing around them and giggles from Kayla, who'd wrapped her arms around both of their legs. "Dr. Richard and Mama do that a lot."

Releasing Fallon, Lance had picked the child up. "That's because they're in love and happy."

The words were barely out of his mouth before he realized his blunder. Fallon made him happy, but they weren't in love. He didn't want to love any woman.

"What do you say, Kayla, we ride the train next?" Fallon asked.

Lance thought her voice sounded the same, and when he placed Kayla on her feet and looked at Fallon she met his gaze with her usual smile. That smile should have reassured him and let him off the hook, yet somehow it didn't. Continuing down the midway, he wondered why and didn't have an answer.

Chapter 6

Fallon was getting in over her head, but like a ball rolling down a mountain, she couldn't stop her growing feelings for Lance. She'd tried, but her heart wasn't listening. She'd seen the shocked way he'd reacted after telling Kayla that Richard and Naomi were in love and happy. Lance hadn't wanted Fallon to draw the wrong conclusion about their kiss. They were two free consenting adults enjoying each other for the little time they had.

Only she wanted more.

"Fallon, what have you done?" she asked herself that night at her apartment as she gazed into the bathroom mirror. She didn't have an answer. Flipping the lights off, she went into the living room to get her key and camera. Naomi had just called and said to come over for a "quiet" dinner. Fallon hadn't told her that she knew about the surprise going-away party. Lance would probably be there; thus she was wearing the stretch magenta-colored dress she'd purchased on the Los Angeles trip.

Leaving her apartment, she went next door and knocked. Kayla opened the door. Standing behind

her was Naomi. When they moved, Fallon saw
Lance. Her heart lurched; her body yearned. His
eyes narrowed and she knew he felt the same way.
But all they had was tonight.

With an effort, she made her gaze move and saw
Ruth Grayson; Catherine and her husband, Luke;
Richard and his parents; and Sierra with Blade and
Rio. Fallon's gaze widened in surprised delight.

"Happy going-away party!" Kayla yelled, blowing the paper horn in her hand.

Fallon hadn't expected so many people. Laughing at her stunned expression, Naomi pulled her
inside and closed the door. The furniture had been
pushed to one side and replaced with card tables
and chairs. Sitting on each table was an arrange-
ment of white gardenias on top of a miniature world
globe.

"I'm going to miss you so much," Naomi said,
dabbing her eyes with a crumpled tissue.

"Me, too." Fallon brushed a knuckle beneath
her eyes.

"Here." Lance handed Fallon his handkerchief.

"Thank you." Fallon dabbed both eyes. "I said I
wouldn't cry."

Richard curved his arm around Naomi's slim
waist. "Brandon volunteered to do the food
since Naomi tears up every time she thinks of
you leaving."

"He said to tell you don't forget you have a standing invitation to the Red Cactus and you never
have to wait for a table," Luke told her.

"I won't." Fallon faced Sierra. "I have another

family member to thank as well. Three magazines—one of them *Luxe Lifestyles*—have asked me to do an in-depth article on great escapes for the rich and famous after seeing the pictures of Naomi's shopping trip for her wedding dress."

"Like I said, we have to take advantage of opportunities that present themselves." Sierra's gaze moved to Lance. "I think you know how to do that."

Once, but Fallon wasn't so sure anymore. Caring for Lance could lead to heartaches, but as she met his stare and felt frissons of heat race through her she knew it could also bring an immense amount of pleasure.

The party was lively and fun. Recounting the fun trip to Los Angeles helped keep Fallon's mind off leaving early the next morning. However, when everyone left except Richard and Lance and it was time to say good-bye, neither she nor Naomi could hold back the tears.

"You'll see each other in five weeks at the wedding," Richard reminded them.

"But then she'll leave, and I won't see her again." Naomi sniffed.

"Yes, you will," Fallon corrected, taking her friend's hands. "I'm not going to lose touch with you. Austin isn't that far and I might decide to do a follow-up story on Santa Fe."

"And I get to help again." Kayla jumped with happiness.

Brushing away tears, Fallon leaned down until her and Kayla's faces were inches apart. "I can't do a story without my research assistant. Now, give me a big hug."

Fallon held the small child close, felt the tears coming again, and straightened. "Good night, and thanks for the wonderful party."

"Thank you for being my friend when I needed one the most." Naomi hugged her again, then stepped back. "Safe travel."

Brushing away another tear, Fallon went out the door Lance was holding open, and then they went to her apartment. "Thanks for coming."

"I have something for you. I'll be right back."

Not giving her time to answer, he went to his car and quickly returned with a box beautifully wrapped with glossy yellow paper and white organza ribbon. "I hope you like it."

She hadn't expected anything. Her hands trembled. "You didn't have to."

"Yes, I did. Open it." He shifted nervously as he stared down at the square box in her hands.

Entering her apartment, Fallon took a seat on the sofa. Her hands trembled as she untied the bow.

"Why don't you just tear into it?"

She was going to savor every second with him. "Mama said a lady should take as much time unwrapping a present as it did to wrap it to show appreciation for the thought that went into the gift." Fallon pulled back the bright yellow paper and lifted the white box top. A soft gasp slipped past her lips.

She looked at Lance, then back at the red crystal heart paperweight. "It's part of the Yates crystal glass collection. It's the one I admired."

He reached over and lifted the paperweight. "I want you to have it."

"It's part of the collection," she repeated. "It's Baccarat. You're selling it as a group."

His hands didn't waver. "It will mean more to you."

Tears sparkled in her eyes as she took the paperweight in her hands. "Thank you, Lance."

His thumb brushed the tears from her eyes. "None of that."

She blinked her eyes rapidly and felt more tears forming. "Sorry. I'm usually not so mushy."

"That's all right. I've had some rough moments myself," he told her.

"I'm coming back for the wedding," she said.

"Five weeks is a long time," he said.

"I know," she whispered.

"You're beautiful and tempting. A dangerous combination." He came to his feet and went to the door.

"You're leaving?" She couldn't keep the disappointment out of her voice.

"It's best." His knuckles grazed her cheek. "If I stay, I'll kiss you, and I'm not sure I'll be able to let you go until the morning, and I'm not sure I'll be able to even then. So close the door, sunshine, and be happy."

Fighting tears, Fallon closed the door.

In the past, Fallon always looked forward to going home, catching up on things with her mother and sister, just relaxing. Usually she couldn't wait. Now, in the taxi heading for her mother's house, Fallon fought tears and misery. She missed Lance so much she ached.

The cab pulled up in front of the single-story brick home she and her sister, Megan, had been able to buy their mother when the real estate market had gone south a few years back. In the past year the housing market in Austin had rebounded strongly, and the house now was worth a lot more than the original price.

After paying the driver, Fallon picked up her suitcase and carry-on. She'd already shipped everything else home. Her steps slow, she went up the short walk overflowing with wood ferns, African daisies, and moss roses, one of her mother's favorite summer flowers. Thoughts of roses had Fallon stopping in her tracks. Tears crested on her lashes.

"Fallon."

When she saw her mother the tears flowed faster. "Mama."

Fallon's mother was out the front door and down the steps in seconds. "Honey, what's the matter?"

The luggage fell from her hands. Fallon wrapped her arms around her mother and just held on. "Mama."

"Honey, you're scaring me. Please tell me what's the matter."

Trying to stop the tears, Fallon lifted her head. "I care deeply for a man and he's too afraid to give us a chance."

"Well, he's a fool, and I'd say you were better off

without him, but obviously you aren't ready to hear that." Her mother picked up the weekender. "Come inside and we can talk."

Fallon picked up the rest of her things and followed. They could talk, but it would solve nothing. Lance's past was the issue, and until he could put it behind him he and Fallon didn't have a future.

Lance had a restless night and was up when Fallon's plane took off early Sunday morning. He'd actually walked outside and looked up at the clear blue sky. He could admit to himself in the stillness of the morning that she had come to mean more to him than he felt comfortable with.

He couldn't clearly define how she fit in his life or even if she should. He only knew that he had enjoyed being with her and that her departure left him feeling on edge and restless. One thing he wouldn't admit to was feeling lonely. He didn't need a woman to make his life complete. Returning inside, he'd gone to his office to work.

Now, hours later, he found himself in the guest bedroom staring at the glass collection. He would have bet any amount of money that he wasn't the sentimental type, yet he'd paid three thousand dollars over the appraised price for the collection. He wasn't even sure why. In all things, he thought, he was practical. He had no use for the crystal.

Leaving the room, he went back to his office. The auction was in less than a week. Making sure it was a success should be his sole focus, yet somehow Fallon kept slipping into his consciousness.

Perhaps it was because it was so easy to recall her vibrant presence here and in every room of the house. She'd wanted the auction to succeed and helped him to ensure that it did—asking nothing in return, even at times ignoring his brusqueness. He knew he wasn't the easiest person to get along with.

Yet she had stuck. For a little while at least, he had been enough. But would she have remained or would she, like those before her, one day leave because he couldn't give them what they needed due to his inadequacies?

He picked up the landline phone and dialed a number he hadn't called in over a year. If not for his aunt, he would have gladly waited another year.

"Hello."

At the sound of his mother's voice, Lance was hurtled back to the young boy who had wanted his mother's love and support after the death of his father, but she had chosen a stranger instead.

"Hello? Is someone there?"

"It's Lance."

Now his mother was the one silent for a long moment. "Gladys said you would call."

No pleasant greeting, no warmth, just cold duty. "Aunt Gladys wants you here for the wedding. Richard is marrying a sweet woman with a little girl."

"Are you seeing anyone special?"

He frowned, surprised by the personal question. They didn't do personal. "No." Whatever was going on between him and Fallon, it wouldn't last and it certainly wouldn't end at the altar. "You can fly to Dallas, then take a direct flight to Santa Fe, or drive."

"I'll tell Jim."

Jim. Always the man she'd married. She acted as if she couldn't make a decision without him. Lance would have thought her abused, but she wasn't. *You do that,* he almost snapped. "Aunt Gladys wants you to come. Call her when you decide. Bye."

"Good-bye, Lance."

He hung up the phone and sat there for a moment staring at it. Was he mistaken or was there something different in his mother's voice? She'd sounded . . . despondent. In the past, her response to him had been as even as his own. Could she be ill?

He reached for the phone to call back, even punched in the area code, before hanging up. He wasn't sure she'd tell him if he asked, which was a pretty clear indication of their poor relationship. He picked up the phone again. This time he completed the call.

"Hello," answered his aunt on the third ring.

"Hello, Aunt Gladys. I just got off the phone with my mother. She didn't sound like her usual self."

"I wondered if I had imagined it."

His brows bunched. "Imagined what?"

"I was so excited when I called to tell her about Richard getting married. She sounded happy; then I mentioned you were in the wedding and back in

Santa Fe. I could tell she was surprised. You hadn't told her you were here, had you?"

"She has my phone number," he replied. His mother could just as well call him.

"Lan-n-c-ce," his aunt said, drawing out his name. Clearly she hadn't liked his reply. "I think she finally realizes that sometimes in life you don't get a second chance. She regrets that you're not close."

He refused to believe that. "You're mistaken. Jim is what she wants. She can't have a conversation without mentioning his name."

"You might not like Jim, but he's a good husband to your mother," Gladys said. "I admit he was too strict with you, but you never wanted him married to your mother and you let him and everyone else know it."

"He wasn't my father."

"And you never let Jim or Irene forget," Gladys said gently. "You were too young to understand things between a man and a woman, and she didn't know how to reach you."

"I understood that in less than a year she had forgotten about her husband and started seeing other men."

"I don't believe she had forgotten," Lance's aunt replied quietly. "I'm telling you this in hopes you'll try to understand now that you've been in a relationship yourself. Your mother wasn't over your father. She was grieving. She tried to fill the void. She loved your father and you. His sudden death devastated her. Sometimes people make decisions they regret and have to live with the consequences."

Lance had difficulty taking it all in. "Are you saying she doesn't love Jim?"

"Only your mother knows how she feels," Lance's aunt said. "I do know she asks about you every time we talk, asks how I think you're doing. But since you haven't been around since you broke up with Ashley, I couldn't tell her much."

A pain he didn't want to remember shot through him. He'd buried himself in work so he could forget. He hadn't wanted to be around anyone he knew because they would have known something was wrong. To prevent that, he'd stayed away the past three years. He hadn't thought how his absence would affect them. "You know I love you and Uncle Leo."

"Yes, we do. But what about your mother?"

It was a loaded question, and one he wasn't sure how to answer. "She hasn't shown that it matters how I feel about her."

"If you looked past your own anger and pain, I think you'd see that she has."

His aunt was wrong and he was tired of talking about it. "I asked her to call you with her decision."

"She would have liked it better if you had said to call you."

Again his aunt was wrong. "I have to go."

"One day you'll stop running. I just hope, when you do, it's not too late. Good-bye, honey."

"Good-bye." Lance hung up the phone. He wasn't running from anything. He just saw no reason to give people another chance to shaft him. Besides, he had enough on his mind at the moment.

He'd decided to do the open house as Fallon had suggested. It would take a lot of additional work and be time-consuming, and that was exactly what he needed at the moment. He hoped it would keep her off his mind.

Somehow he seriously doubted it, but he was willing to give it a shot.

Fallon was in the cheery red-and-white kitchen with her mother when her sister came home from her job as a paralegal. Two years younger and two inches taller, Megan was model-thin gorgeous. She turned heads wherever she went. Fallon was out of her seat and around the table in seconds to give her sister a hug.

"Hi, Megan. Dinner will be ready shortly," her mother said. "You have time to go wash up and change."

"Sounds good, since I worked though lunch again today." Megan wrinkled her pert nose. "If Gordon Russell wasn't such a brilliant lawyer and didn't work just as hard as he demands of others, I'd find another job."

"And it doesn't hurt that he's easy on the eye." Fallon grinned.

"Believe me, that pales after three years and often twelve-hour days." Megan grabbed a bottle of water from the refrigerator. "If I hadn't told him you were arriving today, I'd still be at work."

"Last night she didn't get home until after seven." Her mother opened the stove and pulled out the roast she'd prepared. "Dinner on the table in five minutes."

Megan grabbed her sister's arm. "Keep me company while I change."

In Megan's room, Fallon sat on the bed. "You look good."

Megan's dark brown eyes narrowed. "Unfortunately, I can't say the same about you. Your eyes are red and you have circles under them."

Fallon tried to bluff. "Long hours and the dry air in Santa Fe."

"Somehow, I don't think so." Taking off her ecru-colored suit, Megan hung it up on a padded hanger, then pulled on a pink strapless sundress and sat beside Fallon. "You know how Mama hates to hold dinner, so spill. Who or what has you upset?"

Since Megan could be as persistent as Fallon when she wanted something, Fallon told her, "I met a man, and it didn't turn out the way I wanted."

Megan, always protective despite being younger, hugged Fallon again. "Tell me where to find the scumbag. I know people."

Fallon almost laughed. Megan made friends as easily as she breathed, and since she worked for one of the top criminal defense lawyers in the state, some of the people she encountered had less than savory reputations. "Thanks, but it's my fault. I knew from the beginning he wasn't into a long-term relationship. I told myself I could handle things." She shrugged. "Guess I was wrong."

"Any chance he's as unhappy as you are?" Megan asked.

"I'd like to think so, but it won't make any difference. Lance Saxton is a very self-contained man."

"Dinner is ready, girls," their mother called from the kitchen.

"We're coming, Mama." Megan stood, pulling Fallon with her. "After dinner we'll have a long talk, and if he hasn't called by the time we've finished we'll download a picture of him and use it for dart practice."

"It's not his fault," Fallon insisted. For some odd reason she didn't want her family to think badly of Lance.

Megan grunted and turned Fallon to face her. "Almost every day I hear someone say it wasn't his or her fault. Gordon always reminds them of one thing: you can have the best of intentions, but only the end result matters."

"Gordon sounds as pragmatic as Lance." Fallon wrapped her arms around her waist. "They might have liked each other."

With a frown on her pretty face and worry in her eyes, their mother appeared in the door. "You need to eat, Fallon. You'll feel better."

Megan glanced between the two women. "So Mama knows."

"I cried all over her when I got home," Fallon

confessed. "I'm sorry I put such a damper on the evening."

"You've done no such thing," her mother said, "I'm glad you're home. If he can't see what a wonderful woman you are, then he doesn't deserve you."

"Mama's right. He'd better come through or he might not like the consequences. The Marshall women aren't to be trifled with."

That was the problem, Fallon thought: Lance was of the same opinion.

The open house Thursday night was wildly successful, just as Fallon had predicted. Shortly after ten, Lance waved the last guest good night and went back inside the house. The members of the Santa Fe Historical Society were appreciative of a first look before the auction, and the independent buyers were glad to see the items in person. He'd made sure the pictures in the brochures were top quality, but they had only one view. There was nothing like seeing the pieces for yourself.

Fallon had also been right about the personal notes. A couple of the women had actually become emotional on reading them.

And she wouldn't be back for weeks.

Going inside, Lance went to his office and took a seat behind his desk. He wasn't as bad as Richard about crossing off the days, but he was probably close. He glanced at the clock on his desk. Ten thirteen.

He hadn't called Fallon since she left, but neither had she called him. She wouldn't run after any man, but all he had to do was remember the hunger he'd seen in her eyes in her apartment the night before she left to know she wanted him almost as much as he wanted her.

Yet if that was the case, why hadn't she called? Calling her would give her the upper hand. Women. They created upheaval and uncertainty in a man's life just by breathing. He should just try to forget her.

He gave it his best shot for the next nine minutes by going over the program for the auction before giving up. He'd created the program, had worked with the printer every step of the way; however, he couldn't recall a thing he'd read. Annoyed at Fallon and his own weakness, he reached for the cell phone in his pocket and punched in the phone number he'd memorized.

"Hello."

He frowned. It was a woman, but not Fallon. Fallon's voice was bedroom husky. He shifted in his seat and forbade his mind from going there. In the background, he heard loud music. "I'm sorry; I must have misdialed."

"Were you looking for Fallon?"

"Yes." He didn't know if he should be concerned or not. "Is she available?"

"Who's asking?"

He stiffened. "I might ask the same question."

"Since I know where Fallon is and I have her phone, I believe I win this pissing contest."

"Lance Saxton," he bit out, his irritation growing at the woman's rudeness.

There was a long pause. "You took your sweet time calling. I should hang up this phone. My sister doesn't deserve to be treated like this," she flared, her voice rising.

Sister. He recalled her name was Megan. It appeared she was as outspoken and as no-nonsense as Fallon. Telling Megan to mind her own business ran through Lance's mind before he realized that if she decided to "lose" the phone he'd have no way of contacting Fallon. "I'm calling now. I'd like to speak to Fallon, please."

"Too little, too late," Megan said with entirely too much satisfaction. "We're out partying. Fallon has been on the dance floor since we arrived. She has her pick of guys to take her home. She is having the time of her life and she doesn't—"

He heard a thunk, indistinguishable female voices.

"Lance, is that you?"

He should hang up. But she'd still know he'd called. He had his pride. "I didn't mean to disturb you. I just wanted you to know that your idea of having a preview was spot-on. The last guest left a short time ago."

"I'm glad."

Did her voice lack the excitement he'd heard earlier when she answered the phone? "I won't keep you. I hear the music. You're probably anxious to get back on the dance floor."

"Dance floor? Why would you think that?"

"Your sister. After she told me off, she said you

were out partying and had your choice of men to take you home," he said, trying to keep the annoyance out of his voice. It hadn't taken her long to forget him, and he couldn't stop thinking about her.

"And you believed that I was out partying and picking up men?" She sounded hurt.

There was only one damning answer. "Yes."

"Well, I'm not."

Now she sounded pissed. He had to talk fast or she might hang up on him. "It's your sister's fault. She misled me on purpose." He didn't have any problem throwing Megan under the bus.

"I'll take care of her," Fallon said. "Why did you call?"

Lance knew he had to talk quick and make it good. "I wanted to invite you to the auction tomorrow. I thought it might be a good follow-up piece for your story."

"Is that the only reason?"

Fallon never took things at face value. "I'd like to see you."

"Then it's a good thing I'd like to see you, too."

He finally relaxed. "I'll pay for your ticket and pick you up at the airport," he said. "The guest cottage has two bedrooms." He hoped the last came out casual.

"I can take care of my own travel arrangements and get myself to the auction. You'll be busy tomorrow."

"I can arrange for a car to pick you up and I insist on taking care of the ticket as well," he said. "I would have purchased the ticket already, but I wanted to ask you first. I did reserve you a seat."

"Totally acceptable. You're learning." There was laughter in her voice.

"I'm doing my best," he said, finding that he was smiling as well. "Call when you have things confirmed."

"I will. Thanks."

"I'll wait for your call. Bye." A huge smile on his face, Lance hung up the phone. He had another chance with Fallon, and this time he was making it count.

Chapter 7

Friday afternoon, a long line of cars, trucks, and SUVs were parked on one side of the mile-long driveway leading to the Yates house. Wisely, Lance had hired policemen to ensure traffic control. Once the limo driver Lance had sent spoke with Security, the driver was waved on. Fallon had accepted the car service because she didn't need a rental. Scooting forward in her seat, Fallon saw a huge white tent that obscured the front of the house. People spilled out from all sides.

As they neared, another policeman approached the car and directed the driver where to park. When Fallon got out she noted that there were no other cars, only four golf carts with young men dressed in white polo shirts and black pants, each standing by a cart. Apparently they were there to take people to and from their vehicles.

She strained her neck to see Lance and couldn't. Over the loudspeaker she heard the auctioneer call up the Regency table that held the glass collection from the master bedroom. She wondered if the collection had sold.

"Ms. Marshall?"

Fallon turned to see an attractive middle-aged woman in a black dress with a good-looking young man beside her. "Yes?"

"I'm Carmen, Mr. Saxton's housekeeper and cook. This is my son, Oskar. He'll take your bags and show you to the guest cottage," she said.

Fallon hoped she didn't blush. "I'm not sure I'm staying here."

The dark-haired woman smiled in reassurance. "Mr. Saxton said you might not stay, but he thought you might want to freshen up and have a quick bite since your flight was delayed and you had a longer layover in Dallas than expected."

Fallon felt embarrassed by her own behavior. She was touched by Lance's thoughtfulness. "Thank you. I'd like that."

"Good. I'll get back to the kitchen and the caterers. Mr. Saxton decided to have light refreshments for the guests." With another smile, she skirted the tent and disappeared.

"This way, Ms. Marshall." Oskar, slim and almost six feet tall, picked up her weekender and the garment bag and started in the opposite direction.

Fallon followed him around the tent and through an oversized wooden door in a ten-foot-high adobe wall. Beyond, the landscape was breathtaking. Shrubs were clipped into balls, echoed by round finials. To the left was a long path leading to a pond, and behind were plantings rich in texture and colors of red, burgundy, and orange. A short distance away stood a Pope's urn, named after poet

Alexander Pope. "It's so beautiful here. The grounds are just incredible."

The young man smiled over his shoulder. "My father and I thank you. Mr. Yates knew what he wanted in terms of formality, and my father knew what would grow here with the proper care."

His revelation widened her eyes. "Your father did this?"

"Yes." Oskar stopped in front of a white cottage with red shutters and a profusion of rosebushes by the steps and overflowing clay pots of brightly hued flowers. "He's self-taught, and Mr. Yates took a chance on him. He does other projects now and then, but with four acres he spends his time taking care of this place."

Maintaining a yard this size took hard work and dedication. Her parents might have enjoyed gardening, but she wasn't much of one. "I was struck by the grounds from the first moment I saw them. Your father should be very proud. Do you help?"

He chuckled. "Every chance during the planning and planting, and now just when I'm home from college."

"What's your major?" she asked, liking the friendly young man.

"Landscape architecture."

"You certainly have the genes for it."

"Thank you." He opened the door. "After you."

Fallon stepped inside and was immediately taken by the room. The open area was quaint and beautiful, with an unexpected palette of cool neutrals of eggshell and pale honey. On top of the whitewashed oak floor was a gray-white cowhide rug. The sofa and two side chairs were upholstered in a honey-toned fabric. By a single bookshelf was a beige leather chaise longue. The curtainless windows had cream-colored wooden blinds. On the low coffee table sat a covered tray, a pitcher of iced tea, and a lush bouquet of fresh-cut flowers.

"Lance said you liked quesadillas, so Mama cooked some for you. The driver called when he picked you up in the car, so they're fresh and hot." Oskar placed the garment bag over the back of the sofa and set the weekender beside it. "The main bedroom and bath are through that door. The other bedroom is next to it. Is there anything else you need?"

Fallon gave him points for the diplomatic way he told her about the bedrooms. "I can't think of a thing. Thank you."

Oskar went to the door. "Lance said to tell you to come to the auction when you feel like it. He's running back and forth between the tent and the house showing some special guests pieces before they're brought down."

"I'm not missing any more of this than I have to." She picked up her things and started for the second bedroom. She wasn't going near Lance's bedroom. "If you see Lance, please tell him I'll be out directly."

"I will." The young man's gaze went to the tray before he opened the door. "FYI: Lance and Mama will both probably ask if you ate and enjoyed the food. They both want things to be right for you."

"Got it." It was past two. She'd only had a cup of

coffee so far. Before her delayed flight, she'd been scheduled to arrive at ten thirty. "Thanks again."

He closed the door behind him. Fallon put the luggage down, took a seat on the sofa, and removed the dome off the food. The delicious smells wafted up. Smiling, she picked up the soft tortilla filled with chicken and vegetables, took a bite, and discovered she was starving.

That morning her mother had gotten up to take Fallon to the airport and offered to cook breakfast, but she had been too nervous. Megan's reminder to Fallon that she knew people and showing her the dart-tattered photograph of Lance hadn't helped. While her mother was willing to defer to Fallon's judgment, it was obvious that her baby sister wasn't as forgiving. Fallon had admonished Megan for lying to Lance, but it hadn't seemed to faze her one tiny bit. Like their father, she didn't believe in second chances.

Fallon had lived longer. People made mistakes, just as she had in calling Lance a thief.

Finished eating, she took a quick shower and dressed in a knee-length burnt-orange flowing sundress that complemented her light honey complexion. She decided to leave her camera in the room. Admittedly she was vain enough not to want it to distract from her appearance when Lance first saw her. She combed out her curly hair that reached below her shoulders, reapplied her makeup, and left the cottage.

With each step her excitement grew. She didn't know where the weekend would lead, but she hoped it would bring them closer. She had a strong feeling that his past was standing between them and, until he dealt with that, their relationship would be on shaky ground. Inviting her for the weekend was a good step. She planned to enjoy the time with him and see what happened.

Lance was profoundly grateful for his ability to do two things at once. At the moment, he was listening to the excited comments of a young couple who had just purchased the master bedroom suite and watching the crowd for Fallon. Oskar had told him she had arrived and he'd taken her to the cottage.

Lance hoped she hadn't freaked if she saw his clothes in the closet of the larger bedroom. He'd intended to have them moved, but time had gotten away from him. After thinking about it, he realized his staying in the cottage might give her the impression he expected them to sleep together. While he hoped they would, he wanted her to know she had a choice.

"The suite will be just perfect in our new home," Mrs. Forrester said. "I wanted an antique set with a history."

"You couldn't have made a wiser choice," Lance said, trying not to be disappointed when he didn't see Fallon. "Thaddeus and his wife, Lydia, purchased it on a second honeymoon trip to Europe for their fifth anniversary."

"And their daughter was born a year later." The slender woman blushed the color of her red knit top and smiled. "We've been married two years."

"Congratulations. You make a great-looking couple," Lance said, meaning it. He'd made it a practice never to lie in business. Evade yes, lie no. "It will be delivered to your home in Albuquerque next Thursday. Now, if you'll excuse me, I need to get back. Thank you again for coming, and don't forget the blue ticket you hold will admit you to the refreshments by the loggia."

"Thanks," Mr. Forrester said. "I could use some food. Come on, honey."

"Good-bye." Lance turned and there she was, not two feet away, a smile on her beautiful face. He wanted to take her in his arms and kiss her until everything faded away.

"Hi."

"Hi," he repeated, glad he was able to talk at all. She really got to him. He had finally stopped fighting that truth at least.

She closed the distance between them. "Nice-looking couple."

"They purchased the master bedroom suite." Unable to resist, he caught her hand and pulled her even closer. His gaze went to her tempting mouth and stayed.

He heard her sharp intake of breath, but she didn't pull away.

"If I kissed you the way I want . . ." He drew in a ragged breath and stepped back. "You get settled all right for the time being?" He wanted her to stay at the cottage, but he wasn't going to push.

"Yes, thanks to your thoughtfulness and your excellent staff," she told him.

"Did you eat?"

Her natural smile came again. "Yes. Oskar said you and his mother would ask."

"Carmen likes to take care of people."

"So do you," Fallon said.

"Only certain people." And they were few in his life.

"Excuse me, Lance, but you're wanted in the main library," Karen, one of his assistants for the sale, announced. Like all of his regular employees, she wore a teal-colored polo with "Saxton Auction House" inscribed on the front.

"Please tell them I'll be there directly."

"I'll get out of your way." Fallon tugged her hand.

"Not happening." Taking her elbow, he started back into the house. "I'm not letting you out of my sight so soon." He stopped and stared down at her. "Unless you're tired and need to rest."

"I'm right where I want to be. Let's go."

Oskar was right about Lance being busy and in demand. And wherever he went Fallon went as well. She saw a new, different side of Lance Saxton, not just the moody, mercurial one.

He was cordial, personable, even charming to the attendees. He took as much time with the browser as he did with the person who'd purchased smaller items. It was the same with the people who had winning bids on large-ticket items. He was an astute businessman, but he clearly wanted the person to be happy after the sale.

It was almost dark when Security reported that

they'd seen the last person off the property. The catering truck—which had been parked in the garage—had left as well. So had all Lance's house and business staff.

Lance locked the front door and took Fallon's arm. "So what did you think?"

"It was fast, well organized, and fun." She shook her head ruefully. "I thought those two men would come to blows over the grandfather clock."

In the kitchen, he released her, then went to the refrigerator and pulled out several containers and a pitcher of lemonade. "Our dinner. Hope you like salads. I didn't think either of us would want to bother with the microwave or go out."

She'd already spoken to Naomi and told her she was in town. Her friend understood Fallon would be spending the evening with Lance. Where she'd spend the night wasn't mentioned. "I love salads. How can I help?"

"Table is already set. If you'll grab the ice bucket we'll be set."

Fallon did as asked and followed him outside. She filled their glasses with ice and poured their drinks. Night was just settling. The pool lights were on, giving the area a romantic feel. "It's beautiful and so peaceful here."

"Glad you like it." He pulled out her chair, then took his seat. "The salads are labeled. Please help yourself."

Fallon blessed the food and accepted the container Lance gave her. "Shrimp. Want to share?"

"I'm good with the salmon." He took a bite. "What's next for you?"

"Road trip with the food editor of a national magazine." She grinned. "We're going to eat our way across Texas and Louisiana. She'll spotlight the food and I'll do the local attractions."

"Sounds like your kind of assignment."

She lifted a brow. "Is that your way of saying I like to eat?"

He reached for his lemonade. "I think I'll refrain from answering. It was difficult enough getting you here."

She paused in reaching for her glass. "I'm sorry about Megan. She's younger, but she's fiercely protective."

A shadow crossed his face. "I admit I was annoyed at the time, but I've had time to think and realize she was just trying to protect you. Family should put each other first."

The way he said the last sentence, his narrowed eyes, she wondered if he'd been put first. Then she wondered if the person who hadn't put him first was his mother. In hopes of taking the shadows from his eyes Fallon said, "Megan downloaded a picture of you from my going-away party, enlarged it, and then used it for dart practice."

"How about you?"

"Not once." She stared across the table at him. "Sometimes things just don't work out the way you plan or had hoped for."

His hand flexed on the glass. "Yes."

"So what's next for you?" she asked, wanting the shadows gone from his face.

"I've met several people at this auction who want me to do some private appraisals for them." He picked his fork back up and began to eat. "Some items sounded as if they might be worth taking a look. I'm thinking of having an open appraisal day in a couple of months. It will be appointments only, so it won't get too hectic."

She relaxed. Whatever it was bothering him seemed to have passed. "From the article I read on you, you recently moved into a new building in Tucson."

He straightened. "What article? I haven't given very many interviews."

Her lips twitched. "Would you believe I can't remember?"

"No." He smiled.

"Thought not." Finished eating, she sipped her lemonade. "Actually, it was a couple of days before I came out here. Naomi insisted I read the *Fortune* magazine article to prove I had misjudged you."

"So that, coupled with your plans for the new article, is what changed your mind about me?"

She didn't even think of evading. "Yes. I parked the car close to the front doors so if you threw me out I wouldn't have far to go."

"Yet you came anyway."

"At the time, I told myself it was because of the article, but I also wanted to see you again."

"To apologize?"

She looked at him over the rim of her glass. "To see if I was still attracted to you."

"And?"

"I think you know the answer to that."

His gaze never leaving hers, he rounded the table. With one hand he took her glass and placed it on the table, and with the other he pulled her to her feet. "I've dreamed of kissing you again."

"Don't make either of us wait any longer."

His head lowered, his lips grazed across hers, heating them and her blood. He nibbled, suckled her lower lip into his mouth before his tongue slipped into her mouth to leisurely stroke and tease.

She strained to get closer. As if to answer, his hand cupped her hips, bringing her closer to his hard erection. She moaned, then whimpered as his hand cupped her breast, his fingers squeezing and rolling her nipple.

He jerked her top down and feasted on her nipple, his tongue laving the turgid point. Her senses whirled. She felt herself being lifted, then lowered onto something soft. Then he took her mouth again in a kiss so boldly erotic that coherent thought ceased to be possible.

Heat and desire raged though her. She had to touch him as he touched her. Her hand slid under his knit shirt, stroking and caressing his warm, muscular torso.

His hand slid up her thigh, caressing, kneading.

A coyote yelped, startling Fallon and breaking the mood. She wanted to be with Lance, but . . . She caught his hand.

"I usually like animals, but if I could find that coyote . . ." He stood with his back to her.

Fallon didn't waste any time. She sat up and adjusted her dress back over her breasts. She didn't know what to say. She thought she knew what she wanted. Now she was second-guessing herself.

"I'll walk you to the cottage."

While she hadn't planned to stay at the cottage, she hadn't made any hotel reservations, either. She could bunk at Naomi's place, but she was so embarrassed by her behavior that she didn't look forward to the twenty-minute ride to her friend's apartment. Plus she didn't want to intrude on Naomi and Richard. Lance had to be annoyed with her as well.

Fallon kept her head averted on the way to the cabin. Opening the door, she went inside. "Good night," she murmured, looking over his shoulder. She was too ashamed to look him in the eye.

"I didn't get a chance to move my clothes. They're in the main bedroom. I'll need a change for tomorrow."

"Oh yes. Of course." Her gaze bounced off him. She stepped aside.

Silently Lance went by her and into the bedroom. Fallon stayed where she was. He quickly came back out. "I'll see you in the morning. Good night."

"Good night." Closing the door, Fallon leaned against it. He probably never wanted to see her again, and she couldn't blame him.

Chapter 8

Lance, always neat and meticulous, dumped his clothes on the daybed in the pool house. He'd hoped the night would end differently. He shoved his hand over his head and reached for his belt buckle. He wasn't going to be able to sleep. He was too keyed up to read. He wasn't about to go running in the night and break a leg. That left only one way to work off some of the sexual tension humming though his veins.

Naked, he pulled on a pair of swim trunks and headed back outside. He dove into the water, kicked to the surface, and began swimming the length of the pool. He'd gone several laps before he sensed he was being watched. Wild animals were in the area, but he didn't think any of them could scale the ten-foot adobe wall that enclosed the backyard. Certainly not the coyote that'd ruined the moment.

"Fallon." He peered into the darkness and thought he caught a flash of something white.

After a few moments, Fallon stepped out of the shadows, her arms wrapped around her waist. She wore a white bikini that showed her long legs and full breasts to perfection. Briefly Lance wondered why he was being tortured with what he couldn't have.

"I didn't know you were here. I couldn't sleep and thought I'd take a swim."

So he wasn't the only one fighting pent-up sexual frustration. "What changed your mind?"

"I wasn't sure if you were annoyed with me or not," she said, her head coming up the tiniest bit.

An unsure Fallon was a rarity. "You can always say no." He swam to the edge of the pool and climbed out. Her eyes tracked the glide of water over his skin. The arousal that he had been trying to ease came back with a vengeance. He knew it the instant her eyes widened and she jerked her gaze upward and bit her lower lip.

"I'll race you to the other side. I'll even give you a head start." He turned away, hoping against hope he hadn't scared her. He caught movement out of the corner of his eye.

"I don't need an advantage. On the count of three. One. Two Three." She dove cleanly into the water, her slender arms slicing through the water.

Amazed by her ability, Lance simply watched her before his competitive spirit kicked in. He dove into the water after her, aware that if he caught her it would be because of the length of his strokes. He gave it all he had. He knew she wouldn't want a hollow victory.

"I won," Fallon announced a split second before Lance touched the wall.

He stared over at her pleased face. He wanted to

kiss her again, but he wasn't ready for her to reject him again. "It looks like you should have given me the head start."

"Daddy loved to swim. I've been swimming since I was a toddler." She rested one hand on the blue-tiled edge of the pool. The other undulated in the water as she floated.

"You seem to do everything well," he said.

Unhappiness glittered in her eyes. "Apparently not." She started for the other end of the pool.

Lance followed as she swam the length of the pool. Once. Twice. When she pushed away for a third lap, he was there in front of her. "What is it?"

She glanced away. His hand gently turned her to face him. She looked so sad. This time he didn't think; he just brushed his lips against hers. He wanted her happy. He didn't want her to have regrets about staying the weekend with him.

"Lance." She breathed his name and he was lost. With one hand braced on the edge of the pool, he pulled her into his arms with the other, his mouth hotly devouring hers. Their legs slid against each other, the water giving their bodies an erotic buoyancy.

Fallon wrapped her arms around his neck, pressing against him. She felt the rigid hardness of his arousal against the juncture of her thighs. Her own body quickened in response. His mouth, which she had desperately wanted on hers, was hot and demanding.

Lance lifted his head, their breathing loud in the stillness of the night. Fallon shivered from the fierce desire she saw in his eyes. "Tell me to stop or I won't let you go until the morning."

She couldn't say the words to send him away again. Life offered no guarantees. She wanted to be with him. "Then don't let me go."

"Fallon." Her name was a whispered prayer on his lips. His mouth took her again, worshiped her before becoming more heated and demanding. Suddenly releasing her, he got out of the pool and pulled her up into his arms. "Let's hope I can make it to a bed."

"Me, too." Now that she had made up her mind, she found she liked teasing him. She nibbled on his ear, blew.

"Fallon, please don't do that."

"I like kissing you." She proved it by kissing the curve of his jaw.

Lance entered the cottage with a burst of speed and didn't stop until he was in the master bedroom. Placing Fallon on her feet, he jerked the covers back, then grabbed her and fell into bed with her, his mouth slamming into hers, the kiss filled with passion. His mouth slanted downward to the swell of her breast. He untied the swim top and tossed it aside.

He sucked in a ragged breath at the glorious sight of her high, firm breasts. They'd tempt a saint. He had to taste. His head lowered, taking the turgid peak into his mouth.

She sucked in a sharp breath and clasped his head, holding him closer. He moaned. She was exquisite and tasted like his most forbidden fantasy.

His hand moved downward, sweeping over her trembling stomach to her womanhood, then back up to untie the strings of her bikini bottom. He pulled it away.

Sheathing himself, he brought them together. His hips flexed, moving in and out of her hot, wet body. The tight fit almost sent him over the edge. He cupped her hips and brought them together again and again. Her legs wrapped around his hips, she eagerly met him thrust for thrust.

They went over together. He held her as aftershocks rippled though her body. Nothing had ever touched him as much. He rolled, his arms around her, unwilling to let her go.

Her eyes opened. They were a bit dazed and fully sated. He'd give anything to keep her with him always.

"Are you all right?" he asked, brushing her hair from her damp face.

She smiled, touched her fingertips to his lips. "Incredible, but don't get the big head."

"I'll try not to." He pulled her on top of him, his hand sliding over the slope of her back and stopping on her naked butt. "Let's see if I can do a repeat."

Laughing, Fallon lowered her lips to his. "Let's."

Fallon woke with a smile on her face, her back snuggled against Lance. Not only had they done a repeat, they'd also managed a three-peat. She felt deliciously happy. The night with Lance had been beautiful, and all that she had hoped for.

The early-morning light shone though the wooden blinds. Each time they'd made love had been more powerful and dazzling than the last. She hadn't known it could be so moving.

"You OK?" he asked, his hand stroking her arm.

She angled her head to look at him. He was handsome enough to tempt an angel. He'd been all that she desired. She kissed his chin. "For the umpteenth time, yes."

"Carmen will be here soon to cook breakfast, then the people I hired to help with the auction." He kissed Fallon on the shoulder. "It's going to be another hectic day."

"But then comes the night," she said, surprised by her boldness.

He rolled on top of her. "We don't have to wait that long."

Fallon couldn't keep the huge grin off her face all during the day. It was going to be all right. She and Lance hadn't had a chance to discuss how they'd handle their long-distance courtship, but somehow they'd make it work.

Fallon paused in taking a picture of the woman who'd purchased the chest of sterling silver flatware. "Courtship" was such an old-fashioned word. Fallon wasn't sure why it had popped into her mind. She didn't think it was because she was surrounded by things of a bygone era. More likely, the word seemed to fit. There was still a lot she and Lance didn't know about each other, but now they had time.

"You look happy."

Glancing up to see Lance, she didn't even think; she just kissed him on the lips. "I am."

He smiled back. "Just checking. Things are going so well we'll probably sell out today."

"And we'll have more time to spend together tomorrow," she said, delighted by the prospect.

"That was my thought."

She stepped back. "Then stop goofing off and go sell. I have plans for you."

His eyes darkened. "I asked Carmen to prepare our meal again. Unless you want to go out."

"What do you think?"

He pulled her into his arms and kissed her until she trembled; then he was gone.

Lance went straight to the auction tent. He needed to focus and get his mind off Fallon. She was as addictive as he'd feared. When he wasn't with her he wanted to be, and each time he was he had the compelling urge to kiss and hold her. No woman had ever affected him so strongly.

This was bad. Very bad.

This wasn't forever. He didn't do long-term. Yet he didn't want to think of the day she wouldn't be there. He was getting in over his head. If he had any sense, he'd make up some excuse and get back to Tucson as soon as the auction was over. She'd be disappointed, but she'd understand. Before the thought fully formed, he knew he wasn't going to do that.

As dangerous to his peace of mind as Fallon was,

he also wanted her for as long as he could have her. He'd just have to deal with the fallout later.

Saturday night, Fallon kept looking at her watch. She wasn't supposed to come out of the guest cottage until eight thirty. It was eight twenty-eight. Lance had a surprise for her. She couldn't imagine what. She was pretty sure it wasn't a whom. Both of them wanted to be alone.

She glanced at her watch again and moved toward the door, the tiered hem of the cranberry maxi strapless sundress swirling around her legs. Eight twenty-nine. She couldn't stand the suspense. She'd walk slowly. She was to meet him by the pool.

She reached for the door and stopped. She didn't want to ruin his surprise. She remembered he'd been a bit unsure of himself when he'd told her, which made her care for him more. She loved it when—

Her thoughts stumbled to a halt. *Love.* She loved him.

Closing her eyes, she leaned her head against the door. She'd rolled down that mountain past caring deeply and straight into disaster. Lance wasn't ready for the *l* word. She knew that. Love to her meant forever, marriage. He'd made it no secret that marriage wasn't in his future.

So why hadn't her heart listened?

She jumped on hearing her cell phone. It was probably Lance. She'd talked to Naomi and then her mother and sister that afternoon. She stared at the phone. What if he could tell she loved him? She chastised herself and answered the phone. How would he know when she'd just figured it out herself?

"I'm on my way," she answered, and cringed on hearing the shakiness in her voice.

"You all right?"

"Yes. I was trying not to come early and just lost track of time. I'm hanging up because I can't wait any longer." Disconnecting the call, she hurried out the door. She wasn't going to spoil tonight for them.

She rushed down the path, her low-heeled sandals clacking on the paver stones. She rounded a huge potted plant and came to a complete stop. Her mouth formed a silent O.

Floating spheres of lotus blossom lights bobbed in the pool. Lance stood on the loggia with a long-stemmed red rose in one hand, a wine flute in the other. Instead of the rattan table, there was a smaller one draped with a white tablecloth. On top was a five-tier lit chandelier.

"Say something," he said, sounding nervous.

Tears formed in her eyes. She blinked them away. Somehow she made her feet move until she was within arm's reach of him. "I make my living with words, but this . . ." She extended her hand toward him and the pool and swallowed. "No one has ever made me feel as special as I do at this moment."

"Stop looking at me like that, or I'll spill your wine and we'll miss a great dinner." He handed her the rose and the wine.

Her unsteady hands closed around the stem of the glass and the rose. He lifted his flute. "To second chances."

"Second chances." She sipped, then took the seat he pulled out.

He lifted a domed lid. "Prime rib, baked potato, and asparagus."

Steam tendrils wafted up from her plate. She placed her glass aside as he took his seat and said grace. "Do you have genies in your kitchen?"

"Carmen stayed and cooked." He picked up his knife and fork. "Oskar and his father helped me with the lights."

Fallon still couldn't take it all in. "Nothing could have pleased me more."

"I wouldn't go so far as to say that."

Fallon laughed. "You might have a point."

"I like hearing you laugh." He cut into his beef. "It was one of the things I missed. I'm glad you trusted me enough to come back for the weekend."

"Thanks for inviting me."

He picked up his glass. "How long is your assignment with the food editor?"

"Off and on for a month. She'll have to get back to her magazine from time to time," Fallon explained, sure Lance was going to ask her for dates and times so he could visit her.

He nodded. "I can't wait to read the article you wrote about this place. When do you think it will come out?"

Disappointed, Fallon fought to keep the smile on her face. "In a couple of weeks for the newspaper, and in a travel magazine in two to three months."

"Be sure and let me know so I can get copies."

He stopped eating and stared across the table at her. "You're not eating."

"Just thinking about tomorrow."

"I'm trying not to." A frown on his face, he sat back in his chair. "The time went by so fast."

Fallon perked up a bit. He *did* care. "But I'll be back."

"I'm not sure I can wait that long," he said.

More encouraging words to hear. She'd just have to be patient. He'd say something about them getting together before the night was over. Assured she was right, she picked up her knife and fork. It was going to be all right. She'd worried for nothing.

Fallon woke up in Lance's arms Sunday morning, but this time she wasn't smiling. Doubts that she had pushed aside last night refused to budge this morning. Lance hadn't said anything before they fell asleep about a future for them. She didn't hold out much hope he'd say anything this morning.

The slow glide of his hand down her naked back had awakened her. She would have thought he'd awakened her to make love, but he never deepened the pressure, never touched her anyplace else to inflame her senses.

Misery swamped her. Before now, he hadn't seemed able to touch her without wanting to kiss her or make love to her. Now, she didn't seem to matter. She'd gambled and lost. Pride dictated he never know how much he'd hurt her or that she loved him.

She rolled away from him and got out of bed.

Naked, she felt exposed. She saw the dress she'd worn last night hanging off the foot of the bed and reached for it.

"There's nothing much at the airport to eat. You want to leave early and grab a bite?" Lance asked.

Fallon pulled the dress over her head before turning. The sheet pushed to his waist, he leaned on one elbow and stared at her. After all they'd shared, his eyes were once again impersonal. Perhaps, to him, they'd shared nothing but a few hot moments.

"I'm not hungry." Food was the furthest thing from her mind.

Frowning, Lance threw back the covers and got out of bed, unconcerned by his nakedness. His brows furrowed, he crossed to her. "You feel all right?"

She kept her gaze on his face instead of the body that had inflamed her senses. "I never eat much when I fly. I better get showered and dressed."

"Your plane doesn't leave for another three hours." He frowned down at her.

She picked up her weekender. "I like arriving early. Besides, I promised Naomi I'd call and I want to have enough time to catch up on how things are going for the wedding." This time she made good her escape.

In the bathroom, her arms wrapped around her waist, she sat on the commode. She loved a man who had only wanted a convenient bed partner. She brushed away the tears threatening to fall. She was stronger than that.

Standing, she pulled off her dress and stepped

into the shower. She'd leave him with a jaunty wave and a smile on her lips. Perhaps she should have listened to Megan after all.

Lance had wondered how today would unfold, but never in a million years would he have thought Fallon would be so anxious to leave. Or that he would want so badly to ask her to stay.

He'd already accepted that there couldn't be a future for them, had told her as much in the beginning. Yet he was finding out as he glanced at her while they took the road to the airport that saying something and being able to stick with it were two different things.

This morning, when he'd awakened with her in his arms, he'd felt a blissful peace he'd never experienced before. He'd been content to just hold her. When she'd awakened, he'd wanted to ask her if he could fly out to her assignment, but she had been so anxious to leave he hadn't said anything for fear she'd turn him down. Something had changed between last night and this morning, and he wasn't sure what.

He parked in front of the airport terminal. Fallon got out of the car and arrived at the trunk of his car before he did.

She glanced at her watch. She couldn't wait to be away from him. Unlocking the trunk, he reached for her bags.

"Thanks. I have them." She straightened with her garment bag, camera bag, and weekender.

"I'll take them in for you."

"No need. See you around." On tiptoes, she kissed him on the cheek. "Take care, Lance."

He didn't know what to say to the easy brush-off. It was all he could do not to reach out to her. "I'll call."

She shrugged her elegant shoulders. "Suit yourself, but I'll be on the road and I'm not sure about reception."

His hands slid into the pockets of his jeans. She couldn't have made it any plainer. "Good-bye, Fallon."

Without another word, she walked into the airport terminal. She didn't look back.

Inside the terminal, Fallon went through Security and directly to her gate. Her sunshades firmly in place, she stared out the window. She wouldn't cry. She wouldn't. Swallowing repeatedly, she fought to keep the tears at bay.

She couldn't even blame Lance for the way things ended. He'd made no promises. She'd walked into this with her eyes wide open. She'd foolishly thought that he cared, that after they'd made love he would change his mind.

She sniffed. What did that old song say about love making a fool of you? She certainly qualified, but she'd survive. She'd get over him. At the wedding, she'd show him that he meant nothing to her. Perhaps one day she wouldn't be lying.

Chapter 9

Unable to help himself, Lance had marked off each of the days Fallon was gone. He'd never missed anything or anyone as much or been as anxious to see them again.

Parking in the church's parking lot, he got out of his car. He didn't see Richard's truck, which was understandable, since Lance was thirty minutes early for the wedding rehearsal. He blew out an aggravated breath and leaned against the door of his rental.

His plane from Tucson had landed that morning in Albuquerque. He'd picked up his rental and driven straight to the Yates house. He hadn't stopped until he was back in the cottage he and Fallon had shared. Memories had washed over him, not just the intimate ones but those of hearing her laughter, of her teasing him, of him holding her.

He'd relived the scene of their last morning together over and over and still didn't know why she'd gone to sleep with her arms around his neck and awakened anxious to leave him.

A SUV he recognized as Naomi's pulled up in

the parking lot. Immediately behind were Richard's truck and two other trucks and cars Lance didn't recognize. He straightened, hoping Fallon was in one of the vehicles.

The front passenger door of Naomi's SUV opened and Fallon stepped out. Lance had thought he was prepared to see her again. He wasn't.

He didn't expect the tightness in his gut, the almost overwhelming need to hold her. He'd missed her every day she had been gone, had even searched the Internet to find any tidbit of information on her articles. The one she'd done on the Yates auction had been published and was very well written. He'd received several inquiries directly related to her article, but he'd heard nothing from her.

Their gazes touched. He was moving before he knew it. She turned away and opened the back door. His mother got out. He stopped abruptly. It hit him that he was looking at the first and the last women who had rejected him.

Car and truck doors slammed. People were laughing, talking, and heading toward the steps of the church.

"Hi, Lance. Come on." Richard beckoned with his arm around Naomi's waist, his hand holding Kayla's.

There were more people greeting Lance. He didn't look at the man who'd married his mother to know or care if he'd spoken. Lance did catch his mother looking at him, but his gaze was centered on Fallon, who led the way into the church. Nothing had changed. She wanted no part of him.

* * *

"I can't do this," Fallon murmured. But she glanced back at the happy faces of Richard and Naomi and stiffened her spine. She wasn't ruining this for them because she'd made a mistake.

Naomi spoke quietly to Richard, then went to Fallon and took her hands. "You're trembling."

"I'm fine." Despite her intention, she looked at the door for Lance before she chastised herself and glanced away. She'd worn the dress she wore for her going-away party to show him what he'd lost. A huge mistake, since the dress now hung instead of cupping and tempting. She was a slow learner.

"You should go back to the apartment and rest," Naomi suggested quietly. "Richard will understand."

Fallon's hands tightened. "You said you wouldn't tell him. I know I'm asking—"

"I didn't tell him. I'm just worried about you," Naomi interrupted. "I just wish there was more I could do."

"You're already doing it by being my friend."

"Naomi, we need to get started." There was impatience in the woman's voice.

Fallon glanced around to see Mrs. Lincoln, the wedding planner Naomi hadn't been too thrilled to have but one Richard's mother wanted. Her thin lips were pinched. Since Naomi already loved her future-mother-in law, she'd agreed.

"We're coming," Naomi said; then she turned to Fallon. "If you have to leave, just do it."

"I'm fine for now and, since Mrs. Lincoln is giving

us the eye, we better move it." Taking Naomi's arm, Fallon joined the group at the back of the church, making sure that she was nowhere near Lance. It wouldn't remain that way, since they were paired up, but she'd cross that bridge when the time came.

Lance was fully prepared to ignore Fallon at the wedding rehearsal as she'd ignored him until he really got a good look at her as they waited for their cue to go down the aisle together. She remained beautiful, but she was pale and didn't look well. There were dark smudges beneath her eyes. She didn't fill out the straight dress as he remembered. Had she lost weight?

"Hello, Fallon."

She turned her cool gaze on him. "Hello, Lance. How's the auction business?"

His eyes narrowed at her condescending tone. "Fine. How's the travel business?"

"Couldn't be better. It's our turn."

Lance walked beside her down the aisle and decided to bide his time. Had she gotten ill?

"Mr. Saxton, eyes straight ahead," requested the wedding planner.

Lance complied with difficulty. Something was wrong with Fallon. The thought of her being ill or hurt made his gut knot. She could be pissed at him all she wanted, but he was going to find out what was the matter with her. She was probably too stubborn to see a doctor. They were all going to Brandon's restaurant afterward for a rehearsal dinner; Lance would get his answers then.

*   *   *

Lance found that Fallon was more difficult to corner than he'd thought. She sat at the other end of the tables pushed together at the restaurant. Fifteen minutes after they were seated, she got up, spoke briefly to Naomi, and left. Lance assumed Fallon would return, but after five minutes passed and there was no sign of her he asked Naomi if she was coming back.

"No," Naomi answered, not quite meeting his gaze.

"Lance, please sit down. I'd like to make a little speech," Richard's father requested.

Lance took his seat until his uncle finished, then excused himself and went outside to call Fallon's cell phone. It rolled into voice mail. Returning his phone to his pocket, he went back inside the restaurant. Tomorrow she wasn't going to escape him.

The morning of the wedding dawned beautiful and clear. Despite how busy Fallon was helping Naomi and keeping Kayla entertained, there were moments that Lance slipped into her mind. The most painful moment was standing in the bride's room and seeing Naomi in her wedding gown. Fallon would never have this with Lance, never know the excitement of being a bride.

Fallow swallowed and walked around Naomi to ensure everything was perfect. Despite how badly things had turned out for Fallon, she was glad Naomi had found the happiness she deserved, and was happy to share Richard and Naomi's wedding day with them. "You look amazing," Fallon said softly.

"Stunning," Catherine added.

"Thank you." Naomi smiled. "I feel beautiful." She lifted the voluminous A-line tulle skirt of the floor-length nude strapless gown. The ornately embroidered and beaded bodice continued on both sides of the dress and stopped at her fingertips. The gown complemented Naomi's complexion and whispered softly when she moved. Her hair was swept atop her head and held in place with a jeweled comb.

"Richard's jaw will drop." Fallon grinned.

"Don't make me cry." Naomi fanned her face with her nude elbow-length gloves.

"It's time." Mrs. Lincoln clapped her hands together. "Mrs. Grayson. Fallon. It's time to meet the groomsmen."

Fallon felt her stomach dip and prayed she'd make it through today. Trying to keep the smile on her face, she gave Naomi a hug and followed Catherine out of the room.

Lance had been waiting for this moment since last night. The first sight of Fallon struck him like a closed fist. She was stunningly beautiful. Even the dark smudges beneath her narrowed eyes couldn't detract from that beauty. Despite everything he'd planned, thought, some part of him refused to banish her from his mind.

Fallon didn't meet his gaze as he took her arm and started down the aisle. Beneath their feet were the white rose petals Kayla had scattered. Fallon loved flowers. The flowers he'd given her were dead and forgotten, just as he was to her.

Perhaps because today the church was filled with flickering candles, dozens of flowers, their scent heavy in the air, he felt "something" walking beside her. He couldn't define the feeling and it bothered him.

Richard certainly looked happy, ecstatic actually, Lance thought. His cousin was as anxious as a kid on Christmas morning expecting his first bike. His best man, Luke, who'd been married for a while, clearly loved his wife. Marriage might work for some people, but not for Lance.

When it was time to release Fallon, Lance felt a momentary resistance that oddly didn't surprise him. Taking his place beside Luke, Lance watched Fallon. He frowned on seeing her blanch and almost took a step toward her. Yet even as the thought formed, her head lifted, and she stared toward the back of the church. She was ill. He was positive. As soon as the wedding was over, he was going to find out what was wrong with her.

The organist began playing Wagner's "Bridal Chorus." It would never be played for Lance and Fallon. There was a rustle as the audience stood, then appreciative "oohhs" and "aahhs" as Naomi started down the aisle. She looked radiant and beautiful. Richard looked stunned—in a good way. As if compelled, despite Mrs. Lincoln's strict instructions and him knowing better, Lance didn't seem able to stop watching Fallon.

Lance's concern regarding Fallon grew as the day of the wedding lengthened. Just after the wedding, she'd looked so pale and shaky he'd been fearful that she'd faint. She'd seen him coming toward her and gone to the limousine waiting for the bridal party.

She'd thwarted him again. He'd gone to his car and driven to the Casa de Serenidad hotel, where the wedding reception was being held, and bided his time. He'd waited through the arrival of the bride and groom, the toasts, the first dance, and the food before he got his chance.

Fallon had excused herself from the wedding party and left the room. She'd done so before, but he hadn't felt as if he could follow until now because the bride and groom had just left as well.

This time he'd get an answer. He saw her go into the women's restroom. He leaned against the wall to wait. She came out a few minutes later. Her steps were unsteady. Worried, he started for her. She saw him and stiffened.

"You look sick. Have you been to the doctor?" he asked. He hadn't intended the words to come out so abrupt.

"As a matter of fact I have. He said I'm fine. Now, if you'll excuse me." She took two steps, swayed.

He caught her, more frightened than he'd ever been in his life. "Fallon!"

"I'm—I'm all right." She pushed away from him and rubbed her hand across her forehead. "I don't need your help."

"The hell you don't." His arms circled her shoulders again. "I'm taking you home."

"I—" She slapped her hand over her mouth, pushed out of his arms, and rushed back into the bathroom.

He reached for the door to follow her.

"That's the women's bathroom," an elderly woman said, eyeing him with suspicion.

"I know. A friend of mine is sick. She just went inside."

The well-dressed woman continued to look at him with skepticism. "You just wait here, and I'll go see."

"Thank you." Lance didn't know whether to go get his aunt or—

The door opened and the elderly woman came back out. "She said to tell you that she's fine. She'll call you tomorrow."

He didn't believe either statement. "Thank you. I'll wait."

A frown on her face, the woman looked back at the bathroom door, then back at him. "Maybe it's best. She didn't look well."

Lance's eyes rounded. He reached for the door again.

"Young man, you can't go into a ladies' restroom," the woman protested.

"I'm not waiting out here while Fallon is sick." He turned to the door just as it slowly began to open.

Fallon, looking pale and weak, stood there. He scooped her up in his arms. "I'm taking you home and putting you to bed. Tomorrow you're going to see another doctor."

"Lance, please put me down. People are staring."

"I don't give a damn." He continued down the hall and then outside. Standing her on her feet, his arm securely around her waist, he gave the attendant his valet ticket. "Please hurry. She's ill."

"The hotel has a doctor on call," another valet said while one ran to get Lance's car.

"I've already seen a doctor," Fallon gritted out.

"A quack apparently," Lance said.

The valet jumped out of Lance's car. "Here's your car, mister. I hope you feel better, miss."

The other valet opened the passenger's door. "You sure you don't want me to call the front desk to get the doctor on call?"

"I'm taking her home." Lance would put her to bed at the cottage and take care of her. His aunt probably knew a doctor he could call. He reached for Fallon and she slapped his hand away.

"I'm not going anyplace with you."

"You're sick," he said. Maybe she'd picked up some bug on her last trip.

"I'm not sick, you fool. I'm pregnant." Spinning on her heels, she went back inside the hotel.

Lance felt the earth shift beneath his feet. There was a roaring sound in his head.

"Mister. Mister. You all right?"

Lance glanced between the two young attendants on either side of him holding his arms. "Pregnant."

They nodded solemnly.

Pregnant and she wasn't happy about it. Fear consumed him. "I've got to get to her."

"Mister. Your car."

Ignoring the valet's frantic call, Lance rushed back to the ballroom. He had to find her. If . . . No, he refused to let his mind go there.

Richard and Naomi might have left, but people were having a great time at the reception. They were congregated at the buffet table or the three bars or on the dance floor. The one person Lance sought wasn't there. He didn't even know where she was staying.

He pulled out his cell phone only to replace it. She wasn't going to pick up his call. Shoving his hand over his head in frustration, he made his way to his aunt and uncle's table.

"Aunt Gladys, have you seen Fallon in the last five minutes?" Lance asked, trying to appear calm when he was almost jumping out of his skin.

"No, Lance." Gladys came to her feet. "Are you all right?"

"Fine." He searched the crowd again before turning back to his aunt. "Do you happen to know where she's staying?"

"No," she said, then looked at him ruefully. "You two have a fight?"

He worked his shoulders. "I need to find her."

Something brushed his arm; he turned to see what it was and saw his mother. He frowned.

"Do you want us to help you look for her?" she asked. Her husband stood as well, silently offering his help. They'd briefly spoken to Lance at the reception today. They tended to avoid each other.

As much as he wanted to find Fallon, Lance didn't want anything from his mother or her husband. "No." He faced his aunt. "If you see her, please call me."

His aunt's annoyance with him was obvious. She wanted him and his mother to settle their differences. It wasn't happening. "I will, but we're leaving as soon as Catherine and Luke return with Kayla. She wanted to say good night to her mother and new daddy."

Lance's brows bunched in surprise. "They haven't left?"

Richard's mother leaned closer and whispered, "Naomi wanted to make sure Kayla was all right before they left on their honeymoon. They're staying in the hotel for a couple of days."

Naomi would know how to find Fallon. "What's their room number?" Lance asked, uncaring that he sounded a bit frantic.

"Lance—"

"Please." He took Gladys's arms. "I wouldn't ask if it wasn't important."

"Tell him, Gladys," his uncle said.

"Three ten. The honeymoon suite," Gladys answered.

"Thank you." Lance rushed from the ballroom. He couldn't get to the elevator fast enough. He leaned on the button, then jabbed it a couple of times. "Come on. Come on."

The elevator pinged. Lance started to get on but

stepped back as Luke, Catherine, and Kayla started to come out.

"Hi, Cousin Lance," Kayla greeted cheerfully. "Are you going to say good night to Mama and Daddy, too?"

"Hi, Kayla. Something like that." Ignoring the strange looks Catherine and Luke were giving him, Lance entered the elevator and punched 3. If they'd just left, he might catch Richard before he and Naomi became "involved."

As soon as the elevator doors began to slide open on the third floor, Lance was through them and hurrying down the hall. Locating 310, he knocked on the door, then knocked again. Somehow he'd make it up to them, but he had to find Fallon before it was too late.

Richard opened the door. The indulgent smile morphed into aggravation. He probably had thought it was Kayla again. "This had better be someone dying."

"Fallon's pregnant and I can't find her."

Fallon made it as far as the sofa in Naomi's apartment before she had to sit down. She'd never felt as weak and as tired as she did now. Thankfully, the nausea had subsided. For someone who had never been sick with more than a cold, her body wasn't dealing well with pregnancy.

Neither was she.

Eyes closed, she dropped her head on the armrest and placed her forearm over her eyes. She'd attributed the missed menstrual cycle to stress, worry, and anger—until the nausea began. The food editor Fallon was traveling with suggested that she might be pregnant. She had scoffed at the idea. She'd purchased a pregnancy test to prove she wasn't pregnant.

She wasn't laughing the next morning.

She wasn't sure how long she'd stared at the stick, then she'd cried. She didn't want to be a single mother. Despite the way things had ended between them, she wanted Lance so badly she ached.

The hard knock on the apartment door startled her. She sat up and was hit by a wave of dizziness. She eased back down. The knock came again. This time harder. Fallon didn't particularly care. It couldn't be a friend of Naomi's because a friend would know she was getting married today. Anyone else didn't matter.

"Fallon! It's Lance. Open the door!"

She might have known. He must have tracked Richard and Naomi down. How insensitive of him.

"Fallon. I know you're in there."

Her lashes fluttered open. What did he have to be angry about? He wasn't the one puking his guts out, unable to walk ten feet without getting tired.

"Fallon, open this door. I'm not leaving until we talk."

Obstinate man. Now he wanted to talk, unlike the last time they were together.

"Fallon!"

She sighed. If he kept shouting and beating on the door, someone might call the police. Getting the authorities involved would solve nothing, and there was the little matter that the newspaper often printed the police report. She didn't want everybody knowing her business. She still couldn't believe she'd blurted out she was pregnant in front of the valet attendants. Her emotions were on a roller-coaster ride.

"Fallon!"

He sounded ready to blow a gasket. "Coming." She didn't know whether he heard her or not. Her overriding concern was trying to keep the nausea and dizziness at bay. This time she sat up slower. All she wanted to do was close her eyes and rest. That wasn't going to happen until she and Lance talked. Little by little, she made her way to the door and opened it.

Lance brushed by her as if he expected her to change her mind and lock him out. As good as that sounded, he deserved to know he was going to be a father.

"It it true?"

Instead of answering, she inched her way back to the sofa to lie down. As soon as she stretched out, she felt nausea rise in her throat. It wasn't fair. She'd only eaten a couple of bites of food at the reception. Maybe if she kept swallow—

Clamping her hand over her mouth, she came off the sofa and headed toward the bathroom, hoping she'd make it in time. She wasn't paying Naomi back by throwing up on her newly cleaned carpet, and certainly not in front of Lance. It would be the height of embarrassment.

Fallon had only gone a few steps before she was

lifted and swiftly carried down the hallway and into the bedroom. She'd thought so often of being in Lance's arms again, but never for this reason. He placed her on her feet in the connecting bathroom.

"Please leave."

She didn't have time to see if he did as she requested. She was too busy emptying her stomach until there were only dry heaves. Her hand trembling, she flushed the commode and wondered if she had the strength to stand.

Behind her she heard running water; then she felt a damp, cool washcloth on her face. Once again she was lifted. This time she was placed on the commode seat.

Lance hunkered down in front of her. "Do you think you could manage to brush your teeth?"

She looked at him in his tailor-made tux, looking gorgeous while she probably looked like what the cat had dragged in. She'd washed her face so many times that night, she had absolutely no makeup on. There were dark circles beneath her eyes. Her curly hair had long since lost the sophisticated upsweep and spiraled in every direction.

"Or you can rinse your mouth out."

He was trying to be kind when what she wanted was his love. Not his fault. "I know we have to talk, but not tonight."

His large hand closed over hers. "I'll get that toothbrush. Where is your luggage?"

Relieved, she briefly closed her eyes. "Bedroom."

He left and returned shortly. Silently he helped

her brush her teeth and then picked her up again. "You need to rest." In the bedroom, he sat her on the side of the bed and unzipped her dress. "Can you manage the rest?"

She wasn't sure. "Yes."

Going to her weekender again, he pulled out a pink silk nightshirt and placed it on the bed beside her. "I'll be back in a few minutes." The door partially closed behind him.

Fallon managed to get her floor-length chiffon dress to her waist, but she was too tired to lift her hips and pull it completely off. She lay down on the bed, her legs over the side. He'd have to help her undress.

After all, it wasn't as if he hadn't seen her in her underwear and naked before. He certainly wasn't going to try anything. Their only connection was the baby she carried.

A knock sounded on the door before it fully opened. "It's me."

If she had the strength, she would have laughed. Who else would be there?

"Let me help you."

She envied Lance's easy strength as he effortlessly lifted her up and slid the gown off her legs. If his hands fumbled with removing her demi-bra, she was so relieved to be out of the thing she didn't care. Off came the lacy garter belt that she'd purchased in Los Angeles, thinking about how sexy it looked and about Lance removing it; the sheer stockings followed. Her panties remained.

In a blissfully short amount of time she was in her nightshirt and beneath the covers. She didn't want them to be enemies. "Thank you."

"Do you have any medicine you're supposed to take now?"

"No."

"Go to sleep." He adjusted the covers, the backs of his fingers brushing against her shoulders. "I'm here."

She tried to ignore the comfort of his words, not to let his tender touch matter, but couldn't quite manage. She loved him and had wanted things to work out between them. That they hadn't didn't stop her from loving him. Fighting tears, she closed her eyes. In seconds, she was asleep.

Chapter 10

Lance stared down at Fallon sleeping. She was too pale. She'd lost weight as well. Her pregnancy still shocked him. No matter how badly he'd wanted her, he'd always used a condom. She'd gotten pregnant anyway.

And the only way he'd found out was because she'd become angry with him. No matter how unthinkable, he had to consider that she might have had an ulterior motive for not telling him.

His cell phone rang and he quickly answered to keep from waking Fallon. He stepped into the hallway but kept the bedroom open so he could keep a watch on her. "Hello," he answered without looking at the readout.

"It's Naomi. Is Fallon all right?"

He'd expected the call. Naomi was caught between her loyalty to Fallon and wanting to ensure she was cared for. "Yes. Thank you for trusting me."

"Don't make me regret my decision," Naomi said. "Fallon needs your support, not your anger."

Lance almost looked at the phone. Naomi had

impressed him as a rather meek woman. "She'll have my support."

"You conveniently left out anger, but I'll let it pass. There's ginger ale in the refrigerator, soup and crackers in the pantry. She'll feel better if she eats before she gets up. She forgot her nausea medication this morning because we were rushing so much. "

"I'll see that she won't forget in the morning," he said firmly.

"Lance, Fallon is strong willed. You can't badger her or she'll balk or leave."

The possibility of the latter was what scared him. "She's carrying my child." That he'd never doubted for a moment.

"Yes, she's carrying your child, and it's her body that is going through a lot of changes. She doesn't need any added stress," Naomi said.

He didn't like being told what to do, but he had to remember that if Naomi hadn't helped him he never would have found Fallon. Just thinking of her being alone and ill made his gut knot again. "All right."

"You have Richard's phone number. Call if you need us."

"But you won't need us tonight, will you, Lance?" Richard said into the phone.

Lance heard Naomi's "Richard," then her laugh. They were happy and in love, as Lance had told Kayla. He'd ceased to have hope that he would ever share a similar happiness with a woman.

"No, I won't," Lance told him. "And, Richard, you have quite a woman."

"I know. So is Fallon. Night."

Lance slipped the cell phone back in his pocket and returned to the straight chair he'd gotten from the kitchen. It was uncomfortable, but he'd make do. For the moment, making sure that Fallon and their baby were all right was all that mattered.

Fallon woke up slowly the next morning. She felt drained, her mouth dry. She started to sit up.

"You're supposed to eat first."

She almost screamed until she recognized Lance's voice. As it was, she sat up abruptly, then closed her eyes and lay back down when she felt dizzy.

"Are you all right?"

She barely opened her eyes to see Lance with a glass of pale liquid that had effervescent bubbles and a small plate with crackers. "Better if you hadn't scared me."

"I'm sorry." He held out the glass and the plate. "Naomi said you're to eat before you get up, and then you can take your medicine."

Fallon nibbled on a cracker and sipped the ginger ale. "You shouldn't have bothered her on her honeymoon."

"I had to find you."

She heard a hint of desperation in his voice. "I was going to tell you about the baby."

"When?" he asked, his black eyes narrowed.

When she felt better and could go two hours without being nauseated, she thought. "If you're going to be snippy, you can leave."

"I asked you a simple question that I think, as

the father, I have a right to know the answer to," he persisted.

He wasn't backing down on this. Oddly, she was pleased. No matter how things were between them, she wanted their child to have a good relationship with its father. "I only recently found out myself. It wasn't real to me at first." She lay back in bed and closed her eyes.

"Are you all right?"

"I've been better."

"You're going to keep this baby. You're not going to go to some clinic to get rid of it!"

Fallon's eyes snapped open. She stared at him, the cold anger in his face. She couldn't believe what he'd just said. Slowly she sat up. "What?"

"You heard me." He leaned over the bed, his arms on the bed bracketing her. "You're having this baby. You're not getting rid of it!"

"Of course I'm having this baby." Was he nuts?! "Why would you think otherwise?"

He jerked upright. His expression closed. "You had your life all planned. A baby will change that."

"You think I'd harm my baby to have a career?" she asked, caught between anger and incredulity.

His answer was slow in coming. He slid his hands into the pockets of his slacks. "You said yourself that you'd been better."

"You really don't know me at all, do you?" She closed her eyes, then opened them to stare at him. "And I don't know you. I should have listened to myself."

"About what?"

"Lust will lead to misery and heartache," she said. "Please show yourself out."

"We haven't talked or settled anything."

"I think you've said enough." Sitting up slowly, she slid her legs over the side of the bed and stood. "Are you still here?"

"I'm the father. I have a right to know what your plans are."

"But not to insult me." Stepping around him, she picked up her weekender and went into the bathroom, shutting the door behind her.

He'd messed up. He should have listened to Naomi. One thing he did know about Fallon was that she had a quick temper. If she decided she didn't want him around there was nothing he could do about it. There was only one way he could think of to watch over Fallon and his unborn child.

It was drastic, but what else could he do? It surprised him he would go to such lengths, but he accepted it as the only way.

The bathroom door opened. "You still here?"

"I owe you an apology," he said. "You were right about something else: we don't know each other. I'm asking for the opportunity to change that."

She folded her arms and eyed him skeptically. "And how do you suppose to accomplish that?"

"By getting married."

Her arms came to her sides. "Have you lost your mind?"

"It makes perfect sense." Lance thought it a brilliant idea. Marriage would give him the legal right to his child and keep Fallon with him. He wanted her and he was tired of fighting it. He didn't have to let her know how much he cared. He wasn't going to be vulnerable again. "I can provide the financial support and I can be there for you, just as I was last night."

"No." She left the room and Lance was on her heels every step of the way. If he had mentioned anything about caring for her, she might have been tempted.

"Why?"

She entered the kitchen, intent on fixing herself some chicken broth so she could take her medicine. Opening a cabinet, she reached for the can.

"I already fixed you some soup." He pulled out a chair at the table. "Have a seat and I'll get it for you, and then you can take your medicine."

Fallon sat and watched Lance go the stove, pick up a quart saucepan, and pour soup into a bowl. "I thought you said you couldn't cook."

He placed the bowl of soup and more crackers in front of her. "Heating isn't cooking. We'll finish this discussion once you've eaten and taken your medication."

She took a bite of soup. "Eating won't change my mind. If you want to be a part of our child's life that's good, but I'm not marrying just because I'm pregnant."

"I can't be a part of the child's life if you're one place and I'm in another," he argued.

"Marriage is more than convenience." She lifted the spoon to her mouth only to put it down and head for the bathroom. Finished emptying her stomach, she came out. Lance was standing there with a glass of ginger ale and her medicine.

"Sorry. You were supposed to take it before you got out of bed."

"Not your fault." She took the pill, then pulled off her shoes and lay on the bed.

"You can't get comfortable dressed like that. I'll get your nightshirt."

She didn't think of protesting as he helped her undress and put on the nightshirt again.

"Should I get you something?"

"No, thank you."

Lance stood there, feeling helpless. He didn't like that he couldn't help her feel better or take the unhappiness away. She'd wanted marriage, a family. He'd ruined that for her. At least he no longer feared she didn't want the baby. She didn't want him, either. He'd expected as much, but leaving didn't enter his mind.

Slipping off his shoes, he got into the bed on the other side and pulled her into his arms. He felt a possessiveness for the mother and child that he hadn't expected. He'd take care of them, no matter what.

"We'll figure this out, but I'm not going anyplace. Just remember one thing: I want what's best for you and the baby."

There was no answer. He didn't know if she was asleep or if she had doubts about him. He'd just have to show her.

*   *   *

Fallon woke up in bed alone. She didn't expect to feel lonely. So much for Lance promising to be there. Sitting up, she saw crackers on another plate and a glass of ginger ale in a bowl of half-melted ice. Her stomach wasn't queasy for once. She ate and got dressed again.

Thank goodness she had called the airline yesterday when she started having the frequent nausea and changed her flight out to Monday. Naomi had been with her when Fallon placed the call and insisted she stay at her apartment, where she'd be more comfortable than at a motel.

Fallon had taken her up on the offer. She didn't relish flying ill, and she wanted to be steadier on her feet when she went home. She hadn't told her mother or Megan about her pregnancy. They'd want to hang Lance up by his thumbs and wish that marriage had come first, but they'd love the baby regardless; of that she was sure. She just wished the father loved her a little bit.

The bedroom door opened wider. Lance stuck his head around the open door and came farther into the bedroom. She couldn't hide her surprise.

"You've been asleep for a couple of hours." He looked at the empty plate of crackers and the half glass of ginger ale. "You feeling better?"

"Thanks to you."

He nodded solemnly. "Your pregnancy was a surprise, but that doesn't mean I don't want what's best for our child. I'll do whatever it takes for us to work things out. I don't want you to worry about anything."

She believed him, but something troubled her about their earlier conversation. "You seemed frightened for the baby. Did you lose a child?"

He stiffened. "I don't want to talk about it."

"If you want to be a part of my life that means I'll be a part of yours—no secrets. It's non-negotiable," she added when he remained silent. "How can we get to know each other better if we can't trust each other?"

"Come into the living room." He waited for her to pass, then followed.

Fallon took a seat on the edge of the sofa and watched Lance struggle to speak. He glanced at her, then faced the window.

"I met Ashley Sims when I brokered a deal to open a new restaurant in Atlanta. She was smart, savvy, and vice president of the bank. We clicked professionally and personally. She worked hard and didn't mind the long hours required to reach the top. She never missed a day of work or complained about her hectic schedule. Six weeks later, she moved in."

Fallon didn't want to hear about another woman or that the woman had been able to get Lance to commit and she herself hadn't. But she'd asked for an explanation.

"Two months after she moved in, she complained of having the flu. She'd never been ill, so I took off early to go check on her. She seemed surprised that I was home and insisted I return to work. At the time I thought she just didn't want me to see her ill. The phone rang while she was in the bathroom. It was the doctor's office, checking on her after the procedure."

Fallon sensed what was coming and felt ill. "Lance, I don't want to hear any more."

He continued as if he hadn't heard her. "She aborted our baby. I confronted her. She said it was for the best. A baby would have interfered with our career plans. I lost my child before I even knew of its existence."

Fallon's heart ached for him. She fought back tears. No wonder he'd been scared and accusatory. She took a step toward his rigidly held body, then stopped.

He appeared unapproachable. She knew he wasn't.

Going to him, she wrapped her arms around him from behind and placed her cheek against his back. "Lance, I'm so sorry. I'll protect our baby with everything within me. Believe me."

"I do."

Her eyes misted. She stepped back. He'd stayed last night and this morning out of fear and obligation. "You can leave now. You must have things to do."

He turned with shadows still lurking in his midnight black eyes. "I'm not going anyplace until I know you're feeling better."

"But I do." She just hoped she stayed that way. "In any case, I'm leaving tomorrow morning."

"Not if we're planning our wedding," he said, taking her hands again. "Marriage would solve everything."

She shook her head and retook her seat. "Obviously you haven't been around a lot of married people. I admit the Graysons seem to have it right, but they're the lucky ones."

"Where are you going?" He sat beside her.

"Home to Austin, then to my next assignment," she informed him.

He studied her for a moment. "How long do you plan to stay in Austin?"

"Two weeks, then I'm flying out to Playa del Carmen to do a follow-up on the Navarone Resort and Spas on Riviera Maya. Sierra invited me down there."

"Then you'd want to be at your best." He took her hands again. "I'm asking you to give me the two weeks to get to know each other better, to think about us getting married."

"Lance—"

"Hear me out," he interrupted. "You could have your own room and a cook and housekeeper at your beck and call. You wouldn't have to do anything but rest, relax, and hang around the pool."

"I'm not going to Tucson with you." She pulled her hands free.

"You wouldn't have to. I bought the Yates house."

She stared at him in astonishment. She'd wanted someone to purchase the house who would appreciate and love it. "When?"

He shifted uncomfortably. "The sale was finalized just last week, but I put a contract on the house the day after I first saw it."

"And you didn't tell me when I asked about the owner?"

"I didn't tell anyone, not even Richard. I don't discuss my life."

"So I'm learning." She came to her feet. "You were a tremendous help, but I'd like to rest and make some phone calls."

"You're kicking me out?"

"I wouldn't put it that way exactly."

"But it amounts to the same thing."

"Yes."

He stood, paced in frustration. "What do I have to say or do that will make you stay? I'm just asking for two weeks. You can't tell me you're carrying my child and then leave."

Fallon realized he might say he believed her, and he might, but he was still scared. "I'm sorry, Lance. It wasn't my intention to make this difficult for you. Please try to understand."

"I'm asking for that same understanding. Two weeks where you'll be pampered and fed real food that doesn't come from a can so you'll be ready for your trip to Mexico."

She rubbed her stomach. "Food isn't high on my list now."

"Maybe not now, but soon. You love to eat. Let me take care of you so you'll be able to enjoy Mexico," he cajoled.

Fallon was thoughtful. "When I was there before I didn't get a chance to go scuba diving."

Lance's eyes widened in horror. "You can't be thinking of doing that now?"

"I'll let my doctor decide." She placed her hand on his when his frown didn't clear. "I plan to have a healthy baby. I won't do anything to jeopardize that. I'll keep our baby safe. Don't worry."

"Do you mind giving me your mother's home phone number?"

Because he'd asked and not demanded, she told him the number and watched him put it in his cell phone contact list. "Call me if you change your mind."

"I won't." She opened the door. "Good-bye."

Lance got inside his car, started the motor, but didn't put the car in gear. Fallon was going to have his baby. He was going to be a father. His hand shook when he reached to put the car in gear.

A father. And this time he'd get to see and hold his child, but for how long? He stared at Fallon's closed door. What was he missing? He had hammered through business deals that others thought impossible. He was used to coming out the winner.

Except where women were concerned. His hands flexed on the gear knob. First his mother had chosen Jim Banks over him; then Cissy Douglas had dumped him as her date for their senior prom and gone with the football captain instead; then Melissa Sevens had broken up with him when he was a sophomore in college because he didn't make enough money working at the auction house to take her to "nice places."

He really thought he'd finally gotten it right when he met Ashley and she moved in. Finally he'd found a woman who thought he was enough.

Only she hadn't. If she had, she wouldn't have
gone to the clinic. He'd walked out of his condo
and never returned. Three days later he'd sent a
moving service to pick up his things. According to
the owner of the service, Ashley had already moved
out. That was three years ago, and sometimes the
betrayal felt as if it had just happened. Lance honestly didn't know how he would have reacted if
she'd told him she was pregnant. He just knew that
he would have wanted his child and would have
done anything to keep it safe.

I'll keep our baby safe.

Fallon's words came back to him. He believed
her, but she also planned to go on with her life
without him. That he wouldn't allow. This time
he'd be enough!

He pulled out his cell and dialed Richard's number. It was almost one Sunday afternoon. Perhaps
he and Naomi were talking to Kayla or doing something else innocent.

"I'm really going to kill you," came Richard's
snarled voice.

"Is Fallon all right?" asked Naomi in a breath-
less voice.

So they weren't talking to Kayla. "Sorry. Fallon
is resting. Can I speak with Richard, please?"

"Make it quick."

"I asked Fallon to marry me and she said no." It
still rankled.

He heard a rustling sound. "Did you tell her you
cared about her?"

Lance shifted in his seat. "She's carrying my baby."

"Lance, this is not a business deal. No woman is going to say yes—unless she's a gold digger—to a cold marriage proposal."

"It wasn't that bad," he defended.

"Oh, poor Fallon," he heard Naomi whisper. He looked back at the closed apartment door. At least he didn't think it was that bad.

"She plans to leave tomorrow morning." Just the thought made him restless and on edge. "I purchased the house I auctioned the contents from and asked her to spend the next two weeks with me there so we could get to know each other better and she could rest."

"And probably just as businesslike as you said now." Richard snorted.

"Fallon deserved better."

From the clarity of the comment Naomi had spoken into the phone, Lance didn't think of asking Richard to move so they could talk privately. He'd made it clear last night that he and Naomi had no secrets. They shared everything.

Lance knew that some secrets were too painful to share.

"I want her to stay," was all he could think to say.

"For the baby or for Fallon?" Naomi asked.

He wasn't that inept or stupid. "For both."

"Then she has to feel she matters," Richard said. "You have to convince her to stay."

Lance was shaking his head before Richard finished. "You know I can't do that, and why." He wouldn't be vulnerable to a woman again.

"I also know you were miserable when she left the first time," Richard came back. "You want to chance it again? And this time the stakes are much higher."

He didn't. "I'm not sure I can do as you ask."

"Then you better find out and in a hurry," Richard said. "If you can't say the words, do something to show her until you can."

"Just like you did for me," Naomi whispered.

Lance could almost visualize them kissing and wanted them back on track. They had their happiness. He was trying to get his. "What do you suggest?"

"Since my beautiful wife is shaking her pretty head at me, you'll have to come up with the answer on your own," Richard said.

"It has to come from you or it won't count," Naomi said into the receiver. "Fallon is a wonderful woman. If you can't see that and appreciate her . . . maybe you're not the right man for her."

"No other man is touching her," Lance snapped.

"Since I know your emotions are running high right now, I'll overlook you shouting at my wife. But I wouldn't do it again if I were you."

Lance took a deep breath, then another, and remembered their help again. "Naomi, I'm sorry. Richard, it won't happen again."

"Apology accepted," Naomi said. "Now, get off this phone and make Fallon happy."

"Good-bye, Lance, and lose the phone number unless it's a real emergency."

"But—," Lance began, but Richard had hung up on him again.

He needed help. He'd never dated much, never been around that many men discussing how to treat and handle women, so he hadn't a clue of what to do. Lance put away the phone and started the motor.

Maybe if he went back to the Yates house, he'd think of something.

Chapter 11

Late Sunday afternoon, just after twilight, Fallon
was trying to make herself eat the bowl of canned
chicken noodle soup in front of her without much
success. Just a few more bites and then she'd go lie
down. She'd already packed for her morning flight.

And she'd leave Lance behind. She lowered the
spoon, then placed her hand over her stomach.
"We'll love him even if he won't let himself love
us."

A knock sounded on the front door. Her heart
leaped. *Lance.*

She got up from the table. He'd probably come
back to try to bulldoze her into living at the Yates
house with him for two weeks or to marry him.
She wasn't going to do either, but she admitted to
herself that she'd like to see him before she left.

Opening the door, she saw Lance wearing a white
polo shirt and black jeans. He was carrying a handled shopping bag with the Red Cactus logo. She
didn't think it possible, but her mouth watered.

Lance held up the bag and stepped forward, forc-
ing her to move aside or be run over. "Tortilla and

chicken soup." He continued for the kitchen. "You can have your choice."

Fallon, her hand on her stomach, followed. She watched him take down two bowls and remove the containers of soup. She imagined he'd learned where things were earlier.

"Have a seat," Lance instructed. "Brandon said there's soup on the menu every day."

Fallon, who had been reaching for the back of her chair, abruptly stopped. "You told him."

His gaze on hers, Lance pulled out the chair for her. "Only that you weren't feeling well and I thought you'd like some soup."

Fallon took the seat. "I-I'm just not ready to tell people yet."

"We'll announce it together when the time comes." He placed the two bowls in front of her, then handed her a soupspoon. "Enjoy, but eat slowly."

Fallon was still caught on the announcing together, but the aroma pulled her toward the food. She'd barely eaten in the last week for fear of becoming sick. She was almost afraid to eat.

"Just a couple of bites to see how your stomach likes it." Lance took the seat next to her.

Fallon spooned in a sip of the chicken soup, waited a few moments, then took another sip. So far, so good.

"There was a line out the restaurant door again." Lance braced his arms on the table. "It's a good thing Brandon said to give your name to get a seat. I got dirty looks again, which I ignored."

"I thought you ignored them the night we had dinner there." The soup really was good.

"I tend to ignore things that aren't important to me," he said. "You looked beautiful at the wedding. Did you pick the gown up in Los Angeles?"

She grunted. "I'll ignore the first comment and answer the second. Yes."

He lifted a dark brow. "I'm noted for my ability to discern quality and beauty. You looked great and so did the bride."

"She did, didn't she?" Fallon's face softened; then she giggled. "I hope the photographer got a picture of Richard with his mouth open in stunned amazement."

"He did."

"Good." Fallon dipped her spoon into the bowl and found it empty. She frowned.

Lance reached across the table, picked up the bowl, then rinsed it out. "I'll put up the tortilla soup and the rest of the chicken soup for later." Opening the refrigerator, he poured her a small glass of ginger ale and placed it in front of her.

Fallon picked up the glass and sipped. She had to admit that it felt good to be taken care of and waited on. "Thank you."

Lance finished putting things away and cleaning up the kitchen before taking his seat next to Fallon again. Phase one accomplished. He'd distracted Fallon so she wasn't worried about being sick and had actually eaten. She now had a little color in her cheeks. With rest and care she'd get rid of those dark circles as well.

On to phase two. He pulled out his cell phone and opened the photo app. "I wanted to get your opinion on a couple of things."

Fallon leaned over to see Lance standing beside a tree. "You're doing more landscaping at the Yates—I mean, your house?"

"You might say that." He looked at the photo, then at her. "I remember you saying that your parents planted a tree when they brought Megan home from the hospital. I thought, why wait to celebrate our child. "

"What?" She straightened.

Lance slid the photo file on the cell phone. "Here are the choices of pots at the nursery. They're closed now, but we could go in the morning to select one . . . if you'd like. Francisco thinks we should plant it in the ground, but regardless, he's promised to help take care of it."

"You want to plant a tree?" she asked as if she was having trouble taking it all in.

"Your parents might not have been aware of it, but they started a beautiful tradition that I'd like to continue, only do it a little earlier." Reaching into the handled bag on the floor, he pulled out an embossed raspberry-colored journal and handed it to her. He'd chosen it because it was the color of her knit top when she came to the Yates house. "The Yateses had the right idea about leaving something behind. I thought you could keep track of things for the baby so one day he or she could pass it down to their child."

Tears filled her eyes. "Lance."

His chest felt tight. "Don't cry. It wasn't supposed to make you cry."

She smiled through her tears and hugged the journal to her breasts. "They're good tears." Leaning over, she kissed him on the cheek. "Thank you. Our baby will know what a wonderful father he or she has."

Lance was glad Fallon was looking at the journal instead of at him. He didn't plan on being a long-distance father. A quick change of plans. "It's still light outside. What do you say we take a drive out to the house and pick out a couple of spots for the pot or the tree?"

"I—"

"The trip will be the first note in the journal," he tempted. "It won't take long."

She bit her lower lip in indecision; then she smiled at him again. "All right. Let's go."

Maybe it was feeling better, the good food, or just Fallon wanting to spend part of the last evening in Santa Fe with Lance, or perhaps she just wanted to give him some good memories to replace the horrible ones of losing his first child.

Or perhaps a little bit of each, but against her better judgment, she was going to Lance's house again.

She thought she might feel awkward on seeing the guest cottage where they'd first made love. She didn't. She reasoned it might have something to do with the baby she carried. She wouldn't lie to herself. There were moments that she wished she and Lance had been married when she conceived, but she loved her baby regardless. Motherhood was a scary prospect, but she had eight months to adjust.

Lance kept the conversation going smoothly as they walked the grounds searching for the perfect spot to place the sycamore tree.

"I think it should be by the front door." Lance looked around the garden near the pond.

"I Googled the tree and they can grow eighty feet or more. Let's plant it here in the ground where the tree branches can shade him or her and later their grandchildren can climb," Fallon said softly, her arm circling her stomach.

Lance nodded, swallowed. "Then here it is."

She didn't know if he was thinking of the child he'd lost or the child she carried. He was inches away from her and it seemed like miles. She didn't know if losing his child had made him so self-contained or something else in his past, or a combination of the two. She did know he had a wall built around him that she wasn't sure she could scale.

They had been lovers, but they were practically strangers. Now they were going to be parents. How could they ever hope to be anything meaningful to each other and raise a child together if they didn't talk about their innermost fears, their hopes, and their dreams?

Fallon wanted to touch him, comfort him, and this time she didn't hesitate. She circled his waist with her arm and looked up at him. *We'll always love you.* "What if we get two trees?"

His stunned gaze snapped to hers; then he looked out over the verdant backyard. "Two it is."

"I better get back." Her arms dropped to her sides and she stepped away.

His reaction was immediate.

"Stay. We'll help Francisco plant the trees."

She wanted to. "I think it's best you take me back."

"For whom?" He caught her arms. "What do you want from me? I'm doing the best I can."

The last sentence shocked her. It was more than just him asking her to stay. The pain in his voice went much deeper.

He let her go so quickly she swayed. His hand shot out to steady her, then released her again. "I'll take you back." He stepped aside for her to continue on the winding path back to the car.

His expression was closed, remote, but his eyes were filled with the same pain she'd heard moments earlier in his voice. "Who hurt you?" The words just slipped out.

He flinched. "I'll take you back," he repeated.

She started for the car. He wasn't going to explain himself. She'd waste her breath asking.

She stopped at the wooden door leading into the inner courtyard and looked back to where the trees would be planted, then at him. "Take care of yourself."

His movements agitated, he unlatched the door and closed it when she passed through. Moving quickly ahead of her, he opened the car door.

"Thank you."

As she suspected, the door slammed shut. He was angry. *Well, let him be,* she thought as he got inside and started the engine. Life had dealt him a cruel blow, but he didn't get a pass because of it.

He put the car into a sharp spin and turned around. He shifted gears. The foreign sports car barreled down the road and would have made Faith's brother, Cameron, a NASCAR driver, envious.

"If you plan to speed, let me out and I'll call a cab."

He didn't say anything, but the car slowed. He kept his speed under the posted limit the rest of the way to Naomi's apartment. As soon as he stopped in front, Fallon opened her door.

"I apologize if I frightened you. I wouldn't do anything to harm you or our baby." His hands were clamped around the steering wheel.

She started to just get out, leave him to whatever devils plagued him. She couldn't. "Not intentionally perhaps, but would you have slowed down if I hadn't asked you?"

"I'm not sure."

She blew out a breath. "Well, you better damn well be sure. I don't plan to be a single parent, so take your anger and frustration out someplace else other than in a car." Getting out, she slammed the door and started for her apartment.

He caught her when she was about to enter the apartment. "I only lose my temper with you."

"How lucky does that make me?"

He opened his mouth, then took her into his arms, held her tight. "I missed you when you left.

Both times. And now you're back and you're leaving again and taking our baby."

Her arms automatically lifted to hug him back. She knew what he meant, but her lips still twitched. "It's not like you can carry the baby."

She felt his body shake with laughter. She leaned her head back. "Thanks for the smile. I didn't want to leave with us angry at each other."

"Me, either." His hands flexed. "Can I take you to the airport tomorrow?"

"Pick me up at eight. Good night, Lance."

"Good night." Releasing her, he stepped back. "I'm not giving up on talking you into staying until you walk through Security. Sleep well."

Entering the apartment, Fallon leaned against the door and admitted she wasn't sure she wanted him to give up.

Her cell phone rang. She quickly dug it out of her purse. "Couldn't wait until tomorrow, huh?"

"Fallon?"

Fallon glanced at the readout, although she knew it was Naomi. "What are you doing calling me instead of enjoying that yummy vet of yours?"

"Checking on you, but you sound as if I wasted a call." Laughter came through the phone.

Fallon took a seat on the sofa, her smile fading. "Lance and I are talking, but I'm still going home to Austin tomorrow."

"Oh, Fallon. I'm so sorry. I'd hoped things would work out."

"Me, too." Fallon leaned her head against the cushions. "There's something eating at him, and until he can talk about it openly to me we'll never be able to move past it and see if we can be a couple."

"You want that, don't you?"

Fallon sighed. "I love the stubborn man. But he's also kind, considerate. He was wonderful with Kayla."

Naomi laughed. "She likes her cousin Lance as well."

"He can grow on you," Fallon admitted.

"Then why are you giving up?" Naomi asked. "Where would I be if Richard had given up on me? Miserable instead of in a fabulous honeymoon suite and so in love and happy I want to shout it from the rooftop."

"Just say the word."

Fallon heard Richard's comment and laughed. "You both did good."

"But it wasn't easy," Naomi finally said. "You and Catherine helped me get over my fears of being vulnerable again. Now it's my turn to help you. Kayla is enjoying her new grandparents enough so that I feel we can leave on our honeymoon tomorrow. We'll be gone until Sunday. Stay in the apartment and work things out with Lance."

"I don't know." Fallon blew out a breath and came upright.

"If you leave tomorrow without giving yourself a chance, you'll regret it for the rest of your life. Sometimes we don't get a second chance." Naomi spoke from experience.

"I'll think about it," Fallon said. "Go enjoy your husband and have a great time at Playa del Carmen."

"We will. Good night."

"Good night." Fallon disconnected the call, then leaned back once again on the sofa and circled her waist with her arms. "What do you say, give Daddy another chance or get the hell out of Dodge before I fall even deeper for him?"

Lance had another chance, and he didn't plan to waste it. By six the next morning he was up, dressed, and walking out of the cottage on the Yates estate. For some odd reason he hadn't even thought of moving into the main house. He certainly had the means and the access to furnish the entire place, but he was comfortable in the guesthouse.

Lance made the first of two stops fifteen minutes later. By the time seven fifty arrived, he'd accomplished everything on his list. Parking a couple of doors down from Naomi's apartment, he knocked on the door.

Fallon slowly opened the door. Gone was her smile. Her hair was in some kind of off-kilter ponytail. Her pale face was free of makeup. She wore a yellow knit top and khaki slacks with black house slippers.

"You sick?"

She stared at him as if she'd like to throw him out the window of a very tall building. "What was your first clue?"

Lance didn't' think of answering. "Let's get you some ginger ale and crackers."

"No time." She started for her luggage.

"Fallon, you can't seriously be thinking of flying

when you're ill." He picked up the weekender and held it just out of reach of her outstretched hand.

She gave him that look again. "Pregnancy is not an illness."

"You have your house shoes on," he said, feeling at least that was safe to point out.

She sat in the nearest chair, closed her eyes for a moment, toed off the slippers, and didn't move.

"Where are your shoes?"

"Bedroom, I think."

Lance found the high-heeled sandals and returned. He started to ask if she had any flat shoes, but he wasn't sure of her response. Instead he opened her luggage, found a pair of ballerina slippers, and exchanged them for the heels. Bending, he put the slippers on her feet. "If you'd like, I don't mind changing your flight reservations to tomorrow or whenever you'd like."

"We've decided to get the hell out of Dodge." Fallon came unsteadily to her feet.

Lance was pretty sure she meant her and the baby. He picked up the garment and camera bag and followed her out the door and placed her things in the trunk of his car. "How will Naomi get her key back?"

"I left it on the kit—" Fallon gasped, looked back at Lance, then at the two net-covered trees on the back of a larger black truck.

The look on her face was so astonished, he knew he'd done the right thing. He curved his arm around her shoulders. "I wanted you to see them even if you couldn't help plant them."

"Oh, Lance." She wiped away tears.

Lance really wished she'd stop that. He gave her his handkerchief and motioned for the two men sitting in the truck to join them. "Fallon, you've already met Oskar. I'd like you to meet his father, Francisco Fuente. Francisco, this is Fallon Marshall."

Francisco removed his straw hat. "Pleased to meet you at last, Miss Marshall. I saw you at the auction."

"The gardens at the Yates house are beautiful," she said.

"Thank you." He looked at the trees. "Now, once these are planted they will be even more beautiful."

Fallon burst into tears. The three stunned men looked at one another for help. Lance hugged her, kissed the top of her head. "Please don't cry. I won't give you another surprise if you keep crying."

"I'm sorry if I upset you," Francisco said, his hat pressed to his chest.

Fallon sniffed and shook her head. "You didn't. What you said was just so beautiful."

The older man smiled. "I spoke from the heart."

Oskar laughed and placed his hand on his father's shoulder. "Father would have been a poet if not a landscape designer."

"Gardener and proud of it." He jabbed a finger into his son's chest. "You will be the landscape designer. Now, if you'll excuse us, we better get going."

"Thanks, Francisco. Oskar. I'll see you in a bit." His arm still around Fallon, Lance helped her into his car.

Fallon twisted around in the seat to see the truck head out of the parking lot. "Do they plan to plant them now?"

"Not until I get there. I want to start digging the holes. Francisco said you picked a good location." Lance backed out of the parking space and followed the truck to the street. The Silverado went left and Lance right. "We'll be at the airport in ten minutes." He hoped by then he would have thought of a way to keep her with him.

"Stop the car!"

Lance threw a frightened look at Fallon, saw her holding her hand over her mouth, and sped up to pass the car on the outside lane. Flicking on his signal, he pulled into the parking lot of a fast-food restaurant.

Fallon had the door open before he came to a complete stop. She barely made it to the grass before emptying her stomach. Finished, she tucked her head in embarrassment. "I'm sorry."

"You have nothing to be sorry for." Taking her arm again, he helped her back into the car. "I'm going inside to get you some water to rinse your mouth out and something to drink."

Her eyes closed, she leaned her head back on the headrest. "I don't want anything."

He closed her door. There was nothing in her stomach. If she thought she was flying, she was crazy. She could get mad all she wanted, but he was taking her to the cottage.

Lance ordered the drinks and returned to help

Fallon rinse out her mouth. She took a sip of the 7UP and refused any more. Not sure if he should force her to drink it, he eased her back against the car seat and poured the liquid over the spot where she had been sick. After putting the cups in the nearby trash receptacle, he fastened her seat belt and got back inside the car.

He looked over at her, his heart turning over. He wanted his child, but he didn't want Fallon to be ill. Starting the car, he backed out and continued to the airport.

Fallon was stubborn. He wouldn't put it past her to call a cab if he didn't take her. He wasn't above pointing out to the airline officials once she'd gone through Security that she was ill and shouldn't be allowed to fly. One look at her and she'd be booted off the plane.

He took the entrance to the airport. Of course, the tricky part would be if she'd call him to come pick her up. He might have to rethink that one. He saw the sign for parking, flicked on his signal, glancing at Fallon as he did so. She was asleep, her lips slightly parted.

Lance turned off his signal and kept going. She could be mad all she wanted, but she wouldn't be ill and alone on an airplane.

She was wrapped securely in Lance's arms. They were on the loggia enjoying the moonlight, their hands interlocked over her bulging stomach. "You're all that I need," he whispered, then angled his head to kiss her, slowly deepening the kiss.

Fallon's moan of pleasure woke her. She stared at the lamp in her direct line of vision and knew immediately she was in the cottage. *Lance.* She'd kill him. She remembered just in time to slowly sit up and swing her legs over the side of the bed; when she did she saw the ice bucket with a can of ginger ale and a small plate of crackers.

Being considerate wouldn't get him off the hook. He'd kidnapped her. She pulled the tab on the soft drink and took a sip. It tasted good. So did the crackers. She glanced at her watch and her eyes widened. She couldn't have slept for six hours! On the heels of that was the knowledge that she was supposed to have landed in Austin an hour ago. Her mother and sister had to be worried sick.

Fallon glanced around the room for her purse, saw it and her luggage on a chair, and went to retrieve it. She had to call. She reached for her purse to get her cell phone and saw the handwritten note on a sheet of typing paper.

> *You were asleep when I reached the airport. I called your mother so she wouldn't worry. I called the airline. I postponed digging the hole in case you wanted to help. Go back to sleep if you can, and call when you want to eat. Carmen fixed chicken and potato soup.*
>
> *L*

Taking the note, she got back in bed, noting she was wearing a sleeveless blue nightgown, no bra, and her panties. She could be angry or look at it as faith's way of giving them both a chance to get to know each other better. A movement in the open doorway caught her eye.

"Lance."

He stepped inside the room, a bed tray in his hands. "I thought I heard you get up. Hungry?"

She eyed him and held up the sheet of paper. "What did you tell my mother?"

He placed the tray over her lap and handed her a warm, damp washcloth. "After I introduced myself, I told her that you weren't feeling well and that a friend thought you should postpone your flight, and that you'd call her later today when you felt better."

Fallon ran the cloth over her face, her hands. "Smooth, and what did she say?"

"That if I hurt you again to look for her on my doorstep."

"That's my mother." Fallon picked up her spoon. "Good thing Megan didn't answer the phone."

His mouth tightened. "When your mother mentioned my name Megan got on the phone. Your sister has an inventive way of talking."

Fallon grinned and took a bite of potato soup. "She knows people."

"So she said." He folded his arms. "And something about bodies never being found. That's when your mother took the phone and said they expected to hear from you before the day was over."

"We're close."

"I gathered as much."

"What about your family?" she asked, and

watched his face close. She placed her spoon on the tray. "We talk and get to know each other or I call a cab and catch the next plane out of here."

His gaze narrowed. "The last flight for Dallas left ten minutes ago."

She smiled sweetly. "Here, but not the Albuquerque airport."

He walked to the window. "There's nothing to talk about. You met Richard's parents and my mother and stepfather at the wedding rehearsals."

"Your aunt introduced them to everyone," she said. "I never saw you talk to them."

"You were probably busy." He picked up her tray. "You want anything else?"

"Besides a straight answer? No."

He turned away, then turned back. "Some things aren't easy for me."

"I gather." She got out of bed and retrieved her cell phone.

His hands tightened on the tray. "My mother and I haven't gotten along since she remarried when I was ten, the same month my father had died."

"What happened?" Fallon asked.

Lance's eyes chilled. "Nothing. She just preferred him over me." He left the room.

Fallon followed him into the kitchen. She didn't know what to say. He thought his mother had rejected him, then the woman he loved had rejected his unborn child. He'd been through a lot, and she wasn't sure he was telling it all. No wonder he shied away from commitments.

"I don't know about then, but at the rehearsal and reception a couple of times I saw her watching you. She had this wistful look in her eyes," Fallon told him. "Once she even reached out to touch you."

"You're mistaken," he clipped out.

She wasn't. He'd deny it to the end, but the strained relationship between him and his mother still hurt. "I'm going to call Mama and Megan to tell them I'll be staying in Santa Fe for the time being."

He faced her, the shadows fading from his eyes.

A lump formed in her throat. He expected her to desert him like he thought his mother had. "It seems afternoons are better for me. You think Francisco and Oskar are around so we can plant the trees?"

"I'll call." He pulled out his cell phone.

"I better get dressed." She started from the room.

"Fallon."

"Yes?" She stopped at the door.

"Thank you."

She smiled. He was getting there. "I shouldn't be long."

Chapter 12

The two trees were already at the site ready to be planted when Lance and Fallon arrived. So was a hole digger and two husky men Lance had seen around the estate.

Francisco introduced the men to her and Lance, gave them gloves and a shovel. "You start and we'll finish."

"First, I want to take a picture." Fallon took the shots with hands that weren't quite steady, making sure she got one of Lance. They would be included with the first notation in the journal. She hadn't felt like it last night. Finished, she handed the camera to Oskar. "Could you please hold this for me?"

"My pleasure." Oskar held the camera with both hands.

Lance leaned the shovel against his leg, pulled on the gloves, and looked at Fallon, surprised to find a lump in his throat. "We're doing this together. Ready?"

Fallon slid her hands into the small gloves that probably belonged to Carmen, nodded, swallowed, and placed her hands below his on the wooden handle. "Yes."

Together they cut into the earth, once, twice, a third time before moving to the spot where the other tree would be planted, and repeated the motions. Lance stopped when he felt moisture drop on his hand. He glanced up to see tears sliding down Fallon's cheeks.

He pulled her into his arms with one hand and exchanged the shovel for the camera with Oskar. "Thanks." His arm still around her, they started back to the house.

"I'd like to watch for a bit."

He led her to a bench tucked beneath the trees off the long path leading to the pond. He took her hand. "Are you all right?"

She nodded, then leaned her head against his shoulder. "I was thinking about the child you lost and thought it was a shame that no one ever cried for the loss except you."

"And Richard." Lance blinked a couple of times. "I called him and he came to Atlanta despite the torrential rains and power outages across the city."

She lifted her head. "I'm glad he was there for you."

"I . . . I never told anyone else," he said slowly. "It was too . . ."

"Painful," she said.

"That, and I felt guilty." He glanced away. "Maybe there was something lacking in me that made her do it. Maybe I wasn't enough."

"Maybe she wasn't the woman you thought she

was." Fallon took his face and turned it to her. "She was selfish. She didn't think of you or the child, only herself. She took something from you that can never be replaced. Put the blame where it belongs. You make me want to scream, but from the short time I've known you I know you take your responsibilities seriously and there isn't anything you put your mind to that you can't accomplish."

"You believe that?"

"I'm sitting here when I planned to be in Austin by now. I don't bend easily, if at all." She gestured around the landscaped yard. "Richard said you came from humble beginnings, yet you have this fantastic home and succeeded in everything you've ever set out to do."

"Professionally, yes," he said quietly.

"I admit your interpersonal skills need work, but so do mine. I tend to speak first and think later." She looped her arm through his and looked to where the men were digging the holes for the trees. "Don't sell yourself short. If I didn't think you're pretty fantastic past the good looks, I wouldn't have gone to bed with you and I wouldn't be here now aching for you."

"I don't want your pity." He came to his feet.

"Pity?" She stood as well. "Why would I pity you? You were kicked in the gut, but so were a lot of people with much worse. You not only survived; you flourished. But you're so busy looking at the past, you can't be thankful for where you are or focus on the present."

"Are you finished?"

"For now." Picking up her camera, she stalked off toward the men planting the trees.

Lance sat back down on the bench. Maybe he should have let her call the cab. Even as the thought formed in his mind, he knew he couldn't have. Somehow she had worked her way into his heart even before he knew she carried his child.

She was right about one thing: he couldn't let go of the past. Caring meant being vulnerable. It was safer being alone, yet as he watched the first tree being lowered into the ground and saw Fallon brush away tears even as she raised the camera he had to wonder if he might be wrong. Was finding the person who made your heart glad worth the risk?

Despite her being angry with him, she still cried for the life of his child that had been lost. She was a complicated woman. She'd stayed instead of going to the house and calling a cab. On one hand, he had to admire her for holding her own, even if it would be so much easier if she were easily intimidated.

As if their argument had never happened, she stared at him across the hole in front of her and beckoned him. He honestly thought of not going.

Fallon was getting to him. He thought he could keep her compartmentalized, but he realized that wasn't happening. She was too vibrant. She called to him on so many levels that he was finding, much to his chagrin, he wanted her heart as well as her body.

Her beautiful eyes narrowed, she propped one hand on her slim hip, the other on top of the metal handle of the shovel. Lance stood and started toward her. He was strong. He could be around her and protect his heart from being ripped from his chest again.

He honestly believed that until he reached Fallon and stared down into her eyes glistening with tears. His heart clenched.

He wanted to pull her into his arms, soothe her, and never let her go. He realized he'd miscalculated. It was too late to guard his heart. Somehow she'd already found a place there. He could accept it and convince her to marry him—something he never thought he'd do—or keep fighting a winless battle.

"I told Francisco we'd like to throw the first dirt to start filling the hole and return to finish," she told Lance.

He'd already told Francisco as much. Lance had wanted him and Fallon to be a part of the planting at the beginning and the end. They'd had a shaky beginning and he wasn't sure if the ending would be any different.

"Are you all right?" she asked.

Standing close to her, their bodies touching, smelling her perfume, he came to a decision—he'd do whatever it took to keep Fallon and their baby. But that didn't mean he had to put himself at risk and let her know how much he cared.

"I'm sorry," he told her. "I don't want to argue."

"Neither do I." She smiled up at him. "I think I'll

leave that part out when I write in the journal to-night."

He found himself smiling back. "Don't. It will show what kind of woman you are."

"And that would be?"

"Strong, dependable, courageous, and all in a beautiful package."

Her astonished delight showed in her face and eyes. He took pleasure that he was the cause. "We'll make this a day to remember."

Sure of himself and in control of his emotions once again, he took hold of the shovel she held. Together they scooped up the first turned earth and tossed it on top of the root ball.

Late that afternoon, in the guest bathroom of the cottage, Fallon soaked in the tub filled with scented bath salts and admitted gaining Lance's trust was going to be one of the most difficult tasks she'd ever taken on. He could turn that cold stare on her in an instant, but he also went out of his way to take care of her.

She learned from Oskar that Lance had asked him to pick up the gloves after Lance had brought her to the cottage. He'd wanted them to share the experience together. He'd insisted she return to the cottage and rest in between the plantings. Carmen had arrived soon afterward with a light snack.

He watched over and took care of Fallon. It could be duty or obligation because she carried his child, but she didn't think so. There was something in his eyes when he looked at her that gave her hope.

When she'd returned later, his T-shirt was soiled and wet with perspiration. He'd done more than shovel in dirt. There'd been a look of satisfaction on his face.

A knock sounded on the door. "Are you all right?"

He also worried about her. Another good sign.

"Fallon?"

"Just enjoying the tub. I'm getting out now." Climbing out of the tub, she dried off, moisturized her skin, and put on a strapless sundress, thankful that she always packed a few extra pieces when she traveled. She'd asked her mother to pack her enough clothes for the two weeks and send them.

Opening the door, she found Lance waiting for her. He'd showered and changed clothes. He wore a white knit shirt that delineated the hard muscles of his chest, and a pair of the sinful tight jeans she loved seeing him wear. Her skin heated. The man definitely had a high Y factor.

He reached for her hand. "Carmen left dinner for us on the loggia. Or do you want me to bring it back here?"

She placed her hand in his, felt her pulse leap. "By the pool is fine. What did you tell Francisco about the second tree?" she asked. It had been on her mind for a couple of hours.

Long seconds ticked by before Lance answered, "That I wanted to honor the memory of someone I'd lost."

She leaned into him as they approached the loggia. "You helped them plant the trees. You're going to be sore in the morning."

"I'll survive." He pulled out her chair, poured her a glass of lemonade, then served them baked chicken and brown rice. "We both thought this might be better for your stomach than spicy food."

"The soup last night wasn't spicy, but it still didn't stay down."

Lance frowned. "Maybe you should just eat the rice. Smaller portions are better, too."

"We'll see." Bowing her head, Fallon said grace, then picked up her spoon and ate a bite of rice. "Good." She waved her spoon toward his plate of rice and chicken. "You don't have to eat light because I am."

He picked up his fork. "We're in this together."

"Have you had the open appraisal yet?" she asked.

"It's scheduled for next month." He cut into his chicken. "Word leaked out and we're already getting lots of calls. It's going to be a madhouse."

"I saw you at the auction, remember. You can handle it." She sipped her drink. "And you can't wait."

He almost smiled. "Ninety-nine percent will be worthless, but there's always that chance of finding a valuable piece."

"And you'll treat them fairly," she said with conviction.

"Thank you. That means a lot." His phone rang.

"Excuse me." He reached for his phone, looked at the readout, and frowned.

"Problem?"

"I'm not sure." He accepted the call. "Hello."

"Did you find Fallon?"

"Yes."

"Good. You—you seemed concerned. I hope things are all right."

"Yes."

"I . . . Good night, Lance."

"Good night." He disconnected the call and returned the cell phone to his pocket.

Fallon ate a couple of more bites, then lowered her spoon. "You can tell me to mind my own business, but you have that look again."

He picked up his lemonade, then put the glass down again. "It was my mother."

"And?"

"I was looking for you the night of the wedding reception. She called to ask if I'd found you."

Fallon brightened. "I told you. She's reaching out to you."

He picked up his knife and fork. "Did you tell your mother about the baby?"

He certainly knew how to change the subject. "No. I don't know how."

He put the utensils on his plate and came around the table to hunker down beside her. "Your mother and sister love you. They would walk to Santa Fe to break every bone in my body to protect you. No matter what, they love you. That won't change."

She swallowed, glanced down at her stomach. "I

know. I just don't want to disappoint them. I always thought I'd be married first."

His mouth tightened. "I ruined that for you."

"I could have said no. I take full responsibility for my actions." She moistened her lips.

"I'm not sure how it happened. I mean, I used a condom each time."

Fallon blushed. "We're the failure rate."

"Yeah." He pulled a chair over and sat down. "So, where do we go from here?"

"I wish I knew."

"We could get married," he suggested.

"And then what?" she asked. "You have your business in Tucson and I'm traveling—"

"You still plan to work?"

"For as long as I feel like it," she answered. "I plan to be in Playa del Carmen as scheduled."

"You are not scuba diving!" he said emphatically.

She twisted her head to one side. "How about parasailing?"

"You—," he began, then saw the teasing glint in her eyes. "That wasn't nice."

"You should have seen your face." She laughed.

"It's good hearing you laugh." His hands palmed her cheek. "It's good having you here. I missed you."

Her hands covered his. "I missed you, too."

He had to kiss her. His lips touched hers, a gentle melding of warmth. Heat and desire rushed though him. He deepened the kiss, his hand lowering to mold her breast; his mouth followed.

She moaned his name. He wanted, needed, more. Picking her up, he carried her to the oversized chaise longue and followed her down.

"Lance, we can't."

He shut his eyes tightly and tried to bring his body under control.

"Lance."

"Give me a minute." He stood, raked his hand over his head.

"We—it . . ." Her trembling voice trailed away.

He turned. Her dress was back over her breast, but he could still feel, taste, her hard nipple in his mouth.

"I think I should go to the cottage." She came to her feet. "I-I'll see you in the morning. Good night."

He let her go. It was easier that way. Besides, he was too near the edge. After a few minutes, he followed and knocked on the cottage door.

The door opened. "Lance, it's not going to happen."

"I got the message earlier." He headed toward the master bedroom.

"You haven't moved your clothes into the house yet?" she questioned, trailing after him.

He stopped at the door. "I haven't moved, period. See you in the morning." The door closed behind him.

Fallon stared at the door, then jerked it open and came to an abrupt halt. Lance, his knit shirt off, was bent from the waist, shoving his pants off his long legs. They were halfway down his thighs.

Her eyes rounded on seeing his erection. Her gaze snapped up to his; then she spun away. "Please pull up your pants so we can talk."

"There's nothing to talk about, and since this is my room—"

"Lance, you can't be serious about sleeping here," she said, trying not to imagine him with his pants off. He had an incredible body.

"I am. This bed is comfortable."

Fallon blushed. She knew exactly how comfortable the bed was. "I didn't hear you showering."

"Well, I heard you running the water in the tub and went to the pool house to shower," he said, not sounding too happy.

She had almost turned to ask him why before the reason sank in. The same reason her own imagination was running wild. Besides an incredible body, Lance had a mouth and hands that set her body on fire. She'd hardly been able to form a coherent thought.

She cleared her throat. "You haven't been back since the auction?"

There was a telling silence. "No. I came back for the wedding, just like you did."

Something wasn't making sense. "Why buy the house and not move into it?"

"I haven't had time."

She didn't believe him. She needed to see his face. Taking a deep breath, she turned. Lance leaned against the poster closest to the foot of the bed. His pants were on, thank goodness, his bare arms crossed over his lickable chest. He didn't look happy.

"Then why buy a house you don't have time to furnish or live in?"

His hands dropped to his sides. "Shouldn't you be in bed?"

Did the time they shared at the cottage mean something to him? "I asked you a question first."

He started toward her. "Good night, Fallon."

When he was within a foot, she ducked around him and went still. On the hand-painted floral chest beneath the window was the glass collection from the Yates estate. She couldn't believe it. Her hand trembling, she picked up one of the crystal pieces, an angel, and simply stared at him.

"So I bought the collection. It's no big deal," he said.

Replacing the glass because her hands were unsteady, she went to him. He'd bought them so he could give one to her. But what made her heart beat with joy was that he kept the collection in his room. "You're a fraud, Lance. You try to be hard and rigid, but you're not. You care about people."

"I thought you were in a hurry to go to bed."

"First, I have to do something."

He gazed at her with suspicion. "What?"

She kissed him, letting her body mold itself to his before lifting her head. "I'll be the first to say it. If I didn't care about you, I wouldn't be here. Good night." She certainly had a wonderful start to her journal.

If I didn't care about you, I wouldn't be here.

Lance had thought about what Fallon had said

most of the night. She cared. Caring wasn't love, but it certainly was a huge step in the right direction.

He picked up his watch from the nightstand. Seven-oh-two AM. He wasn't sure what time Fallon got up, but he planned to be there if she wasn't feeling well. She needed someone to take care of her, and that someone was going to be him. Pulling on his briefs, shirt, and jeans, he went to her door.

Indecision held him still. He didn't want to wake her up by knocking, but he didn't want to walk in unannounced. Yesterday was different.

Deciding he couldn't stand outside her door all morning, he slowly opened the door. Fallon was asleep on her side, her hands pillowing her cheek. She looked peaceful. She still had dark circles beneath her eyes, but he was working on that as well.

"I'm not asleep," she murmured, her eyes still closed.

"You—" He stopped himself before he said "sick." "Do you want crackers and ginger ale?" he asked, coming farther into the room.

"How good are you at backrubs?"

His brows bunched with worry as he strode across the room. "You did too much yesterday. I should have known better."

Her eyes opened. "Planting the trees was important. Besides, I'm not sure it had anything to do with my back hurting. It might be the mattress. I can't get comfortable."

The two nights she'd spent with him, they'd been in *his* bed. "You want to move now or wait until tonight?"

"I'm not putting you out of your bed." She turned on her back and placed her arm over her eyes.

"You know you don't have to," he said, not sure whether he was teasing or hoping she'd take him up on his offer.

She grunted.

Lance smiled. "You could give me a complex."

"You're too self-assured for that."

In business and with other people perhaps, but not with Fallon. "I'm up for the day, so you can have the other bed."

"Lance—"

"Don't argue." Throwing back the bedcovers, he picked her up, congratulating himself for not staring at her bare long legs where her gown had ridden up over her thighs. "Wrap your arms around my neck so you won't jostle yourself."

She complied, and he started back to his bed. "I'll get you your morning snack."

"It used to be coffee, waffles, and sausages."

He placed her in his bed and pulled up the covers. She looked perfect there. "I'm sorry you have to go through this."

"Believe me, it's a lot better than it was." She yawned and closed her eyes.

He should let her rest, but he didn't move. "Was it bad?"

She looked at him. "Not so much. I thought I had a bug until the food critic I was traveling with pointed out that it was only in the morning. I purchased a pregnancy test to prove she was wrong."

"You should have called me," he said.

"I could hardly accept it myself. I stared at that stick for a long, long time." She glanced away. "I cried."

Sitting on the side of the bed, he took her into his arms. "I wish I could have been there for you."

She snuggled against him. "I-I think that was part of the reason. I wanted you there."

His arms tightened. He kissed her forehead, then swept his hand down her slim back. "I'm here now, and I'm not going anyplace."

"Your business is in Tucson. I travel," she said unnecessarily.

"We'll work it out. Go to sleep." His hand continued to glide up and down her back. He wasn't ready to let her go. He enjoyed holding her and their child. He'd find a way to keep both.

Chapter 13

Fallon stared from the bright yellow door of the spa back to Lance. She'd awakened a little past ten to find him gone and her snack waiting for her. He'd knocked on the door two hours later with another surprise. They'd driven into Santa Fe to one of the most luxurious spas in the country. "I don't think I'm going to cry this time."

"Good." He slung his arm around her shoulders. "I booked you for the full treatment, but you can change anything. All of their technicians have at least ten years' experience. They can also see you later."

Fallon glanced down at her flat stomach in the sundress. "My mother gained fifty pounds with me. The doctors feared she would develop gestational diabetes."

"What?" Lance took Fallon's shoulders and turned her to him. "Did you tell your doctor?"

"I did." She palmed his cheek to reassure him. "The way I'm going, I'll be lucky to gain ten pounds."

He studied her. "You kept your food down today

and your color is better. We'll just have to watch your diet."

Her brows arched. "Lance, I love to eat and, once I really feel better, I'm going to indulge in all the food I missed."

"We'll see." He reached for the doorknob. "Call when you're ready for me to pick you up."

"Then we can have lunch at the Red Cactus."

"I don't recall seeing baked chicken or fish on the menu."

"Exactly."

"Fallon! Cousin Lance!"

Fallon turned to see Kayla, her fat pigtails bouncing, rushing toward them. "Hi, Kayla."

Hurrying to keep up with Kayla were Richard's and Lance's mothers. Fallon shot a quick glance at Lance. His lips were pressed together in harsh lines. She reached out to touch his arm in a gesture of comfort and a warning to be nice before bending to envelop Kayla in her arms. When Fallon began to lift the little girl, Lance scooped her up.

"Hi, Kayla," he greeted.

Grinning, Kayla looped one arm around his neck. "We're going to the park and I get to swing all I want."

Her hand on Kayla's pant leg, Fallon had to laugh. Naomi was right about Kayla being happy. Indulgent grandparents would put a smile on any child's face.

"Hi, Fallon, Lance," Richard's mother greeted, a bit out of breath. "I don't think I should have given up my exercise class."

"Hello, Lance, Fallon." Lance's mother hung back, her hand gripping the white leather strap of her handbag.

"Hello, Mrs. Youngblood, Mrs . . . ." Fallon faltered and blushed. She couldn't remember Lance's mother's married name.

"Banks," Lance supplied, his mouth curled as if the word was distasteful.

Richard's mother shot Lance a look of annoyance—which he ignored.

"Mrs. Banks," Fallon said, reaching out to touch the woman's arm. She found it trembling. "I apologize for not remembering."

"That's all right." Mrs. Banks's gaze kept sliding away from Lance as if she was starved for the sight of him and as the same time afraid to be caught looking at him. "I see you're feeling better. You didn't look well at the reception."

"Were you ill, Fallon?" Mrs. Youngblood asked, her brow furrowed with concern. "I'm sorry, I didn't notice."

Fallon's guilty gaze swung to Lance.

"She's fine now," Lance said to his aunt. "In fact, she was just about to go into the spa." He placed Kayla on her feet. "Have fun at the park."

Fallon wanted to kick Lance. He didn't have to be rude.

"After the park, we're going to Mr. Brandon's restaurant for my favorite—hamburger. Once I'm finished, I'm having the brownie supreme with ice cream for dessert," Kayla happily announced.

"Aunt Gladys used to take your new daddy and

me to the park and then out to eat," Lance told her.

Kayla looked at Mrs. Banks and caught her hand. "Aunt Irene said it's her threat. When I got my new daddy, I got Aunt Irene and Uncle Jim, too. It used to be just me and Mama, but now I have other people to love and love me back. It's nice having a big family, just like Mama said."

"It certainly is, Kayla," Fallon answered, since Lance's expression was stony. His mother kept blinking her eyes, and his aunt looked as if she wanted to turn her nephew over her knee.

"We should be going." Mrs. Youngblood sent Lance a stern look. "Expect a call from me."

"Good-bye, Fallon. Cousin Lance," Kayla said, reaching for her grandmother's hand.

"Have fun, sweetie," Fallon said. "Good-bye, Mrs. Youngblood. Mrs. Banks, I wish we had had a chance to get to know each other better."

Lance's mother's eyes widened. Her gaze flickered to Lance. "I do, too."

"Fallon, you'll be late, and they won't be able to see you." Lance caught her arm.

She didn't budge. "This is more important."

"No. No," Lance's mother quickly said. "We won't keep you. Good-bye." Holding Kayla's hand, she continued down the street.

Fuming, Fallon swung around on Lance. "You were rude to your mother."

"Don't judge what you don't know," he came back.

"People make mistakes, Lance," she said. "We both know that."

"But she didn't try to correct hers. She shut me out of her life. Well, now I don't need her," he snapped. "Call when you're ready for me to pick you up."

Furious, Lance got into his car and slammed the door. What was his mother trying to prove? She didn't care about him and her "poor me" act might fool his aunt and Fallon, but it wasn't fooling him.

The passenger door opened and Fallon got into the car. "We haven't finished talking."

"Not now, Fallon." He started the motor. "Go back inside before they cancel your appointment."

"I asked a nice-looking woman going inside to cancel it for me." She reached for her seat belt.

Lance switched off the motor and stared at her. "Well, go uncancel. Besides the full-body massage, I scheduled you for a pampering manicure and pedicure with safe nail polish."

Fallon folded her arms. "Not happening."

He blew out an annoyed breath. "Why are you being so stubborn about this? You just met her."

Fallon rested her hands in her lap. "She's your mother, and you won't even look at her. You can't even bring yourself to call her Mother."

He switched on the motor, checked the traffic, and backed out. "You want to stop someplace for lunch before we go back?"

"Now who is being stubborn?" Fallon lifted both

hands in the air. "You might not want to hear this—"

"So don't tell me." He stopped at a red light. His mother really knew how to mess up his life.

"But I think your experience with your mother and then Ashley has colored how you perceive all women," Fallon continued as if he hadn't spoken. "They let you down, so you expect the next woman to do the same."

A cold chill ran through him. He didn't dare look at her for fear she'd know she'd guessed right. A car horn sounded behind him and he pulled off.

"I understand how an unhappy experience can shape your perception," she went on to say. "Before we met for the second time, every time I heard the word 'auction' I was angry. You changed that for me."

Unspoken but implied was that she hoped she'd changed how he viewed women. She probably expected him to say something about how she'd made a difference in his life, but he couldn't. She hadn't realized yet, the fault was in him and not her. He wasn't ready to admit that he didn't have what it took to make a woman happy.

Fifteen minutes later he turned into the driveway of the Yates house. He suddenly thought about the sex of his child. *Lord, please let it be a boy.*

"You don't have anything to say?" she asked.

Lance parked the car in front of the house and stared straight ahead. "No."

He felt her looking at him; then she got out of the car. He saw her go around the side of the house toward the cottage. He just sat there and watched her walk away. He knew what she wanted and he couldn't give it to her.

He'd failed again. He wasn't sure he was strong enough to watch her leave and not beg her to stay. Starting the car again, he drove off.

Lance didn't know what to do with himself.

He'd left the Yates estate and driven around aimlessly until he decided to go to the only place he could think of where he wouldn't be bothered, Richard's ranch. The entrance gate was unlocked as it had been the day Lance had helped move some of Naomi's and Kayla's things there. Since Richard's house was furnished, most of Naomi's furniture remained at the apartment. Thank goodness, or Fallon would have had to sleep on the floor.

Lance parked and wondered where she was, if she felt all right. He opened the car door and followed the path around the single-level house to the back patio. There were colorful throw pillows on the cushion seats atop an outdoor rug with subtle color variation. *Naomi's doing,* he thought as he sat on a cushioned bench, his long legs outstretched, and stared at the distant Sangre de Cristo Mountains. A woman changed a man's life. Richard's was obviously going to be better.

Lance wasn't sure how long he sat there before darkness descended, obscuring his vision of the mountains. Overhead was a half-moon. The night was still and beautiful . . . and he was alone.

In the past, there'd always been work to chase away the loneliness, but he'd left the papers for the new auction he was working on at the cottage. Even if he had them, he was doubtful he could concentrate enough to do any worthwhile work.

Since Fallon walked into his life again, she had always managed to overshadow whatever he was doing. She had that mercurial ability to slip into his consciousness and tug.

His cell phone rang. Without much interest he pulled it from his pocket. Just what he didn't need. "Hello, Aunt Gladys."

"I'm disappointed in you, Lance."

Join the club. "Yes, ma'am."

"Don't you 'yes, ma'am' me. How could you hurt your mother's feelings that way?"

"What about my feelings? No one has ever considered me in this." Too angry to remain seated, he came to his feet.

"That's not the truth and you know it. Leo and I love you. Don't you ever say we don't," she said, her voice unsteady. "We know it was hard on you growing up after you lost your father, but you have to let it go and move on. Forgiveness isn't easy, but living with bitterness and anger is much worse."

"So I'm supposed to forget she always took Jim's side over mine, always deferred to him when he wasn't anywhere near the man my father was." Lance's chest heaved with anger.

"Yes."

The answer was so simple for his aunt and Fallon. "She gets forgiveness and what do I get?"

"Peace. It's what I hoped and prayed for you to have." Her voice trembled.

It was too late. Fallon was probably in Austin by now.

"Your mother is staying until Sunday. I'm having a cookout Saturday afternoon. I expect you and Fallon. No argument. Good night."

He'd be in Tucson by then. "Good night." He disconnected the call and headed for his car. He was going to the cottage to pack and catch the first available flight out the next day.

There was a light on in the front room of the cottage, but Lance wasn't going to fool himself into thinking Fallon had stayed. Her mother and sister would take care of her.

Inside, he went straight to his room. It wouldn't take—

"Don't you know worry is bad for a pregnant woman?"

He whirled and saw Fallon in an easy chair, her feet tucked under her, a book in her hand. "You didn't leave."

"We decided you're worth the aggravation." She crossed her arms over the book. "Did you eat?"

"No."

Coming to her feet, she placed the book on the nightstand. "I had baked fish. You get steak."

Still a bit stunned, Lance followed her out of the bedroom into the small kitchen. On the round table for two was a single place setting. "I'll get it; you rest."

"Sit." She pointed to a straight-backed upholstered chair. "I'll do it."

She wasn't pleased with him. He sat and watched her take a platter from the refrigerator, place it in the microwave, and set the timer. "Are you angry with me about this afternoon?"

Removing the platter, she plunked it down in front of him on the beaded place mat. "You could have called."

He caught her arm when she went to turn away. "I thought you had left me." He didn't care that she could hear the misery in his voice.

Her beautiful face softened immediately. "Nothing is ever solved by running."

He released her and looked at the steak and mashed potatoes on his plate. "You think that's what I do, don't you?"

She placed a glass of lemonade on the table and took the seat across from him before answering, "What I think isn't as important as what you think."

His gaze lifted to hers. She stared back patiently. He'd given her enough reasons to leave, but she hadn't. She deserved to know.

"My mother was the first woman to let me know I wasn't enough. After Daddy died I needed her more than ever. She sold or gave away all of his things. Five months later, she started going out. She met Jim. She married him the same month my father died. He and I never got along even before they were married. One day he told me to take out the trash and I told him to take it out, he was the big man of the house."

Lance's hand fisted. "He took off his belt. He hit me a couple of times before she came running. She took his side and told me to apologize. I refused and was grounded for a week. School was out the next week. I used the money I'd been saving to catch a bus to Santa Fe to Aunt Gladys and Uncle Leo's house."

"Lance, no."

"She and Jim came to get me, but I told them I'd just leave again, walking if I had to. Aunt Gladys and Uncle Leo talked them into letting me stay, and made me promise that I'd go back in the fall. I agreed if I could come every summer." His fingers curled around the icy glass.

"I joined every club imaginable to stay away from the house as much as possible. As soon as I graduated from high school, I left for Tucson, where I was enrolled in college on a partial academic scholarship for the fall semester. My father left me ten thousand dollars for college, which helped a lot. I went home a few times. I guess hoping she'd be the mother I remembered. It never happened."

Fallon's hand covered his. "I'm sorry."

"I won't bore you with the details of Cissy, who dumped me in high school, or Melissa, who did the same thing in college. You know about Ashley." He placed the glass aside, glanced down at his plate, then at her. "I don't seem to have what it takes for women to stick."

"Whatever happened in the past with your mother, I think she regrets it and wants to reach out to you," Fallon told him.

"Aunt Gladys said the same thing."

"I think you and your mother need to talk it out."

"I'm not sure that's possible," he said.

"I do. You just have to find it in your heart to let it go. As for the women, you just picked the wrong women," Fallon said, her voice unsympathetic. "I've had girlfriends in high school and college who always picked the losers instead of the good guys. Your picker was screwed." She handed him his fork. "To be honest, I've dated a few duds myself. I think we both might have gotten it right this time."

He took the fork and picked up his knife. "I know I've never met a woman quite like you."

"I've certainly never met a guy like you. Now eat." She motioned toward the plate.

Lance cut into his steak and began to eat. They still had a chance.

They cleaned up the kitchen together and, once again, Lance followed Fallon. She had gone over what she was going to say a dozen times as she walked back into the master bedroom. "The bed is big enough for the both of us, don't you think?"

"We could give it a try," he answered slowly.

Sitting on the side of the bed, she toed off her house shoes, snapped off the lamp on the nightstand by her, and got under the covers. "Good night, Lance."

She sensed Lance staring at her and tried not to fidget. Lance needed to see there was more between them than just great sex. They had to move beyond the intimacy and show they cared about each other.

On the other side of the room, a drawer opened and closed, then the door to the bathroom. She heard the shower running. Despite her good intentions and her idea of moving beyond intimacy, she imagined the water flowing over his muscled chest, his flat stomach, and lower to . . . Fallon moaned. She tried to think of something else, but the image that leaped into her mind was of the two of them in the shower making love, her legs clamped around his waist as he surged into her welcoming body again and again.

She groaned as desire heated her blood. She'd been crazy to even think this would work. Now she was stuck. Besides, she didn't want him to think she was rejecting him. She'd just have to control herself. She wasn't leaving the bed until it was time to get up.

Thankfully, after a few minutes the water shut off. Imagining the towel gliding over his powerful body wasn't as disturbing. She heard the bathroom door open. The light snapped off on the other side of the bed. The mattress moved. Then silence.

"Do you trust me to hold you until you go to sleep?"

Lance didn't wear pajamas. "Lance, I—"

"I'm wearing pajamas," he said. She thought she heard a smile in his voice.

Pajamas or no, it was courting disaster, but she scooted backward until her hip bumped into his hard arousal. She froze, resisted the urge to rub her hips against him as she'd done that first weekend. "Lance, maybe my idea wasn't such a good one."

"It's the best one I've heard all day." His arm curved over her, pulling her closer. He dropped a kiss on her shoulder. "Go to sleep. I never thought I'd hold you again."

She fell a little bit deeper in love. The old Lance wouldn't have admitted his need of her. She wanted to roll over and crawl on top of him, take him into her body and show him how much she loved him.

Instead, she concentrated on falling asleep. They had come a long way tonight, but they weren't where they needed to be yet. Making love would complicate matters instead of making them better.

"Good night, Lance."

"Night, Fallon."

Wrapping her arms around the arm that was holding her, she drifted off to sleep.

Fallon woke up surrounded by warmth. She smiled, snuggled, and felt a familiar bulge pressed against her hip. It was incredibly arousing. For just a second she was tempted to succumb to the passion awakening deep within her. Their lovemaking had been incredible. Common sense won out. She started to ease away.

The muscled arm around her waist tightened.

She twisted until she stared into Lance's unblinking gaze. The man was gorgeous and mouthwateringly alluring. "Good morning."

"Good morning."

"How long have you been up?" She groaned and momentarily tucked her head at her phrasing.

His sensual mouth quirked. "Thirty minutes or so. It's after eight. This is late for me. I'm an early riser."

"Me, too," she said, trying to ignore the bulge her hip was pressed against. "Getting up early was the reason I was always able to eat breakfast with Naomi and Kayla on weekdays."

"Carmen should be here already." He brushed the hair out of Fallon's face. "She rides in with Francisco."

Fallon's brows bunched. "She comes every day just to cook for you?"

"And take care of the house. When I'm not here, she's on her own schedule." His hand glided up and down Fallon's bare arm. "There are still some furniture pieces I kept in the library I turned into an office."

"I saw that yesterday when I went to get a book to read. You kept the desk and the books."

"I decided I liked the office and didn't want anything changed," he said.

Or was there another reason? Her thoughts moved to a more pressing concern. She couldn't hold back any longer. "Isn't this . . . er . . . uncomfortable for you?"

"It's a small price to pay for holding you. When you left the weekend of the auction I wanted to ask you to stay, but I was afraid you'd say no, so I pretended that your leaving didn't matter." He kissed her shoulder. "I won't make that mistake again."

She leaned her head against his chest. "I didn't help by acting as if what had happened between us didn't matter. My pride got in the way."

"I finally figured out you acted that way because I hadn't said anything to let you know how much the weekend meant to me." His fingers lifted her chin. "I didn't move into the house because this is where we made love. I was holding on to the cottage and the memories because I hadn't been able to hold on to you."

He was definitely getting there. "I'm here now."

"But will you stay?"

She hated the uncertainty bordering on apprehension in his eyes, but she had to be truthful. "I want to, but it depends on how well things go between us."

His frown deepened. "I'm not used to not knowing where I stand."

"Neither am I, but I figure since we're in this together, we'll be all right." She palmed his cheek. "As long as we're honest with each other, we'll get through this."

He stared at her a long time. "What if we do something the other doesn't like?"

She lifted a brow. He could be talking about what he perceived as his mother's betrayal or Fallon's leaving. "Then we tell the other and talk it through. We have to learn to trust each other. If we don't, this won't work."

"And what exactly is 'this'?"

She didn't have to think. "Courting." She laughed at the shocked expression on his face. "That's the word that came to me when I thought about us. It's old-fashioned, but I though it fit."

"You want to be courted?" The frown didn't clear from his face.

"I said the word came to me. You'll have to decide if it means anything to you." She kissed him on the chin and quickly scooted out of bed. "I'm going to use the tub in the guest bathroom."

He sat up. "Do you think you're up to more than your usual for breakfast?"

"Yes. I'd love to go crazy, but dry toast and a hard-boiled egg will have to do for now." She continued to the door. "What are you having?"

"Probably the same. I'll meet you in the front room in twenty minutes."

"Lance, you don't have to have what I have," she protested.

"I'm not eating in front of you when you can't. Now go take your bath so you can eat and take your medicine." Getting out of bed, he went into his bathroom and closed the door.

She was learning Lance could be as stubborn as she could, but since he was being overly considerate, this time she'd let him. Humming softly, she went to take her bath and get dressed.

Chapter 14

Breakfast wasn't as bad as Fallon had imagined. Probably because watching Lance trying to eat a hard-boiled egg was so hilarious. He'd chopped it up instead of picking it up in his hand; then he'd slowly lowered the fork toward the egg as if expecting it to explode.

Fallon's lips twitched as he lifted the tiny fragment of egg white to his mouth. He scrunched up his face and gulped his orange juice.

She decided she cared about him too much to have him suffer. She caught Carmen's eye. The housekeeper smiled and went to the refrigerator. In less than two minutes she placed a fluffy ham and cheese omelet by Fallon.

Lance's eyes widened. "You sure you should eat that?"

"Nope, but I'm sure you can." She traded plates. "If I suddenly start craving sardines and peanut butter for lunch are you going to want to eat the same thing?"

His horrified gaze was her answer. "Thought

not. Now eat. I'm sure you'll think of other ways to share."

Lance looked at the plate, then leaned over and kissed her. "Thanks. I can't stand boiled eggs."

She bit into her egg, chewed, and swallowed. "There isn't a food that I don't like. Comes with traveling so much, I guess. I've even eaten octopus," she said, then straightened.

Lance was immediately out of his chair and by her side. "Are you all right?"

"Miss Marshall." Carmen hovered on the other side of her.

"Sorry." Fallon glanced from one to the other. "A few days ago, even yesterday, if I had thought of eating octopus I would have been running to you know where." She looked at Lance's omelet.

He slid it closer. "You want to eat just a bite?"

She shook her head. "I'm going to wait for dinner." She spoke to Carmen. "Nothing boiled or baked for the main dish, please, please."

Carmen smiled. "And perhaps cheesecake for dessert."

Fallon's expression brightened. "You think we could eat around five?"

Lance laughed. "A definite possibility."

In his office in the Yates house Lance worked on the papers for the next auction so Fallon could rest some more. In the "before Fallon" period of his life, business had always come first. It had been his way to gain financial independence, a way to prove he had worth.

Now, looking at Fallon dozing on the small sofa with an open book on her chest, he was content at the moment just to watch this woman who was growing more and more important to him sleep. She'd come unexpectedly into his life, changing it in a way he'd never thought possible.

Your picker was screwed.

Only Fallon would phrase things in such a way. She lit his dark places. She was his light, his sunshine. He'd called her that once. He'd probably suspected then how important she would be in his life and refused to admit it. He'd kept his office intact because they had shared their first kiss there.

He leaned forward in his chair and braced his arms on his desk. Unlike Francisco, Lance wasn't the poetic type. He was practical in all things. Yet it wasn't practical or wise to care for a woman who wasn't sure if she was sticking around.

Lance's eyes narrowed in determination. He'd make sure she stayed. He might not know about women, but he was valedictorian of his high school graduating class and graduated from college summa cum laude. He could figure this out. He'd chance another call to Richard if he thought it would help.

Courtship. She wanted to be courted. He might have tried to do an Internet search on the subject if he thought that would be of any use. Yet Naomi's words kept coming back to him. He had to think of it himself.

What would make Fallon happy? His pen tapped

on the sheets of paper on his desk. He hadn't done so badly with his "surprises" thus far. Yet he instinctively knew it couldn't always be about buying her things. He liked seeing her happy and he planned to keep her that way.

"You're staring and frowning," she said without opening her eyes.

He laughed. He was doing that more and more. "How can you tell with your eyes closed?"

"Trade secret." She opened her eyes and sat up. "How long was I out that time?"

"Not long." He went to sit beside her. "You want to go for a walk and check on the trees?"

"I'd love to. At least I won't fall asleep walking." She came to her feet, replaced the book she'd been reading, and glanced around the library/office. "This is one of my favorite rooms in the house. It's restful and it has a lot of history."

"Mine, too." He caught her face between his hands. "History like our first kiss."

"Yes." She laughed. "I had a brain overload."

"Let's see if I can duplicate it." His mouth lowered slowly, giving her time to move away if she wished. She didn't. Their lips met, clung, opened. His tongue leisurely stroked hers, tasted the sweetness of her mouth. Her hands trembled and closed around his wrists. He moved his mouth over hers, hungrily exploring until she trembled. He wasn't much steadier.

Lifting his head, he stared into her face, watched as her eyelids slowly fluttered open. Her eyes were dazed.

She licked her lips. "I'd say you upped it a notch or two."

"I aim to please."

She stepped back and reached for his hand. "Let's go for that walk."

As he kissed her hand joined with his, they left the library, going outside through the front door instead of through the kitchen. "Carmen wants to surprise you for dinner," he explained.

"She's wonderful," Fallon said.

"So is the whole family." He opened the high wooden gate leading to the inner courtyard.

"You won't get an argument from me."

His cell phone rang. "Excuse me. It's from a member of my staff." Lance frowned, then, said, "You're cutting out. Hold on." To Fallon he said, "I'll have to go back to the house and finish this call."

"You go on. I'll be fine."

He kissed her on the cheek and started back the way they had come. Fallon stared after him for a bit, a smile on her face, wondering if he realized how often he was kissing her, touching her. With each occasion, he showed he cared. Soon she hoped he'd be able to say the words.

She continued down the path, past the bench and fountain to where the two sycamore trees were planted. Francisco was already there, watering them.

"Good morning, Francisco."

"Good morning, Miss Marshall. You're looking more like your old self every day."

"I'm definitely feeling better. Can I do that?"

He handed her the water hose. "We laid miles of underground pipes for the sprinkler systems and faucets. Took us months just to prepare for the planting."

"It paid off." Fallon glanced around. "It's like an unexpected oasis here."

Francisco stared at a five-foot-tall stone urn and pedestal. "That was the first piece Mr. Yates bought."

"His death was so tragic, even more so because the Yates line ended with him," she said. "Even if Lance hadn't found his mother's notes, you could tell she wanted her son to marry and have a family."

"I came to work for him after she passed, but he always spoke warmly about her and his grandparents. Mr. Yates was always looking and hoping to find a woman to marry, but like I told him, he looked in the wrong place." Francisco took the water hose and went to the other tree.

Fallon thought of Lance and his horrible experiences with women. "Some men do. You don't seem like one of them."

He looked at her and smiled. "I knew Carmen was the women for me when I saw her when I was eighteen and she was sixteen. She was the bright star in my life. Every goal I've ever set has been with her in mind."

"My parents said the same thing when they first met. They just knew." She reached for the water hose again. If only it had been that simple for her and Lance.

"Before Mr. Yates left on that ski trip, he told me

he thought he might find the woman for him."
Francisco took off his hat, replaced it. "He was a
good man, but life didn't smile on him. I pray he's
finally found the peace he didn't find here. People
took advantage of his goodness and his money.
They won't do that to Mr. Saxton."

True, but Lance is probably just as lonely. "How
long have you known Lance?"

"Six weeks after Mr. Yates's death Mr. Saxton
showed up with three other men. That's when my
family and I learned about Mr. Yates's financial
troubles. Carmen and I had stayed on and worked
without pay because we respected and cared for
Mr. Yates. He loved this house and the gardens, always said he felt at peace here." Francisco's mouth
flattened into a hard line. "One of the men, a banker,
ordered us to leave immediately, called us squatters.
If Carmen hadn't been standing there I'm not sure
what I would have done, I was so angry."

"I don't blame you. That was an irresponsible
and ridiculous thing to say," Fallon said, incensed.

He nodded. "Mr. Saxton said the same thing. He
asked the hotshot banker who would take care of
the house and gardens as well as we had. I don't
know what happened, because we left, but two
weeks later Mr. Saxton came to the house and
hired us to continue as we had been. If he hadn't
and paid us the back wages, Oskar would have had
to drop out of college."

"He's a good man," she murmured. Too bad he
didn't think so at times.

"But not an easy man." Francisco took the water

hose, then hit the button to roll it up automatically. "But my Carmen tells me, neither am I."

"Easy is boring," Fallon said, her lips twitching.

"So my wife says." He tipped his hat. "Good day, Miss Marshall."

Lance simply watched Fallon for a long minute. The midday sun shone through the trees and framed her exquisite face and body perfectly. He wished he could keep the . . . He took out his phone, found Photo, and pressed the button. She turned at that moment. He took another picture.

"Got you."

Her lips pursed, she quickly approached, reaching for his phone. "Give me that. I look horrible."

He held the phone over his head. "You look beautiful. If I wasn't afraid you'd delete the picture, I'd show you."

She folded her arms. "You show it to anyone and I'm going to be very annoyed with you."

"It's just for me." As soon as the words were out of his mouth he had to wonder if this and memories were all he'd ever have of her.

"All right." She gestured toward the trees. "Francisco and I watered. They look good. They'll really sprout out in the spring."

His chest felt tight. "You'll deliver in the spring."

Her eyes rounded, she glanced down. "Y-yes."

He pulled her into his arms, placed his chin on top of her head, felt her tremble. "I'll be there, and you and the baby will be fine. Please don't be scared."

"I'm not—not really. It's just . . ." Her voice trailed off.

"Just what?" he urged. "Tell me so I can help."

He felt her shrug her shoulders and moved his hand up and down her back in a comforting gesture. "I guess it's all starting to be more and more real. I went to a doctor in New Orleans who confirmed the pregnancy, but I'll need to get one in Austin, think about birthing classes."

"They have excellent doctors here and in Tucson," he said carefully.

Slowly, she lifted her head, her gaze level. "My doctor will be in Austin."

Not if Lance could help it. "When you make the appointment, I'm going with you."

"I'd like that."

"Good." His arm remained around her shoulder as they returned to the house. He stopped a short distance from the garage. "You feel up to a drive?"

She glanced up at him. "Is there a destination or are we just driving?"

"I had another call; that's why it took me so long," he explained. "It was Sierra. She asked for my help with planning a fund-raising auction. We're meeting her at one of your favorite places in Santa Fe, the Red Cactus."

Her mouth gaped. Fallon took two steps back from Lance and glanced down at her clothes. "You expect me to meet one of the most fashionable women in the country, not to mention richest, in wrinkled Bermuda shorts and blouse?"

"You look fine to me." Maybe there were a few

wrinkles from her lying down, but nothing major. He reached for her arm. "Sierra won't care what you have on."

Fallon batted his hand away. "Men are clueless at times. What time were you to meet her?"

"A little over an hour from now. I wasn't sure how you felt, so I wanted to give you time to feel better, since I wanted you to go with me. Since you're feeling all right I thought we'd go early and grab—" He was talking to Fallon's back.

"Give me ten minutes."

Lance stared after her. *Women.* Thank goodness, it looked like his picker had finally gotten it right.

Fallon's ten minutes turned into fifteen, then twenty. She wasn't usually fussy about clothes, but she wanted Lance to be proud of her.

I wanted you to go with me.

She tucked the words into her heart and slipped on another sundress, this one apricot colored, with a fitted bodice and flared hem. Her mother had sent mostly casual clothes. The last two dresses and the pants hadn't fit right. Fallon had lost weight.

A knock sounded on her open door. "You all right?"

"Yes." Turning, she went to stand in front of him. "I'm sorry it took so long."

His warm gaze ran over her. "I'm not. You look beautiful. I almost hate to share you."

Nothing could have pleased her more. She kissed him on the cheek. "Thanks. I needed that. Let's go."

Twenty minutes later, they were standing in front of the podium of the Red Cactus. Fallon gave her name and the hostess immediately picked up two menus. "I could get used to this," Fallon said in an aside.

"I'm meeting Sierra Navarone," Lance told the young hostess. "Please let me know when she arrives."

The woman paused. "Are you Mr. Saxton?"

"Yes."

The dark-haired woman smiled. "Sierra is already here. Please follow me."

The woman wove her way through the crowded restaurant to a large booth with banquette seating in red tufted leather. With Sierra was Ruth Grayson on one side of the booth. Facing them was a stunningly beautiful young woman wearing a cream-colored Chanel suit and a triple strand of pearls. Fallon immediately thought class, culture, and old money.

After greeting everyone, Lance and Fallon took a seat in the oversized upholstered chair at the end of the booth table. Fallon eyed the chips and salsa and wondered if she dared try to eat any.

"Lance, thank you for coming," Sierra said to him. With a twinkle in her eyes, she said to Fallon, "It's good to see you're still taking advantage of opportunities."

"Life is more interesting that way," Fallon said.

"I agree." Sierra smiled. "I'd like you both to meet Skylar Dupre, event director for Navarone Resorts and Spas."

"Hello," Skylar greeted warmly, her cultured

voice crisp, with a Boston accent. "It was nice of you to meet us on such short notice."

"My pleasure," Lance said. "If there's anything I can do to help with the project Sierra mentioned, I'd be more than happy."

"Thank you, Lance." Mrs. Grayson placed her hands on the wooden table. "Since you've had experience with auctions, I wanted your input on the one we're planning. Although I trust Skylar's judgment and expertise in this matter."

"Thank you, Mrs. Grayson; your faith and confidence mean a lot." Skylar faced Lance. "But Mr. Saxton has gained a sterling reputation in Tucson and beyond in a very short time for his expertise in auctions. I'm willing to listen to anything he has to say to make the fund-raiser for the music department at St. John's a huge success."

"I'm at your disposal, but do you mind if we order first?" Lance asked. "Fallon's breakfast wasn't that great."

"Of course." Mrs. Grayson signaled a waiter.

Fallon didn't know if she wanted to kick or kiss Lance. Since she was eyeing the chips again, she had a pretty good idea.

"Did you try to cook, Lance?" Sierra teased.

"I wouldn't subject her to that kind of punishment," he said.

"Yes, Mrs. Grayson?" the waiter inquired.

"Sam, we'd like to order," she told him. "In the meantime, please ask Brandon if he can send out a couple of appetizers for our guests. This is the first time Skylar has eaten here."

The young man's gaze moved to Skylar. He blinked, straightened his narrow shoulders. "I certainly hope it won't be your last."

"I'm sure it won't," she answered, the corners of her mouth curving upward.

"What would you like to drink?" the waiter asked.

Skylar smiled easily at the mesmerized man, Fallon thought. Apparently Skylar was used to the effect she had on men. "Fallon and Lance, please order first."

"Vegetable soup and lemonade," Fallon ordered, and couldn't ignore the astonished expression on Sierra's and her mother's faces. They both were aware of Fallon's usually hearty appetite.

"We've planned for a special dinner tonight, so we're eating light," Lance explained smoothly. "I'll just have chips and lemonade."

"I admire your restraint." Skylar picked up the menu. "I've heard for months about the food here. I think I'll have the combination chicken/beef fajitas. Pepsi."

"Make mine the same. Fajitas and Pepsi, that is," Sierra said with a mischievous grin.

"I'll have the Cobb salad with smoked salmon, and lemonade." Mrs. Grayson handed Sam her menu.

"I'll get those out as soon as possible." The young man moved away.

Sierra picked up a chip, then scooted the basket across the table in front of Fallon. "Skylar, I think you can add another one to your list."

"Sierra, you're imagining things. Mr. Saxton—"

"'Lance,' please."

"Lance, and please call me Skylar. As Sierra told you on the phone, I came up with the idea to have a fund-raising auction at Sierra and Blade's home and invite a very select guest of people with the financial means to bid on high-ticket items donated from celebrities, businesses, and collectors."

"The castle?" Fallon almost whistled. "The media has wanted a look at your home since you moved in. People will come just to see the house."

"The house will be a strong draw, but I also want them to purchase," Skylar said, her brows furrowed.

Sierra wrinkled her nose. "It was maddening at first . . . until Blade bought up all the surrounding property around us. Nothing gets on our property without Rio's permission."

Fallon couldn't resist any longer and reached for a chip. "Rio impressed me as very efficient."

"Security is paramount," Lance said. "You'll have some very high-profile people and valuable merchandise."

"That won't be a problem with Rio in charge," Skylar said with complete confidence. "As Ms. Marshall said, Rio is very good at what he does."

"Too efficient at times," Sierra muttered.

"That's because you can't get by him," Mrs. Grayson said.

Sierra shot an annoyed look at a nearby table where two men sat. "What do I need with bodyguards in my brother's restaurant?"

"So Blade won't worry," Mrs. Grayson and Skylar answered in unison.

"And that's the only reason I let Rio get by with this." Sierra munched on another chip. "But one day, Rio and I are going to have a heart-to-heart."

Mrs. Grayson frowned. Skylar looked worried. Fallon had heard that Sierra liked having her way, but Rio looked like a man who wasn't easily pushed . . . if at all.

"Your drinks and appetizers." The waiter served their drinks and the appetizers. "Brandon said to let you know that your food will be right out."

"Thank you." Mrs. Grayson said grace. "Please help yourself. Fallon and Lance, Brandon likes to see people eat at his restaurant."

Sierra picked up a mini-taco. "He gets testy if they don't."

Unable to resist, Fallon picked up another chip and dunked it into *queso*. "Good food is one of my weaknesses."

"Mine, too," Sierra agreed, her eyes twinkling again. "Among other things."

Fallon's lips twitched. Sierra was terrible and oh, so right. She was referring to Blade, of course. Fallon had to admit some men changed all the rules. But Sierra had Blade's love; Fallon was a long way from getting Lance's.

"I can certainly see why Brandon has such a great reputation as a chef." Skylar sank startling white teeth into a mini-quesadilla. "We're planning a party with food and dancing early in the evening before the auction. It will give people time to view the pieces and enjoy the evening."

"I would suggest setting aside a room for the items and discreet guards." Lance placed his folded hands on the table. "You might not have to worry about theft, but there's always breakage to consider or a party crasher."

Skylar shook her head. Hair, as rich and luxurious as sable, framed her exquisite face. "Party crashers won't be a problem. All of the guests will be vetted before the event and checked at the entrance of the estate for identification and again before they enter the house. So will the trunks of their cars. The invitation is person specific, with clear instructions. No guests allowed unless cleared a month before the auction."

"Rio again," Lance said.

"He doesn't like surprises," said Skylar.

"Blade, either." Sierra picked up a nacho. "If the fund-raiser wasn't for Mama, he would have just written a check and said no."

"Blade understands how important this is to my students," Mrs. Grayson said. "After the auction is over, the college will be able to not only purchase new instruments but increase scholarships as well."

"Mrs. Grayson, auctions can go either way," Lance warned.

"Ours will be successful," she replied easily.

"It certainly will." Skylar picked up her glass. "To success."

"Failure isn't an option. To success." Sierra

picked up her glass and the women saluted one another.

"Hi, everyone." Brandon arrived with a tray of food. Directly behind him was the waiter with platters as well.

"Hi, Brandon, thanks again for the priority seating." Fallon dipped another chip into *queso*. "Excellent as usual."

"Thanks, Fallon." Brandon placed the sizzling fajita platter in front of Skylar. "The plate is hot. Please be careful."

"I will. This is my first time eating here, Brandon, but you have a right to be proud." Skylar reached for her flour tortilla. "If I wasn't flying out tonight, I'd come back tomorrow."

Brandon straightened and folded his arms across his wide chest. "You ladies are going to make my male waitstaff unhappy when you leave. A couple of them are wondering if they stand a chance."

"Not with Fallon they don't," Lance snapped, and scooted closer. "She's taken."

Since Fallon loved the stubborn man and was carrying his child, she chose to ignore Lance's possessive attitude. Besides, it gave her bruised ego a little boost to know Lance was a bit jealous.

"How about you, Skylar?"

"Navarone keeps me too busy to think about dating."

Fallon used to think the same thing and now look at her, pregnant and in love and trying to be part of a couple.

"Speaking from experience, when the right person comes along, whatever certainties you have about love and romance will be turned upside down," Brandon told Skylar.

"He's right," Sierra agreed. "Blade changed everything for me."

"Skylar, you will find that out as well," Mrs. Grayson said softly.

Brandon groaned. Sierra grinned.

Skylar frowned and glanced from Mrs. Grayson to Brandon to Sierra. "Did I miss something?"

"No, you didn't miss a thing." Mrs. Grayson picked up her lemonade and just smiled.

Chapter 15

"That was a power luncheon if there ever was one," Fallon said from the passenger seat of Lance's car.

Lance had to agree as he headed out of town and back to the house. "They'll let nothing stand in the way of them succeeding."

"That's the only way it can be for women who want to do well." Fallon folded her arms across her chest. "You have to know what you want and have the single-minded determination and unshakable confidence to go after it."

Lance wished he had the nerve to ask if what she wanted included him. She cared. If she didn't, she wouldn't let him sleep in the bed with her. By doing so, she'd shown him that she also trusted him. This morning he'd seen desire flare in her eyes, but she hadn't acted on it. Hot sex wasn't what she was looking for from him. If he wanted to keep her, he'd better find out what it was, and quick.

"They invited us to attend the auction so we'll get to see how well things work out for them." He tried to sound casual instead of anxious that she wouldn't be with him by then.

"It's two months away," she mused. "I could still wear my bridesmaid dress and not look like walking death this time."

He couldn't tell from her statement whether she still planned to be with him or not. He turned into the driveway of the house. One thing was certain: he didn't like to think of her being around all those influential men and his ring not on her finger. His hands tightened on the steering wheel. "Men won't be able to keep their eyes off you."

She looked at him out of the corners of her eyes. "Sierra is beautiful and vivacious, but no man attending would be stupid enough to show any interest in her. On the other hand, Skylar has that stunning beauty to go along with her obvious cultured breeding and buckets of money."

"They're attractive women, but they can't compare to you." He stopped by the garage and turned off the engine. He sensed her staring at him. "What?"

"You really think that?"

His mouth flattened. "I do. Men will be trying to pick you up, but they'll have to get past me first."

Fallon rolled her eyes. "Not that. I meant the part about Sierra and Skylar not comparing to me—not that I think you're right or anything," she quickly added.

Didn't she know how utterly beautiful she was? His finger gently lifted her chin. "No woman can hold a candle to you in beauty, in charm, in courage. The beauty attracted me, but the charm and courage are just as compelling."

"Oh, Lance." Her smile trembled. "I can tell you've been around Francisco."

His brows knitted. It was important that she know he meant every word and that they came straight from his heart. "He had nothing to do with this. I just told you what I feel."

She kissed him on the lips, then pulled back with a sassy grin. "If I'm not careful, you'll give me the big head." She got out of the car.

Lance did as well. "Why don't you go rest? I'll check and see how Carmen is progressing with dinner."

"I can't wait." She made a face. "I ate two bowls of chips at lunch. Thank goodness, no one seemed to notice."

He had, and that's why he was going to make sure Carmen had prepared a great dinner. "Of course not. Besides, Sierra said Brandon gets testy if people don't eat. Go rest. I'll probably do some paperwork, so you can call your mother and Megan and Megan can threaten me some more."

"She doesn't mean it."

"I'm not so sure, but I'm not going anyplace, so her threats won't work." He kissed Fallon's hair. "Go rest. I'll come get you for dinner."

"I think I'll work on finishing the article. I'll tell Mama and Megan you said hello." Fallon walked away, waving over her shoulder.

Lance grunted and started for the house. Megan didn't like him. *Tough.* Thank goodness, Fallon was independent enough that she didn't need her sister's approval to be with him.

Opening the front door, he went straight to the kitchen and found it empty. Frowning, he looked in the oven. Nothing. He started for the refrigerator just as his cell phone rang.

"Carmen, where are you?"

"At the hospital. My mother-in-law fell," came the shaky reply.

"Is she all right?" he asked. He'd met Francisco's mother a couple of times and thoroughly liked her. She lived alone and had six doting children and numerous grandchildren who adored her.

"Yes. Just bruised, but Francisco is a nervous wreck from the scare. I can't come back and finish dinner."

Lance glanced around the kitchen as if expecting food to appear. "Of course. I'll order something."

"Oh no. Miss Marshall was looking forward to eating at home. I'll walk you through everything."

"What do you mean?"

"You're going to grill the meat and vegetables and finish the garnish on the cheesecake."

The phone fell from Lance's hand. He simply stared at it.

Fallon read over the article she was writing again, deemed it darn good, and saved it to her file. Stretching her arms over her head, she worked her shoulders. The piece was solid and should please the exacting editor who had been on tour with Fallon when she learned she was pregnant.

Fallon glanced down and rubbed her stomach. It was still hard to believe that she had a life growing in her that she and Lance had created. Megan was suspicious of Lance already. If she knew that Fallon was pregnant, Megan might really "send somebody" to teach him a lesson.

With Megan, it was hard to tell if she was serious or if it was another example of her droll humor. At least her mother seemed willing to give Lance the benefit of the doubt. All bets would be off, however, when she and Megan learned that Fallon was pregnant and no wedding was planned. And there wouldn't be unless Lance told her he loved her. It was all or nothing.

Her stomach grumbled, causing her to glance at the clock. She blinked and came out of her chair. Five thirteen. They'd been back since around two. Dinner was supposed to be served by now. Lance was probably starving.

She was out of the cottage in seconds and heading for the house. Knowing him, he had probably peeped in on her, seen her working, and gone back to his office. She cut across the terrace to the loggia and opened the back door leading to the kitchen and came to an abrupt halt. The aroma of grilled meat made her mouth water, but she couldn't believe who was standing at the stove.

Lance, his shirtsleeves rolled up, an apron around his waist, stood over the grill on the stove with tongs in his hand. "Lance."

His gaze jerked toward her, then back to the grill. "The meat thermometer says it's done."

"Good. Place the pork tenderloins in the oval serving dish to your right."

Fallon recognized Carmen's voice coming from the phone. She was on speaker. What shocked Fallon more was Lance placing the meat on the platter. What was going on?

"Done, and we have company."

"Miss Marshall, would you excuse us so Lance can finish cooking?"

Fallon's gaze went from the food to Lance, whose gaze kept skittering away.

"Has she gone?"

"She's still here."

"Miss Marshall, if you please."

"Can I help?" Lance didn't know how to cook.

"No. I have it under control."

It certainly looked like it. Fallon reached for the doorknob. "It smells good, and I bet it tastes even better."

He finally looked at her. "Carmen assured me there are antacids in the cabinet."

"We won't need them. I'll be in the cottage waiting for your call." Fallon opened the kitchen door.

He nodded and said, "What's next?"

There was a slight pause. Fallon slowly closed the door, hoping to hear what Carmen obviously dreaded.

"You have to take the cheesecake out of the pan, flip it onto a cake plate, put more graham crackers on the side, and garnish it."

Fallon didn't have to see Lance to know he hadn't taken the news well. His groan said it all.

* * *

Lance stared down at the raspberries and strawberries on top of the cheesecake and smiled. It didn't look half-bad. The graham crackers on the sides weren't even. Somehow he'd stuck his thumb in the sides a couple of places, but it tasted good—thanks to the thumb incidents he'd licked the cheesecake off.

The timer went off. He placed the cheesecake back in the refrigerator, took the dinner rolls out of the oven, and upended the pan into the bread basket Carmen had left. If she hadn't marinated the meat, prepared the vegetables for him to grill, and left service dishes, he would have been lost. He'd tasted the pork tenderloin. It wasn't bad. There was no way he was going to let Fallon get sick eating poorly cooked or bad-tasting food.

He picked up the phone and called Fallon's cell phone. Once he put the bread in the oven, Carmen had finally agreed to hang up. All of the family was there with her mother-in-law, and Francisco understood how important the dinner was. He'd even come online a couple of times to ask Lance how it was going. He realized they'd moved beyond employee-employer to friends.

"Hello."

"Dinner is ready. I just have to set the table."

"Already done with dishes from the cottage. I'm just outside the door. I'll help you carry everything out."

Lance hung the phone up just as Fallon came into the kitchen and straight to him.

She swallowed. "You are wonderful to do this

for me. Every time I think you can't surprise me more or make me feel special, you do." She stepped back. "What should I do to help?"

"How about a kiss?"

She didn't hesitate to wrap her warm arms around his neck and press her soft curves against his body, press her hot mouth against his. His arms brought her closer as his mouth devoured hers. Her tongue explored the recesses of his mouth, tempting him to lay her on the floor and take her hot and hard. With a strength he didn't know he had, he eased her away.

"We better stop before my brain overloads," he said, his voice rough.

"Same here. What happened to Carmen?" she asked.

He told Fallon about Carmen's mother-in-law falling. "She's just bruised, but Francisco wanted to be with her."

"That's understandable. It's his mother."

All mothers weren't deserving of love and devotion, Lance thought, but he wasn't going there. "You grab the bread and vegetables, and I'll get the rest. Carmen left a big tray." Together, they got the food outside. Fallon insisted on serving him; then she said grace. Anxious, Lance watched her place the first bit of pork into her mouth.

"Delicious." She speared a grilled mushroom, then a tomato from her marinated salad. "Lance, I think you missed your calling. Everything is scrumptious."

He was surprised how pleased and proud he felt.

"Carmen marinated everything and talked me though it."

"But you had to do the actual cooking." She cut into her meat. "It couldn't have been easy."

He shrugged and finally picked up his knife and fork. "You deserved a good meal, and I didn't think you'd want to go back out."

"You're right." She plucked a roll from the bread basket. "I can't imagine a more wonderful dinner."

"There's one thing." He came to his feet. "Excuse me for a moment." Grinning all the way, he went to get the cheesecake. Who said you had to wait for dessert or cut it a certain way? He grabbed a knife from the cutting block, a couple of saucers, and went back out. "Close your eyes."

"Is it what I think it is?"

"Maybe." He was grinning like a kid with a new bike. "Open."

Fallon opened her eyes, then gasped. "It's beautiful."

Lance placed the garnished cheesecake on the table, cut out a large slice, and set it by her plate. "Take a bite."

Fallon cut into the cheesecake with her fork and lifted it to Lance's mouth. "You first."

His lips closed over the fruit topping. "Carmen's quite a cook if I can't mess it up." Taking Fallon's fork, he fed her a bite.

"Delicious."

"Just like you." He shook his head, took his seat, and picked up his fork. "How did the writing on the article go?"

"I finished it."

"Good. The one you did on the auction was fantastic." He picked up his glass. "You're a wonderful writer."

Pleasure spread across her face. "I like what I do and I hope it shows in the writing. I have several more to finish before I fly to Playa del Carmen."

He placed the glass on the table without drinking. Giving up what you enjoyed doing wasn't easy. "So you're still going?"

"Yes."

Lance picked up his fork, but he no longer felt like eating. She was leaving him, and there was nothing he could do to stop her.

"You know they recommend a diving partner, someone you trust to go down with you." She speared an asparagus, chewed. "You interested?"

His head lifted. He stared at her across the table. She read him too easily, but for once he was glad. "You're not going scuba diving."

"How do you plan to stop me?" she challenged, switching to eating cheesecake.

There was only one way and they both knew it. But even if he went, he wasn't sure she'd listen. The important thing was that she wanted him with her. He cut into his tenderloin. "I'll think of something when the time comes."

Fallon laughed. "You can try, but my money is on me. My father called me strong willed."

She was certainly that, but she was also incredibly giving and she lit up Lance's life as nothing had before. "We'll see about that."

"I plan to go home first to see my family and find a doctor," she said slowly.

"I want to be there when you tell them about the baby." His eyes narrowed. "Megan already doesn't like me. She won't make it easy for either of us."

"Probably." Fallon pulled her cheesecake in front of her. "But I like you, and so will Mother."

Fallon had said the words that meant so much to him so easily. "You want another slice?" Only fragments remained on her plate. When she didn't answer he cut another slice and put it on her plate. "You don't want Carmen to think you didn't like it."

"You shouldn't tempt me this way."

"It's the only way I can tempt you," he murmured.

Fallon cocked her head. "I wouldn't be so sure about that. You're a hard man to resist."

He was definitely hard all right. Sleeping together in the same bed tonight would test his control to the limits, but he'd do whatever it took to keep Fallon's trust and be with her.

Fallon tried to act casual as they walked back to the cottage after cleaning up the kitchen. She couldn't quite manage. The kiss they shared had made her tremble with desire. She tried to push the need to the back of her mind, but it kept coming back.

A secretive glance at Lance, his shoulders hunched, his hands in the pockets of his slacks, and she knew he was experiencing the same problem.

Usually neat, he'd untucked his shirt when they began clearing the table. The reason was obvious: he was trying to hide his growing desire.

Sleeping together tonight wasn't a good idea—unless they planned to do more than just sleep.

Lance opened the door and Fallon entered the cottage. She didn't stop until she was in the master bedroom.

Lance looked everywhere but at her. "I think I'll take a walk. You go to bed. I'll be back."

She touched him on the shoulder as he turned away. He looked down at her. She saw desire swirling in the black depths of his eyes, but she also saw tenderness and caring. Even before they'd made love, he'd gone out of his way to please her. Tonight, he'd spent hours on the phone cooking so she wouldn't be disappointed. He'd shown her he cared so many times, that it wasn't just sex, just as he was doing now.

"I don't think a walk will fix what's bothering you." She slid her arms around his neck. His eyes widened; his hands bracketed her waist. Perhaps she was the one who should show she had faith in him. "Let's see if this will."

His hands on her shoulders stopped her. "I-I'm on the edge here. If I kiss you I don't know if I can stop."

"I don't want you to stop."

His eyes shut tightly, then opened. "You just started feeling better. Maybe—"

"Maybe you should stop talking and kiss me."

She grinned. "I'll be gentle with you. Promise. Let me show you." She leaned forward and pressed her lips against his.

With a shaky groan, he pulled her to him. She fitted her softness to his hardness. The gentle kiss heated and mating tongues became demanding. His arms tightened around her, bringing her closer, as if he was starved for the taste of her.

He kissed her as if he'd never get enough. She kissed him back the same way. This was what she wanted, what she needed.

His head lifted, his breathing labored, his gaze searing. She trembled. Only this man could scatter her thoughts and fill her heart with love.

Reaching around her, he grabbed the comforter and flung it aside. Clothes were quickly cast aside. Taking her in his arms again, he placed her on the bed, then followed her down. His mouth fitted itself to hers. His hands tenderly caressed and stroked her breasts, her stomach. She squirmed beneath him.

His hands explored the soft curves of her body, his lips following. He'd never needed anything more than to make this woman his forever. His lips brushed against her nipple, causing her to arch and moan.

Slowly his hands skimmed downward, past her thigh and back up to her woman's softness. She twisted restlessly against him, her hands clutching his shoulders.

He slid his hand under her hips and brought them together. Her legs wrapped around his waist, and she buried her face in the crook of his neck. Together they found the slow tempo and moved their bodies in perfect harmony.

Again and again he surged in and out of her until they went over together. She gasped and clung to him in ecstasy. He clung to her for a long moment before finally having the strength to roll to one side, taking her with him.

"Are you all right?" he asked.

"Better than all right." Her words were breathy. She kissed him on the shoulder.

"You're right. That definitely beat a walk." His breath shuddered in and out, but he had a smile on his face. His hand stroked up and down her sweat-dampened back.

A pleased smile on her face, she climbed on top of him. Her finger traced the lower curve of his lip. "I'm always right."

Chuckling, he shook his head, then framed her face with his hands. His face grew serious. "I want this to work between us. I'm trying to find my way. I don't have any parameters or experience to go by." He blew out a breath. "If I get it wrong a time or two, give me a swift kick, but please don't walk away."

If she hadn't been in love all the way, she would be now. He needed her and was still afraid that she'd walk away as others had. He couldn't see that he had her, that all he had to do was forget the past and let himself love her.

"Fallon."

She saw the uncertainty in his face and leaned

over to kiss him. "I told you, I fight for what I want."

His eyes closed briefly. "You have me."

Not in the way she wanted, but she prayed that would come. Her hands closed around his manhood, felt it pulse and expand. Air hissed though his gritted teeth. "I certainly do. Now, let's see what I can do with you."

Lance woke up with a smile and made sure Fallon had one as well. He kissed her awake, made sure her nausea was gone, then loved her slowly, completely. Afterward they made love in the shower. She was her old playful self. By the time they left the cottage for the main house, it was close to nine.

Carmen was in the kitchen. Francisco had come to work as well. Lance and Fallon were happy to learn Ms. Fuente was doing better. Carmen's mother-in-law was sore that morning, but thankfully she had no broken bones.

Before they took their seats for breakfast, Fallon praised both Carmen and Lance for the wonderful meal the night before. Carmen graciously gave the credit to Lance. He gave the credit back to her. "My skills are limited."

"I wouldn't say that," Fallon said with a straight face.

Lance was glad the orange juice wasn't in his mouth. He placed the glass aside. Fallon certainly made life better. He planned to take every opportunity to be with her. "Carmen, do you think you could fix a picnic basket for us for lunch?"

"Yes, Mr. Saxton," she said. "This time, I'll do all the cooking."

Fallon's eyes had widened with delight. "I haven't been on a picnic since I was a little girl."

"Then it will be my pleasure to take you."

"Yes, Mr. Saxon," she said. "This time, I'll do all the cooking."

Fallon's eyes had widened with delight. "I haven't been on a picnic since I was a little girl."

"Then it will be my pleasure to take you."

Chapter 16

Not only did Lance take Fallon on a picnic, but over the next few days he took her on a tour of places outside of Santa Fe that she had missed. It was fun being with her, seeing her smile. He looked forward to the night, when they would make love and she would go to sleep in his arms. At the same time he dreaded it because it meant her time of being with him was winding down. He planned to go with her to Playa del Carmen, but what happened after that?

Sitting on the deep-cushioned seat of the outdoor bench near the pool Friday afternoon, he went over his plans. "Let's see. I've made all the travel arrangements to Austin, including a hotel, and booked a seat on the flight you're taking to Playa del Carmen. Did I leave anything out?"

"No, but I don't want your business to suffer because you're with me," she told him.

He twisted his head to look at her. "It's not. My people can work independently or I wouldn't have hired them. I was here off and on for weeks preparing for the Yates auction and the auction house got along well without me."

"Still, I worry."

He kissed her hand. He kind of liked that she cared enough to worry about him. "Well, don't. I have this covered. Maybe it would help you feel better if you visited the auction house. I'd like to introduce you to the employees, in any case. What do you say we go Monday?"

"Monday?"

"We could spend the day or a couple of days there, whatever you like," he coaxed. He wanted her involved in every facet of his life. She needed to know how important she was to him.

"I'm not sure I have anything appropriate to wear," she finally said.

Lance barely kept from pumping his fist in triumph. "We can go into town this afternoon and get whatever you need."

"You need to work on the auction," she told him. "I can drive myself."

"I'll give you my credit card."

Her brow arched. "I'll pay for my own clothes."

"Whatever you say." He came to his feet and reached for her hand. "I'll get the car keys for you."

Fallon purchased a stylish red suit, a black sheath, and shoes for the trip. She freely admitted to herself that she wanted Lance to be proud of her when he introduced her to his employees. If they decided to go out at night, she had the black sheath.

She realized she was taking a chance that things would work out between them. She just believed that everything he did for her showed his feeling went deeper than caring. He just couldn't say the words. Introducing her to his employees meant he wanted her in his personal and professional life.

Her ringing cell phone intruded on her thoughts. Quickly placing her purchases in the trunk, she sat in the driver's seat and answered the call. "Hello."

"Fallon, this is Mrs. Youngblood, Richard's mother. I wonder if I could have a moment of your time?"

Fallon tensed. "Is Kayla all right?"

"She's fine. In fact, I got your phone number from her, since I didn't want to intrude on Richard and Naomi's honeymoon," Mrs. Youngblood answered. "I'll come straight to the point. I want Lance and my sister, Irene, to settle whatever differences they have so we can be a family again."

"Mrs. Youngblood, I'm not sure you should be discussing this with me."

"I'm not asking you to get in the middle. Heaven knows how Lance would feel about that. I am asking you to see that he comes to the cookout at our house tomorrow afternoon. I asked him to come, but I don't think he plans to. Has he mentioned it?"

"No." They were planning on driving to Ghost Ranch, fifty miles north of Santa Fe.

"I thought not." Her disappointment came clearly through the line. "Please help me help them. Irene is miserable. I caught her crying this morning.

She says it's nothing, but I don't believe her. I can tell that Jim is worried, too. Lance hasn't called once. Every night Naomi and Richard call Kayla at bedtime. It's a reminder to Irene that she's lost Lance and, if he does have children, she won't be a part of their lives."

His aunt was right. Fallon placed her hand on her stomach. She wanted her child to have a loving relationship with his or her grandparents. Lance needed to let go of the past and move on. She just wasn't sure he could. "I'll try."

"Thank you." There was relief in Mrs. Young-blood's voice.

"I'm not promising anything," Fallon quickly said, not looking forward to the conversation with Lance.

"He'll come if you ask him."

"How can you be so sure?"

"I saw how he looked at you at the wedding re-hearsal, and how worried he was when he couldn't find you later. He cares about you. We couldn't be happier about you two."

Caring wasn't loving, but Fallon wouldn't lose hope that he'd get there one day.

"Good-bye, Fallon. We'll expect to see you any-time after twelve."

"Good-bye, Mrs. Youngblood." Fallon ended the call, already dreading talking with Lance.

Fallon fully intended to broach the subject of go-ing to his aunt's house for the cookout, but when she opened the door to the cottage and saw several arrangements of flowers sitting around the great room she forgot all about it.

"Do you like them?" Lance moved from the other side of the door and took her packages.

"They're beautiful." She moved to the long-stemmed dark red roses, touched the velvet petals with unsteady fingers, smelled the haunting scent. From there, she went to the woven basket of pink azaleas, the creamy orchids, the fat white hydrangeas in a square vase, before stopping at a terrarium.

"Like I said, I thought flowers were overdone." His hands rested on her waist. "Until I met you. I figured I better make up for lost time."

She blinked back tears. "You did that and more."

His eyes narrowed as he brushed a tear away with his knuckle. "If you cry, you won't be able to enjoy what else I have waiting for you."

Fallon brushed the heel of her hand across both eyes. "No crying."

Holding her hand, he took her into the master bedroom to a massage table. "The spa gave me an idea. I purchased some scented oils. I'm going to give you a massage."

She shivered with decadent anticipation at the thought of his hands on her naked body. "And I get to give you one as well."

His nostrils flared, his eyes narrowed. "That's the idea. First, we have a non-alcoholic sangria and I get to feed you chocolate-covered strawberries." He handed her a chilled flute with raspberries floating inside and picked up one for himself.

"What comes next?" she asked, sipping her drink to ease her dry throat.

Lance placed both glasses back on the small table and took her in his arms. "We get to feast on each other." His greedy mouth took hers and everything ceased to exist but the two of them for a long, long time.

Before dawn Saturday morning Lance woke up feeling as if he could conquer the world. The reason was the sleeping woman in his arms. It was going to work out between them. He was sure of it. Depending how the day went, he planned on asking her to marry him again. Until his ring was on her finger, there was always the possibility that she might walk out of his life and take their child. Just the thought churned his insides.

She cared about him, but that wouldn't make her stay if he did something she didn't like. She was independent and self-assured. She was also loyal and loving. He'd use those qualities to bind her to him. He enjoyed seeing her eyes light up, the trembling smile. He wanted her in his life and he was going to do everything possible to make it a reality.

Kissing Fallon on her bare shoulder, he pulled her closer and drifted back to sleep, silently praying that she would always be by his side.

Saturday morning, Fallon put off talking to Lance until they were almost to the car. He'd been so playful that morning that she hadn't wanted to spoil the day for him. Last night had been incredible. The things he'd done to her with the rose still made her face heat up and her body clench. He was an excellent lover, an astute businessman, a loyal friend. He could be a wonderful husband and father, but not until he forgave and moved on.

"Lance, there's been a change of plans."

Stopping, he grinned at her. "Ghost Ranch isn't going anyplace. I'd much rather go back to the cottage, too."

"Actually, I want us to go to your aunt's house for the cookout," Fallon said.

The smile slid from his face. "Did you talk to her?"

Fallon flinched from the anger in his voice. Instinctively she knew he meant his mother. "Your aunt. She called me yesterday while I was out shopping. She said your mother is miserable. She caught her crying."

"What about all the times I cri—" His mouth flattened into a hard line. "So you're taking her side."

"No." A wave of apprehension swept through her. She'd been afraid of this. "I'm not taking her side. It's you I'm worried and care about. You won't move past it. If you had, you could say her name and talk about her without becoming angry."

"Think what you like."

"Lance, I want our baby to have the love and support of an extended family," Fallon said patiently. "I don't want him or her to not know your mother. I also don't want our child to think that avoiding an issue instead of working through a problem is the right way to handle anything. Face it and move on."

"You calling me a coward?" he asked, his voice rough and tinged with unmistakable pain. "Are you?"

"I—" She faltered. She didn't want to hurt him any more than she apparently had.

"Are you?" he snapped.

"Not in the way you think. It's your emotions you run from when you think you'll be vulnerable. You don't want to be hurt again, so you hide your feelings, mask them behind anger, laughter, teasing, intimacy," she said softly. "My guess is that you'd rather walk over hot coals than face rejection again."

A muscle leaped in his jaw. "You think I had an ulterior motive for making love to you."

"If I thought that I wouldn't have stayed." She gently touched his arm. "I do think you're afraid to let down your guard with me, to be completely honest about how you feel. Because of the past, you don't trust women easily—if at all."

"I don't need psychoanalysis," he grated.

In spite of his anger, her face softened. "Our baby needs his or her father to be a man he or she can look up to. That's what I need, too."

"Get in the car."

Fallon didn't ask where they were going. She had pushed him to the limits. In the passenger seat, she buckled her seat belt. Lance was furious, but he drove within the speed limit to the highway.

She felt his gaze on her and met his stare. The anger was gone, and in its place was a bleakness that broke her heart. "You can do this. Let it go."

He pulled out on the highway, taking the road back to town and away from Ghost Ranch. Fallon wished she could relax, but she couldn't. She'd pushed Lance hard. He'd kept his anger under control with her. Fallon wasn't so sure if he'd do the same with his mother.

Lance was livid. His aunt and Fallon expected him to forgive and forget. It wasn't that easy. He remembered as if it were yesterday. The incidents were indelibly marked in his mind. The punishments, the grounding, being made to feel like an outsider in the home he'd lived in since he was born.

Yet nothing came close to the pain he felt when Fallon said their baby needed a father to look up to. The old taunt of not being enough came rushing back. Once again, his mother was trying to ruin his life.

Lance turned into a residential street of one-story adobe homes and stopped in front of one painted yellow. In the yard were groupings of cacti, since his aunt and uncle traveled so much. Lance had good memories of this house. That was about to change.

The door opened on the passenger side. He slowly turned to Fallon. "Remember, you asked for this."

"Lance—"

Ignoring her calling him, he rounded the car and took her arm. "We can go through the side gate."

"Don't be angry. Just remember Kayla is here," Fallon said. "She likes you."

Lance opened the wooden gate. "I'm glad somebody here does."

Fallon's eyes narrowed. "If I thought you really believed that, I—"

"Cousin Lance! Fallon! You came!" Kayla was across the yard running at full speed and going straight to Lance, arms wide.

"Hi, Kayla," Lance greeted. "You save us any food?"

"We have burgers and chicken and ribs. Aunt Irene said you liked ribs." Kayla flashed a smile. "I told them Fallon likes all kinds of food."

"That's right. Now give me a hug." Fallon took Kayla into her arms, but Lance supported most of the weight.

"Here you go, Kayla." Lance placed the child on her feet.

"I better get back to helping Gramps and Uncle Jim. They said they cook better when I'm around. Bye." Kayla ran back to the two men and the smoking stainless-steel grill that was at least five feet long.

Lance noted that Jim gave a halfhearted wave. Leo spoke and motioned Fallon and Lance over. "In a minute!" he yelled. "We're going inside."

Jim started around the grill. Lance's uncle's hand on Jim's arm stopped him. Lance grunted. This was between him and Irene.

"You might want to keep going to the front room." He went up the two steps leading into the kitchen.

"Lance, don't let your anger rule you. She's your mother."

"Not since my father died." Lance opened the back door.

In the kitchen were his aunt and mother. Both glanced up. He was surprised to see the beginning of a smile on his mother's face, and then it was gone. "Hi, Aunt Gladys. Do you mind taking Fallon into the front room? This won't take long."

"Lance," his aunt and Fallon said at the same time.

He held up his hand, his gaze still on his mother, one hand gripping a wooden spoon, her lower lip trembling. "Save the wounded act."

He thought he saw her flinch and was annoyed to feel a bit ashamed. He reasoned it was because Fallon and his aunt were still there. Regardless, he cared about what they thought of him.

"Gladys. Fallon," his mother said softly. "Please excuse us. Lance deserves his say."

"Remember." Fallon placed her hand over her stomach, then took his aunt's arm and pulled her from the room.

Irene stuck the spoon back into the potato salad, then came within five feet of him and stopped. It took a few seconds before he realized she was studying him. "Looking for flaws?"

She swallowed. Shook her hair with wings of gray that hadn't been there the last time they met before the wedding. "Before the wedding it had been ten years and five months since I last saw you. You look taller, but maybe it's because you're broader in the shoulders."

He didn't want to remember, but he did. He'd gone home for Thanksgiving and left an hour later after he and Jim almost came to blows. "If you had wanted to see me more often, you shouldn't have started dating six months after we lost Daddy."

She glanced away. "Jim is a good man. I'd hoped you two would be friends."

Lance folded his arms. "Not likely after he took a belt to me."

"He hit you twice across your legs. You were wearing jeans. The next day when you were in your shorts there were no marks." She took a step closer. "The licks hurt your pride more than anything."

"You took his side just as you always did, the way you're doing now," Lance told her.

"I wanted you to respect him as your stepfather. To respect authority, to learn that you can't always have things the way you want." She reached out to him, then let her hand fall. "You were understandably angry when your father died so suddenly and so tragically. I didn't want that anger spilling over and getting you into trouble."

"You can lie to yourself if it makes you feel better. It won't wash with me. You never loved Daddy, and you were glad to get rid of me every summer," he said tightly. "I've succeeded without you. I don't need or want you in my life."

"That's enough!"

Lance spun to see her husband, Jim, in the back doorway with his fists clenched. "You want to hit me again? This time, be prepared for a fight."

"No." His mother placed herself in front of Lance and faced her husband. "It's all right. Let it go."

"No. He's got to know the truth. I won't have him treating you like this. You've cried enough over him," Jim said, his voice tight with anger.

Lance's mother paled. "You promised."

"I won't see you hurt any longer for something you had no control over," Jim said. "I love you too much."

Lance's mother began crying, the sounds heart-breaking. He moved his shoulders as if to throw off his need to comfort her. "Is this some little act you two whipped up for my benefit?"

Jim reached into his jean pocket and pulled out a little blue book and held it in front of Lance. "Take it and open it. It's your mother's savings account book. You'll see that it was her and not your father who gave you the ten thousand dollars for college."

"I don't believe you." Lance snatched the book, then looked at the weekly deposits into the account. The week he'd gone to college there had been a withdrawal of ten thousand dollars, almost depleting the account.

He was stunned. "Why?"

Jim answered, "Because she knew you wouldn't

take the money if it came from her, and she wanted you to think your father had provided for you. He was a good man, but he wasn't a businessman. The house had a second lien that doubled the house payments five months after he died. She wasn't going out as you thought; she was working. She didn't tell you because she didn't want you to worry. Your father was making good money and could have paid the note if he'd lived. He didn't. He left you and your mother heavily in debt. You worshiped your father so much, she didn't want you to know."

"Jim, that's enough," she pleaded, and faced Lance. "I realize I waited too long to try and repair the damage I did to you by trying to shield you. All I can do now is ask that you try and forgive me. Don't shut me out of your life." The tears flowed down her cheeks.

Lance tried to take it all in. He didn't know what to say.

"I guess I have to apologize as well." Jim's voice was gruff. "I hit you out of anger. Your mother was trying so hard and all you did was talk back and sulk. I thought you were ungrateful. Irene said you were hurting and confused, but I thought she made too many excuses for you. Every summer, when you went away, for the first few days she'd cry. She should have dusted your behind and made you stay with us."

"I didn't want you to hate me any more than you already seemed to." She sniffed. "You were always away from home. I was to blame for that. I'm sorry, but I thought I was doing what was best for you, helping you grow up to be a good man."

Lance thought of Fallon's comment about the type of father their baby needed. He stared at the savings account book. The truths he was so sure of were crumbling around him.

"If you can find it in your heart to start over again, you know how to reach us." Jim curved his arm around his wife's trembling shoulders. "Let's go, Irene. Kayla is anxious to put the sauce on the ribs."

Irene looked at Lance with watery eyes. "You used to like my barbecue ribs. You and your father would go through a slab in nothing flat."

He remembered. Those had been happy days. "You sold his things."

She swallowed. Hard. "The memories were too painful. I thought giving his belongings away would help. I sold the comic book collection and whatever I thought could earn money to help with the house payments. I knew you wanted them, but I was desperate. We were already behind on the mortgage payments by then."

"If you were so in love with Daddy why did you marry Jim the month he died?" Lance asked, his voice tight.

She looked up at her husband. His face was stoic. "For reasons that will remain between us. I loved your father, but he was gone. I thought we both needed a man in the house. I thought it would be a new beginning." Her head momentarily bowed. "I was wrong."

"We'll be outside." Jim opened the door and placed his hand in the small of his wife's back.

"Good-bye, Lance. Thank you for coming and listening," his mother said. Jim closed the door behind them.

Fallon had heard the argument and confession of Lance's mother and stepfather. She'd tried to shield Lance and ended up hurting him instead. Fallon asked his aunt to let her see him alone. Gladys went out the front door to go around the back.

Lance stood in the kitchen with his fist clenched. Fallon saw the edge of blue paper—the savings account book. He looked up. His eyes were dazed.

"Lance." Quickly she crossed the room and curved her arms around his waist, placed her head on his chest. "It will be all right."

His arms were slow to hold her, and when they did they were loose.

A chill ran through Fallon. His mother and stepfather's revelation shook all of Lance's beliefs to the core. Everything he had believed about them was wrong.

"I need to get out of here."

Fallon straightened and took his hand. "Let's go."

He glanced toward the back door, then down at her, and started for the front of the house. He stopped briefly to open her car door. Once they were inside the car, he pulled off.

Fallon ached for him. He'd just been blindsided. He needed to talk, but that wasn't the way Lance handled his problems. He kept them caged inside him. Perhaps it was time someone opened that cage door.

"We weren't trying to, but we heard everything," she told him, trying to find her way.

He stopped at a signal light. He stared straight ahead.

Her cell phone rang. She saw it was his aunt. "Hello. . . . I'm not sure. I'll call you later." She ended the call. "Mrs. Youngblood wanted to know how you were doing. After your mother helped Kayla slather the sauce on the ribs, she said she had a headache and went inside."

Lance turned into the driveway of his home.

"You both are hurting," Fallon said. "Perhaps, in time, you can help each other heal."

Lance stopped in front of the house. Fallon got out of the car, expecting Lance to get out as well.

The front passenger's automatic window slid down. "I'll be back." The car took off. Fallon was left staring at it.

Lance went back to his previous thinking spot, Richard's ranch. This time Lance saw the man taking care of the livestock while Richard was away. Since he'd seen Lance helping Naomi and Kayla move and at the wedding, he waved at Lance and continued to the barn.

On the patio, Lance took a seat under the shade of a gnarled tree, clasped his hands, and stared downward. He had been so sure his mother had chosen Jim over him, that she'd stopped loving him.

He'd been wrong. So, where did that leave him? He honestly didn't know. If he'd misread his mother and Jim, could he trust his judgment with Fallon?

He had some tough decisions to make. If he chose wrong, he risked not only his heart but his sanity as well.

Fallon tried not to agonize about Lance. He'd texted her three times since he'd been gone. Each time it had been the same message. *Don't worry.* It was impossible not to. His mother had called twice, concerned that by getting Lance to see her, she might have caused problems for them.

Although Fallon wasn't sure, she'd told his mother and Mrs. Youngblood that things were fine between them. With all her heart, she prayed that was the truth. She tried to occupy her mind for a bit with catching up their baby's journal but found she couldn't concentrate. Somehow she knew that if Lance didn't come to terms with his past tonight he never would, and it would be over for them forever.

The doorknob twisted and she was across the floor. As soon as Lance opened the door, she was in his arms. "You're finally home."

"Sorry if I worried you."

She tried to keep the smile on her face. His arms loosely held her. "That's all right. Let's go to bed."

"We have to talk first." He led her to a Queen Anne upholstered chair.

Fallon's apprehension grew. "What about?"

"Us." He rubbed the back of his neck, then began

to pace in front of her. "I thought I had the answers where my mother and stepfather were concerned. I didn't. I misread both of them."

"That wasn't your fault," Fallon said. "They didn't tell you everything."

He nodded. "Despite their good intentions, I had a rough childhood after I lost my father."

Her heart went out to him. "Your mother called twice. She's worried about you. You need to call her."

He blew out a breath. "Yeah. Well. It can wait."

"Lance, what's more important than helping your mother?"

"Figuring out where we stand." He took her hands. "Mother's confession made me realize that trying to shield someone isn't always the right thing to do. It also made me realize you have to be honest even if it makes you vulnerable. I finally figured out what it is you want from me."

Fallon's heart thudded in her chest.

"I woke my lawyer up. He'll be here tomorrow. I'm writing out a new will that leaves everything to you and our baby," he said.

Her chest felt tight. "I don't care about the money."

His smile was sad. "I know you don't, but after hearing about the financial problems my father and yours left behind I don't want to make the same mistake. Regardless of what happens to me or how things turn out between us, I want you and our baby to be safe and secure."

"You sound as if you won't be around regardless." Misery echoed in every word.

"That depends on you and how much faith you have in me." He brushed her hair from her face. "The doubts are gone. I'd trust you with my life, and to care for our baby."

"Always."

"Here goes." A ragged breath shuddered over his lips. He took her hands in his, his gaze direct and penetrating. "I love you, Fallon. I want to be a part of your life and the baby's life. I want us to get married. To be a real family."

Her eyes widened. She opened her mouth and nothing came out.

His world tilted. His hands flexed on hers. His resolve strengthened for her and the baby. He'd make this work. He loved them too much to lose them. "You don't have to love me back; just don't leave me. Let me be with you. Always. You and the baby are all that I need."

"Oh, Lance. You did it." Tears streamed down her cheeks. She sniffed, palmed his cheeks. "I could never leave my heart."

Finally able to breathe normally, he kissed her tears away. This time they made his heart beat with joy instead of fear.

"I love you." Leaning forward, she kissed him gently on the lips. "If I hadn't, I wouldn't have gone to bed with you when I came back."

His heart thumped in his chest. "Then you'll marry me?"

"Yes! Oh yes!"

His world righted itself. He'd picked right. Laughing, he gathered her in his arms and kissed her until his head swam. "Who do we tell first? Your parents or mine?"

Her smile grew. He was finally free. The past was where it belonged, in the past. "Let's do a three-way telephone call and tell them both at the same time."

"Later." He scooped her up. "First, I'm taking you to bed."

Read on for an excerpt from Francis Ray's next book

All That I Desire

Coming soon from St. Martin's Paperbacks

Prologue

Skylar Dupree, Event Director for Navarone Resorts and Spas, had never been impulsive. But now as she watched the approach of two couples and one lone man from the second-floor turret window of Navarone Castle, Skylar contemplated taking the biggest gamble of her life.

As the pampered only child of divorced, over-protective parents, Skylar had wanted for little in her life. What she now desired—what she'd longed for, dreamed of, the past two years—might be impossible to attain. And cost her a job she loved.

Unlike her highly successful parents in Boston, she wasn't cut out to be a lawyer. When a family friend showed her an ad for an assistant to the events director for the Navarone Resorts and Spas headquartered in Tucson, Arizona, she had jumped at the opportunity.

Six weeks after she'd been hired, she met Blade Navarone at the grand opening of his latest resort. With him were his two personal bodyguards. One in particular, Rio Sanchez, caught her attention the instant she'd seen him.

He was tall, fallen-angel handsome with razor-sharp cheekbones, long curly black hair that he wore tied at the nape of his neck, and flat black eyes. Much to her surprise, since she had loads of male friends but nothing serious, Rio piqued her curiosity and heated her body.

The other man, Shane Elliott, might socialize, but Rio never did. He always kept himself apart, always watching. He seemed unapproachable. Hard. She'd observed more than one woman start toward him only to stop a few feet away, then beat a hasty retreat. She well understood why.

Rio was handsome enough to draw women, but the unblinking flat eyes made any sensible woman feel as if she might be getting in over her head. Skylar felt that way herself.

In the two years she'd known Rio, she'd caught him watching her a couple of times. The problem was she couldn't be sure if it went deeper than just doing his job.

Skylar wanted to know the man behind the unreadable façade that never smiled, to make him stop looking through her, calling her Ms. Dupree. It was more than her wanting him to notice her or treat her differently than he did all of the other people, besides Blade and Shane. She didn't think Rio had anyone.

Blade and Shane had wives, but who comforted Rio? With his broad shoulders, quick reflexes, and reported skills as a fighter, Rio acted as if he didn't need or want anyone.

She might have believed that if she wasn't looking at Rio with Blade and Shane and their wives. As always, Rio walked apart, unsmiling as the two couples laughed and held hands. She didn't know there were tears on her cheeks until Ruth Grayson, Blade's mother-in-law, handed her a tissue. "No man should walk this earth alone," she said, and excused herself.

Skylar might have been embarrassed, but she liked Mrs. Grayson and knew she could keep a confidence. Skylar looked out the window again and came to a decision; Rio wouldn't walk alone any longer if she could help it. It would be risky, emotionally and professionally.

If Rio felt she'd crossed the line professionally, she'd be out on her ear. She would be risking everything for a man who had never smiled at her, had never given her any indication that he felt anything more for her than the stones surrounding the castle—except for those two occasions.

Suddenly Rio looked up at her. She felt the familiar leap of her heart, the warmth curling through her, the need to touch, to soothe. She smiled. He didn't smile back, just continued inside behind the others. He was a tough man. That was all right. She turned from the window.

One day he would smile back.

Chapter 1

Skylar Dupree wasn't the risk-taking type, but neither was she the type of woman to falter once she'd made up her mind. The only other time in her twenty-six years she had dared to do anything remotely defying tradition was leaving law school. Yet that had been more for self-preservation. Her parents were pragmatic; she tended to be more easygoing and laid-back.

Skylar paused on the curved stone staircase of the thirty-five-room castle. Easygoing wasn't going to cut it this time, not if she wanted to grab Rio's attention.

Just the thought sent her heart rate skittering out of control. Rio could look straight through you with hard, unblinking black eyes. He exuded danger. Nothing seemed to bother him. She could count on one hand the number of times she'd seen him smile, and those times had been when he was with his closest friends, Blade and Shane. As far as Skylar knew, he'd never bestowed a smile upon anyone else, let alone his laughter.

The task she'd chosen for herself was scary.

Since Shane's marriage, Rio was now head of security for Blade's business as well as Blade's personal bodyguard. Even Rio's security team had a healthy fear of the man reported to be deadlier than a viper, and just as stealthy. She'd heard one of his men refer to him as "smoke" because of his elusiveness.

Skylar had flown in that Sunday afternoon from Navarone Resorts and Spas' headquarters to go over the final preparations for a charity auction and ball to benefit the music department of St. John's College, where Mrs. Grayson was the department chair. The auction was two weeks away. The big draw to get the right people to come was that the auction would be held in Navarone Castle, a place heretofore off limits to anyone but close family and friends.

Much had been speculated about the home of the billionaire, which had a real moat, a working drawbridge, a helipad, and a lake. Sierra, Blade's wife, might have owned the castle before her marriage, but Blade ensured their privacy by buying up all the surrounding property within fifty miles. A person might get on the property, but with constant patrols, they were quickly escorted off, giving Navarone Castle even more of an air of mystique.

Continuing down the stairs with her iPad clutched to her chest, Skylar stepped into the open room. Sitting in the comfortable great room with sky-blue leather chairs and love seats were Blade, Sierra, and her mother on one side. On the other were Shane and his wife Paige. Rio, arms folded, standing by the immense stone fireplace, looked up. Her heart did a fast jitterbug.

Rio looked incredibly handsome in a long-sleeved white shirt with the cuffs rolled back to show strong wrists. He had a silver watch on one arm and a wide silver band on the other. His jeans delineated the long, sleek muscles of his thighs and made Skylar's mouth go dry.

In Tucson he'd always worn tailored clothes, the same as Blade. Here, Rio was more casual. The curly black hair she'd dreamed of running her fingers through was held at the base of his neck with a silver clip. His bronzed, hard body was honed to perfection.

There was nothing in his midnight-black eyes that indicated he desired or felt anything at all for her. Skylar stared back at the flat eyes that seemed to see right through her and stiffened her spine.

One day he'd look at her with desire.

"Hi, Skylar." Sierra rose from her seat and went to greet her. "I'm sorry we weren't here to meet you."

"That's all right." Skylar smiled. She and Sierra had hit it off immediately. "I enjoyed looking around the castle again. You have a beautiful home."

"Thanks." Sierra glanced back at Blade. "We like it."

Skylar's smile increased. One place she'd bet was off limits was the grotto downstairs that was Sierra and Blade's secret place.

"Please have a seat." Sierra took the other woman's arm. "Can I get you anything?"

"No, thank you," Skylar said, and then greeted everyone as she took a leather chair. Everyone spoke. Rio nodded his head.

"Is everything going as planned?" Ruth asked.

Skylar knew Ruth could have asked that question earlier but hadn't. Mrs. Grayson also didn't let on she'd seen or talked with Skylar earlier. She smiled her thanks.

"Yes, Mrs. Grayson. In fact, we're ahead of schedule. As planned, the auction will be by invitation only. Thanks to Lance's help, a printed color catalog with the starting bid for each item has already been sent out."

"Good thing," Sierra interjected. "Because he and Fallon are off on their honeymoon."

"Still discussing if she'll be able to go scuba diving due to her pregnancy." Blade glanced at Sierra. "She's almost as strong-willed as another woman I know."

"Aren't you and Lance the lucky ones?" Sierra grinned and kissed Blade on the cheek.

Skylar cut a sideways glance at Rio. His arms remained crossed, his gaze somewhere over her head. He wasn't going to make this easy. Back to the business at hand.

"I personally called everyone to ensure they received the catalog and still plan to attend." Skylar pulled out the guest list and stood to give it to Rio. "This week, four of the invitees asked if they could bring a guest. It was to be expected that some would ignore the one-month time limit to invite a guest. I know you'd want to check the people out before I committed."

Rio crossed to her in his effortless stride that reminded her of a stalking cat. Long, lean fingers took the list without looking at it. "Thank you." His voice held no inflection.

Trying not to sigh, Skylar retook her seat. She needn't have bothered wearing a tangerine-colored dress that complemented her complexion and hazel eyes. However, she wasn't giving up.

"The items will be arriving by special courier or delivery service starting Tuesday. I'll be here to check and sign them in. I'll return each day until we have all the items in place," Skylar told them. "We've already selected the room where they'll be displayed."

"That's too much trouble," Sierra said. "It would be easier and make more sense if you stayed here."

"I couldn't agree more," Blade said.

"I couldn't," Skylar said, surprised by the invitation. While they were planning the auction, she'd always flown in and out of Santa Fe.

"We have plenty of guest rooms." Sierra leaned against Blade. His arm immediately circled her slim shoulders. "We're leaving for a new Navarone property in the morning; you're welcome to stay here."

Skylar didn't know what to say. She was very aware that a lot of trust had gone into the invitation. If Rio stayed, she might run into him more. The thought no sooner materialized than she discarded it. She was not going to impose on Blade and Sierra's kindness to go after Rio.

"It won't be any trouble," Skylar finally said. "I don't mind the drive."

"We won't take no for an answer," Blade told her.

"You're staying and that's final," Sierra said firmly as if the matter was settled.

"Please." Ruth leaned forward in her seat. "What you're doing is to help my music department. We'll benefit from your hard work. I'll always be thankful. You could have passed when I asked if you had any ideas of how to raise funds. You didn't. You even offered to take vacation time to help."

"I appreciated the professionalism, but as I said then when you mentioned what you would be doing, using your vacation time won't be necessary," Blade said, his gaze direct.

Sierra patted his knee. "He's even gotten over being a little miffed that you thought you had to ask. He forgot all men are not as wonderful as he is."

Blade smiled at his wife, then Skylar, and she breathed a bit easier. She well remembered the harsh look on his face that day in his office. She hoped never again to see it directed at her and remained silent.

"Stay," Blade said. "It would make up for my poor behavior."

Blade wasn't above apologizing. He just seldom had to. Shane had a grin on his face as he held Paige's hand. No one had to tell Skylar that Blade's love for Sierra and hers for her mother were the reason behind the apology.

Skylar recalled Ruth's words: "No man should walk alone." Her gaze went to Ruth again, as she wondered if she was trying to give Skylar a gentle push in Rio's direction.

But as Blade's bodyguard, Rio went with him everywhere or was at least nearby. Was he staying this time? She had her answer seconds later.

"To ensure the auction pieces remain safe, Rio is staying," Blade told her.

"I should be going with you." Rio unfolded his arms, his attention on Blade and Sierra.

Sierra lifted both hands in a fighter's stance. "Don't worry, Rio. I promise to take down anyone who looks suspicious."

Shane was the only one who laughed. He ignored his wife's nudge.

"You checked out the island; the men there were trained by you or Shane. You and Shane made sure my name is buried so no one outside the company knows we own the property," Blade reminded him. "From the vantage point on the island you can see a boat for miles. We'll be safe."

"That's why I should be there—to make sure."

"I want you here." Blade rose to his feet and went to Rio. "This is important to Mrs. Grayson. There's some valuable merchandise coming. I trust you to ensure it's kept safe."

Rio remained silent. Skylar's eyes and everyone else's were on Rio and Blade. No one, absolutely no one—outside of Sierra—went against Blade's orders. She sensed Rio might be the second. Protecting Blade and Sierra was more than a job to him.

Shane went to the two men. "I'll fly down with them and check it out."

Rio's gaze slowly tracked to Shane's and stayed there for a long moment before returning to Blade. "If you'll excuse me, I'll begin checking on the list."

Skylar blew out a breath as Rio's long strides took him from the room and up the stairs to the command center on the second floor of the front wing of the castle.

"You shouldn't tease him," Ruth said to Sierra.

"Who said I was teasing?" Sierra lifted innocent eyes to her mother.

Ruth shook her head once, then stood and pulled a set of keys from the pocket of her denim skirt. "Come on, Skylar. I'll drive you to your hotel to get your things."

Sierra stood, her arm going around her mother's waist. "Since I've seen how Skylar packs, I'll send a driver with the SUV."

Ruth smiled at Sierra, then Skylar. "She likes clothes as much as you do."

"You never know what you might need." Sierra spoke to Skylar, "We'll wait dinner for you."

Skylar smiled. Sierra and her mother weren't taking no for an answer. "I graciously accept. I'll be back as soon as I can."

In less than fifteen minutes Skylar had checked out of the Casa de Serenidad hotel. Thank goodness she had been so anxious to get to the castle that she hadn't begun to unpack. Outside, she climbed into the SUV, and they headed back to Navarone Castle.

Skylar wasn't the impatient type, but she was anxious to get back. She wondered if Rio ate with his men or Blade and Sierra. Everyone had someone, except him. But he didn't seem to need anyone. He certainly wasn't afraid to speak his mind—to anyone.

"Back again," the driver said, startling Skylar out of her deep thoughts.

"Thank you." She got out of the vehicle and walked to the back. She almost winced at the amount of luggage being unloaded. Besides the large trunk, she'd brought five large suitcases. It had taken her weeks to decide what to wear in hopes that Rio would stop looking through her and be just a little bit interested. With him staying and checking in the merchandise with her daily, it might just happen.

"Mrs. Navarone instructed me where to place your luggage. Please, go on in."

"Thank you again, Jefferson." Skylar picked up her overnight kit.

"I can take that as well." The driver closed the back. "Don't worry, Eli is sending someone to help. Besides, we're both used to helping Mrs. Navarone load and unload for trips."

Skylar placed the case on the stone driveway and laughed. "That's very kind of you. Thank you."

The driver tipped his hat. "No problem."

Skylar went up the steps and rang the doorbell. There was a keypad for a code, but she didn't know it.

The door opened. Eli Patterson, the house manager, stood there in his black suit, freshly starched white shirt, and shiny leather shoes. Of medium height, he had a lined, fatherly face and a balding head.

"Hello, Mr. Patterson," Skylar greeted.

"Hello, Ms. Dupree. I'll assist with your luggage," he told her. "Mr. Navarone asked that you see him immediately in his office as soon as you returned. This way."

Unsure of what was going on, she followed the house manager past the wide foyer, then left to an arched door at least fifteen feet tall. Opening the door, he stepped aside.

Thanking him, she entered the office, an immense room lined with bookshelves, a fireplace, and tall windows with silk burgundy draperies. On the slate floor were hand-woven area rugs. Blade sat behind an antique mahogany desk with ball-and-claw feet. Her eyes narrowed on seeing Shane and Rio standing on either side of him.

"Thank you for coming, Skylar. Please have a seat." Blade indicated the chair in front of his desk.

Skylar took a seat in the straight-backed upholstered chair in a deeper shade of burgundy than the curtains, demurely crossed her legs, and placed her clutch in her lap. She'd learned not to jump to conclusions just because she was summoned by Blade, and not to ask questions.

"One of the men on the list you gave Rio is Sherman Tennyson, a venture capitalist. Several months ago, Tennyson used my name to entice backers into buying property. The deal folded." Blade's black eyes hardened. "A lot of good men lost money. Tennyson put the word out that it was my fault."

"No." Skylar's voice was barely above a whisper as she placed her hand on her galloping heart. People who made huge mistakes at Navarone were out the door.

Shane picked up the story. "Blade has been able to overcome the lies, but Tennyson lost a lot of his credibility, along with money he could ill afford to lose."

Blade's fist clenched on top of his desk. "Tennyson hates my guts and the feeling is mutual."

Skylar came to her feet. "Mr. Navarone, I just checked to ensure he had the funds to purchase if he chose. I apologize."

Blade waved her apology aside. "There's no need to apologize. You foiled Tennyson's plan." He leaned back in his chair, the sides of his mouth kicking up. "You didn't just okay the names as he probably expected because the auction is in two weeks and he has money. Instead you had the foresight to give Rio the list of names before committing. You did well."

"I agree," Shane said. "Good thinking."

From Rio there was nothing. Trying to keep from looking at him, she retook her seat. "Should I call Mr. Hampton, the man who had asked if Tennyson could attend?"

Blade's smile was like the sharp edge of a knife. "I'll take care of it. That's all."

Eternally thankful she wasn't the unfortunate man, Skylar came to her feet. "I'll go change for dinner. Good-bye."

"Good-bye," Blade and Shane said.

She told herself not to turn, but a force stronger than her will had her glancing over her shoulder at Rio to see if there might be a spark of admiration. She saw nothing but eyes devoid of warmth. Unconsciously she narrowed hers before turning to leave the room.

Stubborn man! He might not know it, but he'd only made her more determined!